the cold war swap

also by Ross Thomas

The Seersucker Whipsaw

Cast a Yellow Shadow

The Singapore Wink

The Fools in Town Are on Our Side

The Backup Men

The Porkchoppers

If You Can't Be Good

The Money Harvest

Yellow-Dog Contract

Chinaman's Chance

The Eighth Dwarf

The Mordida Man

Missionary Stew

Briarpatch

Out on the Rim

The Fourth Durango

Twilight at Mac's Place

Voodoo, Ltd.

Ah, Treachery!

the cold war swap

Ross Thomas

THOMAS DUNNE BOOKS
ST. MARTIN'S MINOTAUR ᴥ NEW YORK

THOMAS DUNNE BOOKS.
An imprint of St. Martin's Press.

THE COLD WAR SWAP. Copyright © 1966 by Ross E. Thomas, Inc. Introduc-
tion © 2003 by Stuart M. Kaminsky. All rights reserved. Printed in the
United States of America. For information, address St. Martin's Press, 175
Fifth Avenue, New York, N.Y. 10010.

www.minotaurbooks.com

Library of Congress Cataloging-in-Publication Data
Thomas, Ross, 1926–1995.
    The Cold War swap / Ross Thomas.—1st St. Martin's Minotaur ed.
        p.   cm.
    ISBN 0-312-31581-3
    1. Bars (Drinking establishments)—Fiction.   2. Americans--
Germany—Fiction.   3. Bonn (Germany)—Fiction.   4. Defectors—
Fiction.   5. Cold War—Fiction.   I. Title.
PS3570.H58C65 2003
813'.54—dc21
                                                      2002191951

First published by William Morrow & Co., Inc., in 1966

D 10 9   8   7

introduction
by Stuart M. Kaminsky

Ross was forty years old when he wrote his first novel, *The Cold War Swap*, in 1966. Coming from a career as a soldier, reporter, and political campaigner, he leapt onto the literary scene with that first attempt at fiction and won himself an Edgar Allan Poe Award for Best First Mystery.

The principal settings for Ross's first novel were two cities in which he had worked, Bonn and Berlin. The cities are portrayed vividly with a postwar noir style that sets a tone of quiet despair in which the characters will do almost anything to survive. And the beauty of Ross's characters in this dark world is that they are colorful and alive and they seldom plan ahead. Critics have compared Ross's work to that of Raymond Chandler, not in subject matter but in style. I've always thought of Ross as the American Eric Ambler by way of Elmore Leonard. Ross was the master of colorful, unpredictable characters, thieves, scoundrels, drunks, assassins, madmen, fools, bureaucrats, and confused and bewildered professionals.

In *The Cold War Swap* as in so many of his novels, it is sometimes difficult to tell if we are meant to take the characters seriously or if the author is leading us down a series of streets, alleys, and dark rooms with no idea himself of who or what will be around the next corner.

Is McCorkle, who sits in his shady bar in Bonn and drinks, broods, and smokes to generic excess, the comic side of Rick in *Casablanca*? Is Maas, the fat, sweating villain, the comic side of Sidney Greenstreet in *The Maltese Falcon*? Is Padillo Zachary Scott's distorted mirror image in *The Mask of Dimitrios*?

The book is a nonstop tale of blunders by both sides of the Cold War, a constantly changing attempt by mistaken spies and agents to hatch schemes they never quite put together. Is this book a soft laugh at the Cold War novel? I like to think that it is.

Men stagger into hotel rooms and fall dead. Bullets slowly kill off most of the cast. The best character in the book, Cook, the rich alcoholic, leaves the stage with the reader feeling that Thomas has played a dark joke on us, removing the character most full of life when we need him most.

There are things in *The Cold War Swap* that would seem badly outdated in other hands. In fact, there are dozens of books with the same theme, the rescuing of scientists from behind the Iron Curtain. Most of them are forgotten not because of their subject matter but because their pages were not peopled by the memorable, colorful characters of a Ross Thomas.

A caricature in other hands became a vulnerable human in Ross's books. The two gay defectors in *The Cold War Swap* move from near cliché to sympathetic humanness. Waas, the vile fat opportunist, is given his best shot and gradually becomes a basically bad man whom we can truly understand.

I knew Ross, a very soft-spoken, generous, quiet man who displayed none of the flamboyance of his characters. Ross was almost nondescript, seldom smiled, traveled everywhere with his wife, and quietly took in and turned to brilliant fiction the quirks and quivers of those around him, from the small, enthusiastic Mexican band that couldn't carry a tune to the Italian taxi driver who displayed his pride in his mastery of the English language by destroying it.

Ross listened. He took no notes. He didn't seem to be there, didn't ask questions. He observed. He imagined.

Ross could turn a phrase with the best of our ilk and not draw attention to it. Ross could surprise us with a sudden turn that left us bewildered and in the palm of his hand, wondering what would happen to the survivors.

The man was a masterful storyteller.

He once told me that he had no idea what his characters were going to do when he sat down each day to write, no idea of how fate might step in. He said, "I often wonder what's going to happen next and that's what makes it interesting for me and, if I'm lucky, for the reader."

He was more than lucky.

the cold
war swap

CHAPTER 1

He was the last one aboard the flight from Tempelhof to the Cologne-Bonn airport. He was late and became flustered and sweaty when he couldn't find his ticket until the search reached his inside breast pocket.

The English stewardess was patient and even smiled sweetly as he finally handed it over with mumbled apologies. The seat next to mine was vacant and he headed for it, banging a shabby briefcase against the arms of the passengers as he bumbled down the aisle. He dropped into the seat with a snort, not tall, squatty, maybe even fat, wearing a heavy brown suit that seemed to have been cut by a tinsmith and a dark-brown hat of no particular shape or distinction other than the fact that it sat squarely on his head with what seemed to be a measured levelness.

He tucked his briefcase between his legs and buckled his seat belt but didn't remove his hat. He leaned forward to peer out the window as the plane taxied to the end of the runway. During take-off his hands blanched white at the knuckles as they squeezed the arms of his seat. When he realized that it wasn't the pilot's first time up he leaned back, produced a package of Senoussi and lighted one with a wooden match. He blew out the uninhaled smoke and then glanced at me with that speculative look which stamps a fellow traveler as something of a conversationalist.

I had been in Berlin for a three-day weekend, during which I had managed to spend too much money and to acquire a splendid hangover. I had stayed at the Hotel am Zoo, where they make Martinis as good as any place in Europe with the possible exception of Harry's Bar in Venice. They had taken their usual toll, and now I needed to sleep during the hour or so that it takes to fly from Berlin to Bonn.

But the man in the next seat wanted to talk. I almost sensed his mind working for the gambit as I leaned back as far as the chair would recline, my eyes closed, my head throbbing in close harmony with the grind of the engines.

When his opener came, it wasn't original.

"You are going to Köln?"

"No," I said, keeping my eyes closed, "I'm going to Bonn."

"Very good! I too am going to Bonn."

That was nice. That made us shipmates.

"My name is Maas," he said, grabbing my hand and giving it a fine German shake. I opened my eyes.

"I'm McCorkle. Delighted."

"Ach! You are not German?"

"American."

"But you speak German so well."

"I've been here a long time."

"It's the best way to learn a language," Maas said, nodding his head in approval. "You must live in the country in which it is spoken."

The plane kept on flying and we sat there, Maas and I, making small talk about Berlin and Bonn and what some Americans thought of the German Situation. My head kept on aching and I was having a rotten time.

Even if it hadn't been cloudy, there is not much to see between Berlin and Bonn. It's drear and it's drab, like flying over Nebraska and Kansas on a February day. But things got brighter. Maas rummaged through his briefcase and produced a *Halbe Flasche* of Steinhaeger. That was thoughtful. Steinhaeger is best when drunk ice cold and washed down with a liter or so of beer. We drank it warm out of two small silver cups that he also furnished. By the time the twin-spired Dome of Cologne came into view we were almost on a "du" basis—but not quite. Yet we were good enough pals for me to offer Maas a ride into Bonn.

"You are too kind. Surely it is an imposition. I thank you very much. Come! A bird cannot fly on one wing. Let us finish the bottle."

We finished it and Maas tucked the two silver cups back into his brief case. The pilot set the plane down with only a couple of bumps and Maas and I filed out past the mild disapproval of the two hostesses. My headache was gone.

Maas had only his briefcase, and after I had collected my one-suiter we headed for the parking lot, where I was pleasantly surprised to find my car intact. The German juvenile delinquents—or half-strongs—can hot-wire a car in a time that makes their American counterparts look sick. I was driving a Porsche that year and Maas crooned over it. "Such a wonderful car. Such machinery. So fast." He kept on murmuring praise while I unlocked it and stowed my case in what is optimistically called the backseat. There are several advantages to a Porsche that I find no other car has, but Dr. Ferdinand Porsche did not design it for fat people. He must have had in mind the long, lean racing types, such as Moss and Hill. Herr Maas tried to get into the car head first, instead of butt-first. His brown double-breasted suit gaped open and the Luger he wore in a shoulder holster showed for only a second.

I took the Autobahn back to Bonn. It's a little longer and less picturesque than the conventional way, which is the route used by the junketing prime ministers, presidents and premiers who have reason to come calling on the West German capital. The car was running well and I held it to a modest 140 kilometers an hour and Herr Maas

hummed softly to himself as we whizzed by the Volkswagens, the Kap-
itans, and the occasional Mercedes.

If he wanted to carry a gun, that was his business. There was some
law against it, but then there were some laws against adultery, murder,
arson and spitting on the sidewalk. There were all sorts of laws, and I
decided, somewhat mellowed by the Steinhaeger, that if a fat little
German wanted to carry a Luger, he probably had very good reasons.

I was still congratulating myself on this sophisticated, worldly-wise
attitude when the left rear tire blew. With what I continue to regard as
masterly self-control I kept my foot off the brake, hit the gas pedal
lightly, oversteered a bit, and brought the car back into line—on the
wrong side of the road perhaps, but at least in one piece. At that point
there is no divider in the Autobahn. We were equally lucky that there
was no traffic coming from the opposite direction.

Maas did not say a word. I cursed for five seconds, at the same time
wondering how well the Michelin guarantee would pay off.

"My friend," Mass said, "you are an excellent driver."

"Thanks," I said, pulling the knob that unlocked the front lid where
the spare was kept.

"If you will indicate where the tools are stored, I will make the
necessary repairs."

"That's my job."

"No! At one time I was a quite competent mechanic. If you do not
mind, I will make the reparations."

The Porsche has a side mount for the jack, but I didn't have to tell
Herr Maas. He had the blown-out tire off in three minutes, and two
minutes later he was giving the spare's last lug a final jerk with the
wrench and slapping on the hubcap with the air of a man who knows
he has done a competent job. He didn't take off his coat.

The hood was up and Maas rolled the blowout to the front of the
car and wrestled it into its nook. He banged the lid down and got back
into the car, butt-first this time. Back on the Autobahn, I thanked him
for his efforts.

"It was nothing, Herr McCorkle. It was my pleasure to be of assistance. If you would be kind enough to drop me off at the Bahnhoff when we arrive in Bonn, I will still be in your debt. I can obtain a taxi there."

"Bonn's not that big," I said. "I'll take you where you want to go."

"But I must go to Bad Godesberg. It is far from Bonn's center."

"Fine. That's where I'm going too."

I drove over Victoria Bridge to Reuterstrasse and then to Koblenzerstrasse, a double-laned boulevard dubbed the Diplomatic Racetrack by the local wags. Of a morning you could see the Chancellor gliding grandly in his Mercedes 300, heralded by a couple of tough motorcycle cops and the White Mouse, a specially built Porsche that preceded the entourage, shooing the common folk aside as the procession made its solemn way to the Palais Chambourg.

"Where do you want to go in Godesberg?" I asked.

He fumbled in his suit pocket and produced a blue notebook. He turned to a page and said: "To a café. It is called Mac's Place. Do you know it?"

"Sure," I said, shifting down into second for a red light. "I own it."

CHAPTER 2

You can probably find a couple of thousand spots like Mac's Place in New York, Chicago or Los Angeles. They are dark and quiet with the furniture growing just a little shabby, the carpet stained to an indeterminate shade by spilled drinks and cigarette ashes, and the bartender friendly and fast but tactful enough to let it ride if you walk in with someone else's wife. The drinks are cold, generous and somewhat expensive; the service is efficient; and the menu, although usually limited to chicken and steaks, affords very good chicken and steaks indeed.

There were a few other places in Bonn and Bad Godesberg that year where you could get a decently mixed drink. One was the American Embassy Club (where you had to be a member or a guest); another was the Schaumberger Hof, where you paid expense-account prices for two centiliters of Scotch.

I opened the saloon the year after they elected Eisenhower president for the first time. What with his campaign promise to go to Korea and all, the Army decided that national security would not suffer appreciably if the Military Assistance Advisory Group housed in the sprawling U.S. Embassy on the Rhine did without my services. In fact, there was some mild speculation as to why they had called me up for the second time at all. I wondered, too, since no one had asked me to advise or assist on anything important during my pleasant twenty-month stay at the Embassy, which is to be turned into a hospital if and when Germany's capital is ever moved back to Berlin.

A month after my discharge in Frankfurt I was back in Bad Godesberg, sitting on a couple of cases of beer in a low-ceilinged room that once had been a *Gaststätte*. It had been gutted by fire, and I signed a long lease with the owner on the understanding that he was to provide only the basic repairs; any additional redecorating and improvement would be at my own expense. I sat there on the beer cases, surrounded by boxes of fixtures, furniture, and unpacked glasses, nursing a bottle of Scotch, and filling out on a portable typewriter my eighth application in sextuplicate for permission to sell food and drink—all by the warm glow of a kerosene lamp. The electricity would take another application.

When he came in, he came in quietly. He could have been there only a minute or he could have been there ten. I jumped when he spoke.

"You McCorkle?"

"I'm McCorkle," I said, keeping on with my typing.

"You got a nice place here."

I turned around to look at him. "Christ—a Yalely."

He was about five-eleven and would have weighed in at around 160. He dragged up a case of beer to sit on, and the way he moved reminded me of a Siamese tom I had once owned named Pajama Cord.

"New Jersey, not New Haven," he said.

He wore the uniform well: the crew-cut black hair; the young, tanned, friendly face; the soft tweed three-button jacket with a button-down shirt and regimental-striped tie that sported a knot the size of a Thompson seedless grape. He also had on plain-toed cordovan shoes that gleamed blackly in the lamp's light. I didn't see his socks, but I assumed that they weren't white.

"Princeton, maybe?"

He grinned. It was a smile that almost reached his eyes. "You're getting warm, friend. Really the Blue Willow Bar and Grill in Jersey City. We had a dandy shuffleboard crowd on Saturday nights."

"So what can I do for you besides offering a beer case to sit on and a drink on the house?" I passed him the Scotch and he took two long gulps without bothering to wipe the neck of the bottle. I thought that was polite.

He passed it back to me and I took a drink. He waited until I lighted a cigarette. He seemed to have plenty of time.

"I'd like a piece of this place."

I looked around at the shambles. "A piece of nothing is nothing."

"I'd like to buy in. Half."

"Just like that, huh?"

"Just like that."

I picked up the Scotch and handed it to him and he took another drink and then I had another one.

"Maybe you'd like a little earnest money?" he said.

"I don't think I mentioned it."

"I've heard it talks," he said, "but I never paid much attention." He reached into his jacket's inside breast pocket and pulled out a piece of paper that looked very much like a check. He handed it to me. It was a check and it was drawn in dollars on a New York bank. It was certified. It had my name on it. And it was exactly half of the nut I needed to open the doors of Bonn's newest and friendliest bar and grill.

I handed it back to him. "I don't need a partner. I'm not looking for one."

He took the check, stood up, walked over to the table where the typewriter was, and laid it on the typewriter. Then he turned and looked at me. There was no expression on his face.

"How about another drink?" he asked.

I handed him the bottle. He drank and handed it back. "Thanks. Now I'm going to tell you a story. It won't take long, but when I'm through you'll know why you have a new partner."

I took a drink. "Go ahead. I've got another bottle in case we run dry."

His name, he said, as he sat there talking in the cluttered, half-lighted room, was Michael Padillo. He was half Estonian, half Spanish. His father had been an attorney in Madrid who chose the losing side during the civil war and was shot in 1937. His mother was the daughter of an Estonian doctor. She had met Padillo senior in Paris in 1925 while on a holiday. They were married and he, the son, was born the following year. His mother had been a striking, even beautiful, woman of considerable culture and accomplishment.

After the death of her husband she used her Estonian passport to reach Lisbon and eventually Mexico City. There she survived by teaching piano and giving language lessons in French, German, English and, occasionally, Russian.

"If you can speak Estonian, you can speak anything," Padillo said. "She spoke eight without accent. She told me once that the first three languages are the hardest. One month we would speak nothing but English, the next month French. Then German or Russian or Estonian or Polish and back to Spanish or Italian and then start the whole thing over. I was young enough to think it was fun."

Padillo's mother died of tuberculosis in the spring of 1941. "I was fifteen then and I spoke six languages, so I said to hell with Mexico and headed for the States. I got as far as El Paso. I became a bellhop, a guide, and a part-time smuggler. I also picked up the fundamentals of bartending.

"By mid-1942 I decided that El Paso had offered all it was going to. I got a Social Security card and a driver's license and registered for the draft although I was still under age. I swiped a couple of letterheads from two of the better hotels and wrote myself glowing recommendations as a bartender. I forged the managers' names on both of them."

He hitchhiked through the Big Bend country of Texas up to Albuquerque, where he caught 66 all the way to Los Angeles. Padillo talked about Los Angeles in its palmy, scared, war-feverish days of 1942 as if it were a personal but long-lost Beulah Land.

"It was a crazy town, full of phonies, dames, soldiers and nuts. I got a job tending bar. It was a nice place, they treated me well, but it only lasted a little while before they caught up with me."

"Who?"

"The FBI. It was August of 1942 and I was just opening up. The pair of them. Polite as preachers. They showed me their little black passbooks that said sure enough they were with the FBI and asked if I would mind coming along because the draft board had been writing letters to me for the longest time and they kept coming back marked 'address unknown.' And they were sure it was a mistake, but it had taken them five goddamn months to trace me and so forth.

"Well, I went downtown with them and gave a story of sorts. I made a statement and signed it. I was mugged and fingerprinted. And then they took me in to see an assistant U.S. attorney general and he gave me a lecture and a choice. I could either join up or go to jail for draft evasion."

Padillo joined the Army and applied for cooks and bakers school. In late 1942 he was happily running the bar of an officers' club at a small Infantry Training Replacement Center in north Texas, not too far from Dallas and Fort Worth, before someone, browsing through his records, discovered that he could speak and write six languages.

"They came at night," he said. "The top sergeant and the C.O. and this jerk in civilian clothes. It was all very bad, late TV. The olive-drab Packard, the silent ride to the airport, the tight-lipped pilots glancing at their watches while they paced up and down under the wing of the C-47. Pure corn."

The plane landed in Washington and Padillo was shuffled from office to office. "Some of them were dressed in civilian clothes, some in uniform. I seem to remember that they all smoked pipes that year."

They tested him on his languages. "I can speak English with either a Mississippi or an Oxford accent. I can talk like a Berliner or a Marseille pimp. Berlitz would love me.

"They sent me to Maryland then, where I learned some tricks and I taught them a few I'd picked up in Juárez. It was all very gung-ho with assumed names and identities. I said I was a towel boy in a Mexican whorehouse. The rest of the guys never busted me, but they liked to ask detailed questions about my occupation."

When the Maryland training was over, Padillo was hustled back to Washington. It was a house on R Street, just west of Connecticut Avenue. They told him the colonel wanted to see him. "He looked very much like the Hollywood actor who used to play the colonel in all the VD movies they showed you in basic," Padillo said. "I think it embarrassed him.

"He told me that I could make a very important contribution to what he called the 'national effort.' If I would agree to do so, I would be discharged, given American citizenship, and a certain amount of money would be paid to an account in my name at the American Security and Trust Company. I could collect the money when I got back.

"So I asked him back from where.

" 'Paris,' he said, sucked on his pipe, and stared out the window. He was having a fine time for a former assistant professor of French at Ohio State."

Padillo spent two years in France with the underground, most of the time in Paris, where he operated as American liaison with the Maquis. After the war they shipped him back to the States. He collected his money from the bank, was handed a draft card that said he was 4-F, and received a discreet pat on the back from the General himself.

"I headed for L.A. It was still wacky in 1945, but it wasn't like it was. But perhaps the reason I liked it is because it was so goddamned phony. I'd had enough of reality.

"I also had enough money so I could hang around the strip for a while. I got a few jobs as an extra and then started bartending in this small place on Santa Monica. I was even buying in when they came. You know: young, single-breasted suits, hats. They had a little job, they said, that would take two or three weeks. In Warsaw. Nobody would ever know I was gone, and there was a couple of grand in it for me."

Padillo ground his cigarette out on the floor and lighted another. "I went. That time and maybe two dozen times more, and the last time they came around in their dark suits and their fraternity-house manners I told them no. They just got even more polite and reasonable and kept coming back. They started dropping hints about the fact that some question had been raised in Washington about the validity of my citizenship, but they were sure that if I took on this one more job everything could be straightened out.

"I got back part of the money I had invested in the place and headed east. I was working in Denver at the Senate Lounge on Colfax and they found me there. So I went to Chicago and from Chicago to Pittsburgh and from there to New York. In New York I heard about this place in Jersey. It was nice and it was quiet. Some college kids, some neighborhood traffic. I made the down payment."

It was completely dark outside. The kerosene lantern gave off its soft warm glow. The Scotch bottle was getting low. The silence seemed thick and thoughtful.

"They came once more, and that time they weren't polite. So now I'm doing to you what they did to me. I need a cover in Bonn, and you've been thoughtful enough to provide a perfect one."

"What if I say no?"

Padillo looked at me cynically. "Been having a little trouble getting the necessary permits and licenses approved and issued?"

"A little."

"You'd be surprised how easy it is if you have the right connections. But if you still insist on saying no, the odds are five hundred to one that you'll never sell your first Martini."

"It's like that, huh?"

Padillo sighed. "Yes. It's exactly like that."

I took another drink and shrugged a shrug I did not feel. "O.K. It looks as if I have a partner."

Padillo looked down at the floor. "I'm not sure I wanted you to say that, but then again I'm not sure I didn't. You were in Burma, weren't you?"

I said yes.

"Behind the lines?"

I nodded.

"There were some tough boys there."

I nodded again. "I learned a little."

"It might come in handy."

"How?"

He grinned. "Tossing out the drunks on Saturday night." He got up and walked over to the typewriter, picked up the certified check and handed it to me again. "Let's go over to the club and spend some of this on getting stoned. They won't like it, of course, but there's not a hell of a lot they can do about it."

"Should I ask who 'they' are?"

"No. Just remember you're the cloak and I'm the dagger."

"I think I can keep that straight."

Padillo said, "Let's get that drink."

We got drunk that night, but before we entered the club's bar Padillo picked up a phone and made a call. All he said was "It's all right." Then he cradled the phone and looked at me thoughtfully. "You poor bastard," he said. "I don't think you really deserve it."

CHAPTER 3

During the next decade we prospered, adding such symbols of success as a touch of gray at the temples, a series of fast expensive cars, another series of fast expensive young ladies, bench-made shoes, London suits and jackets, and a comfortable inch or so around the waists.

There were also those certain days when I would drop down to the place around ten in the morning to find Padillo already sitting at the bar, a quart of dimple-bottle in front of him, staring into the mirror.

All he ever said was "I got one."

All I ever asked was "How long?" He would say two weeks or ten days or a month and I would say: "Right." It was very clipped, very British, just like Basil Rathbone and David Niven in *Dawn Patrol.* Then I would help myself to the bottle and we would both sit there, staring into the mirror. I think it always rained those days.

We had made a good business team after Padillo taught me the fundamentals of saloon-keeping. He was an excellent host, and his ease with languages made the place a favorite with the embassy staffs in Bonn, including the Russians, who sometimes came by in twos and threes. I ran the business end, and our accounts at Deutsche Bank in Bad Godesberg grew pleasantly fat.

To compensate for Padillo's "business trips" I occasionally flew to

London and the States, presumably in search of new ideas. I came back loaded with catalogues of kitchen equipment, eye-catching contemporary furniture, and cocktail-time gimmicks. But we didn't change the place. It just grew a little shabbier and a little more relaxed. The customers seemed to like it that way.

The trip to Berlin presumably had been on business. I had gone there to see about a bartender who could mix drinks American style. He was working at the Berlin Hilton, but when I told him he would have to live in Bonn, he refused. "Those Rhinelanders are jerks," he said, and went on carving up Mr. Hilton's oranges.

Herr Maas kept up his chatter as I drove through the narrow streets of Godesberg and parked in one of the two reserved spaces in front of Mac's Place that Padillo had managed to wrangle from the city fathers. We got out and Herr Mass was still murmuring his thanks as I held the door for him. It was three-thirty in the afternoon, too early for the cocktail hour. Inside the place was as dim and dark as always, and Herr Maas blinked to adjust his eyes. At table number six in the far corner a man sat, a glass before him. Maas thanked me once more and headed toward him. I moved to the bar where Padillo stood watching Karl, the bartender, polish some glasses that didn't need polishing.

"How was Berlin?"

"Very wet," I said, "and he didn't like Rhinelanders."

"A home-town boy, I take it?"

"Very."

"Drink?"

"Just some coffee."

Hilde, a cocktail-hour waitress, came up and ordered a Steinhaeger and a Coke for Herr Maas and the man he came to Bonn to meet. They were the only customers in the place.

"Who's your friend?" Padillo asked, nodding toward Maas.

"A fat little man who carries a big fat gun. He says his name is Maas."

"I don't care for guns," Padillo said, "but I care less for the company he keeps."

"Know him?"

"Just who he is. Vaguely attached to the Jordanian Embassy."

"Trouble?"

"Something like that."

Karl slid my coffee over to me.

"You ever hear of a seven-layer mint frappe?" he said.

"Only in New Orleans."

"Maybe that's where this chick was from. She comes in at lunch and orders one. Mike never taught me to make no seven-layer mint frappe."

"*A* seven-layer mint frappe," I said automatically. A war orphan, Karl had picked up his English just outside the Army's huge PX in Frankfurt, where, in his early teens, he had made a precarious living by buying cigarettes from soldiers and selling them on the black market. He was a good bartender, but his grammar needed a little polish. His Americanese had virtually no German accent.

"So what did you do?" I asked.

He didn't get the chance to say. Padillo grabbed me by the left shoulder, kicked my legs out from under me, and slammed me to the floor. I turned as I fell and glimpsed the pair of them, faces covered with white handkerchiefs, running toward the table where Maas and his friend sat. They fired four shots and the sound hurt my sinus cavities. Padillo had fallen on top of me. We got up in time to see Herr Maas darting out the door, his shabby brief case banging against his fat legs. Hilde, the cocktail waitress, stood frozen in a corner, a tray forgotten in her hand. Then she screamed and Padillo snapped at Karl to go over and shut her up. Karl, pale under his sun-lamp tan, moved quickly from around the bar and began talking to the girl in what he intended to be soothing words. They only seemed to make her more upset, but she at least stopped screaming.

Padillo and I went over to the table where Herr Maas and his late friend had sat. The friend was sprawled back in his chair, his eyes staring fixedly at the ceiling, his mouth slightly open. It was too dark to see any blood. He had been in life a small, dark man with smooth black hair that was combed straight back in a pompadour with no part. His features were sharp with a hooked nose and a weak chin that seemed to have been in need of a shave. He may have been quick in his movements, volatile in his talk. Now he was just dead—only a dummy that presented problems.

Padillo looked at him without expression. "They'll probably find four slugs right in his heart in a two-inch group. They seemed like pros."

I could still smell the shots. "You want me to call the Polizei?"

Padillo looked at me absently and gnawed some on his lower lip. "I wasn't here, Mac," he said. "I was down in Bonn having a beer. Or up on Petersberg checking the opposition. Just so I wasn't here. They wouldn't have liked me to be here, and I've got to catch a plane tonight."

"I can fix it with Hilde and Karl. The kitchen help's still on their afternoon break, aren't they?"

Padillo nodded. "We've got time for a quick one before you call." We walked over to the bar and Padillo went behind it and took down the dimpled bottle of Haig. He poured two stiff ones. Karl was still over in the corner making soothing noises to Hilde, and I noticed his hands were patting the right places.

"After I catch that plane tonight, I should be back in ten days, maybe two weeks."

"Why don't you tell them you've come down with a bad cold?"

Padillo took a swallow of his drink and smiled. "I don't much care for this trip. It's a little more than routine."

"Anything else I should know?"

He looked as if he wanted to say something; then he shrugged. "No. Nothing. Just keep me clean. Give me two minutes and then call the cops. O.K.?"

He finished his drink and came around from the bar. "Have fun," I said.

"Same to you."

We didn't shake hands. We never did. I watched Padillo go out the door. He didn't seem to walk as quickly as he once had. He seemed to stand just a little less straight.

I finished my drink, walked over and helped comfort Hilde for a moment, and fixed it up with her and Karl about how Padillo wasn't there when the small dark man had had his last drink of Coca-Cola. Then I walked over to the bar, picked up the phone, and called the police.

After that I sat down at the bar and wondered about Padillo and where he was going. I thought about that, but not too much. Then I wondered about Herr Maas and his slight, dark friend and about the masked pair who came in and stopped him from living. By the time the police arrived I was wondering about myself, and I was glad when they came so I could stop that and start lying about something else.

CHAPTER 4

They arrived in grand style: their oogah siren heralded their arrival by a full two minutes—plenty of time for a competent second-story man to make it down the back stairs and out into the alley. Two jack-booted, green uniformed troopers burst in batting their eyes against the dark. Number one stalked over to the bar and asked if I was the citizen who had telephoned. When I said yes, he turned and proudly announced the fact to number two and a couple of men in civilian clothes who had also moved in. One of the non-uniformed policemen nodded at me and then they all went over to look at the body.

I glanced at my watch. Seventeen minutes had passed since the dark little man had been shot. While the police were looking at the body for clues or whatever they do I smoked a cigarette. By now Karl was behind the bar again and Hilde was standing near the door crumpling her apron.

"You fixed it with Hilde?"

Karl nodded. "She hasn't seen him all day."

One of the two plainclothes men detached himself from the group that was fiddling with the body and moved to the bar.

"You are Herr McCorkle?" he asked, giving my name a fine gutteral pronunciation.

"That's correct. I called just after it happened."

"I'm Lieutenant Wentzel."

We shook hands. I asked him if he would like a drink. He said he would have a brandy. We waited while Karl poured it, said *prosit*, and he drank. Then back to business.

"You saw this happen?" Wentzel asked.

"Some of it. Not all."

He nodded, his blue eyes direct and steady, his mouth a thin straight line that offered neither sympathy nor suspicion. He could have been asking about how the fender got dented.

"Please, would you mind telling me what happened just as you remember it? Omit nothing, no matter how trivial."

I told it to him as it had happened from the time I left Berlin, leaving out only Padillo's presence, which I suppose was something less than trivial. While I talked the technical crew came in, took pictures, dusted for fingerprints, examined the body, put it on a stretcher, threw a blanket over it, and carted it off to wherever they take dead bodies. The morgue, I suppose.

Wentzel listened carefully but took no notes. I guessed that he had that kind of mind. He never prompted or asked a question. He merely listened, occasionally glancing at his fingernails. They were clean, and so was the white shirt whose widespread collar was plugged by a double-Windsor knot tied into a brown-and-black tie. It didn't do much for his dark-blue suit. He had shaved sometime during the day and he smelled faintly of lotion.

I finally ran down, but he kept on listening. The silence grew and I resisted the temptation to add a little frosting here and there. I offered him a cigarette, which he accepted.

"Uh—this man Maas?"

"Yes."

"You had never seen him before?"

"Never."

"But yet he managed to meet you on the plane at Tempelhof, became friendly with you, secured a ride with you to Godesberg—in fact, to exactly the same destination—and here you observed him running from your establishment after his companion had been shot. Is this not true?"

"That's what happened."

"Of course," Wentzel murmured, "of course. But do you not think, Herr McCorkle, do you not think it is something of a coincidence—indeed, an amazing coincidence—that this man should sit next to *you*, that *you* should offer him a ride, that he should be going to *your* establishment, where he was to meet a man who was to be killed?"

"It had struck me that way," I said.

"Your partner, Herr Padillo, was not here?"

"No; he's away on a business trip."

"I see. If this man Maas attempts to get in touch with you by some fashion, you will notify us immediately?"

"You'll be the first."

"And tomorrow would it be possible for you to come down to our bureau to sign a statement? It will be necessary for your employees to come also. At eleven hours, shall we say?"

"Good. Anything else?"

He looked at me carefully. He would remember my face ten years from now.

"No," he said. "Not for the present."

I offered the other three a drink; they looked at Wentzel, who nodded. They ordered brandy and drank it at a gulp. It was just as well. Karl had not poured the best. We shook hands all around and Wentzel marched off into the afternoon. I stared at the corner table where Maas and his friend had sat. There was nothing there now. Just some tables and chairs that almost looked inviting.

If it weren't for money, I told myself, I would sell out and go to Santa Fe or Kalispell and open a bar where the only problem would be how to get old Jack Hudson back to the ranch of a Saturday night. But there is a lot of difference in saloon-keeping. Here in the shadow of the Siebengebirge, in the purple shadows of the seven hills where once lived Snow White and the Seven Drawfs and where Siegfried slew the fearsome dragon, I was more or less the Sherman Billingsley of the Rhine. A community fixture, friend and confidant of minister and jackanapes alike. Respected. Even admired.

I was also making a great deal of money and could probably retire at forty-five. The fact that my partner was a spook for busybodies who flitted about looking under God knows what rocks for the blueprints of the Russians' next spaceship to Saturn was incidental—even trifling. And the fact that my place was actually our place—the spooks and I— and the fact that they used it, for all I knew, as an international message center with the secret codes imbedded in the Gibson onions—all this would only serve as cocktail conversation over a couple of tall cold ones at the Top of the Mark in the good days to come.

And the fact that two masked desperadoes burst into the saloon, shot some little man dead, and then walked out followed by a fat stranger I met on a plane would only serve to lend an air of international glamour and intrigue: a decided asset. It was like postwar Vienna in the movies, where Orson Welles went around muttering so low and fast you couldn't understand what he was saying except that he was up to no good.

There was the money. And the good cars. And the imported clothes, the thick steaks, and the choice wines that came gratis to my table, the gifts of friendly cellars from the Moselle, the Ahr and the Rhine. And then there was the fact that Bonn abounded in women. With that cheery thought I took down my mental "for sale" sign, told Karl to watch the cash register, checked to see that the chef was sober, and went out into the street, bound for the apartment of an interesting young lady who went by the name of Fredl Arndt.

CHAPTER 5

It was around six-thirty when I arrived at Fräulein Doktor Arndt's apartment, which was on the top floor of a ten-story *hochaus* that commanded a splendid view of the Rhine, the Seven Hills, and the red crumbling ruins of the castle called Drachenfels.

I rang her bell, told her who it was over the almost inaudible intercommunication system, and pushed open the thick glass door as she rang the unlocking buzzer. She was waiting for me at her door as I stepped out of the elevator, which happened to be working that day.

"*Guten Abend*, Fräulein Doktor," I murmured, bending low over her hand, a continental touch that had taken me a few rainy afternoons to perfect under the watchful eye of an old Hungarian countess who had taken a shine to me when she had learned I ran a saloon. I had brushed up on my manners while the countess had run up a sizeable bar bill. We had parted, mutually satisfied.

Fredl smiled. "What brings you around, Mac? Sober, I mean."

"There's a cure for that," I said, handing her a bottle of Chivas Regal.

"You're in time for the early show. I was going to wash my hair. After that I was going to bed."

"You already have an engagement then?"

"Solo. For a girl on the wrong side of thirty in this town it's the usual way."

While it was true that the female population greatly outnumbered the tired but happy male population of Bonn that year, Fredl wasn't one of those who sat by the phone hoping that it would ring so she could go to the junior prom. She was distinctively pretty in that European way that seems to wear almost forever and then changes slowly into beauty. And she was smart. The Fräulein Doktor title was real. She covered politics for one of the Frankfurt papers, the intellectual one, and she had spent a year in Washington, most of the time on the White House assignment.

"Fix us a drink. It makes the years slough away. You'll feel like sixteen."

"I was sixteen in 'forty-nine and part of a teenage gang that played the black market with GI cigarettes to work our way through school."

"At least you weren't a loner."

She retired with the bottle into the kitchenette. The apartment was a large one-room affair that boasted a small balcony for the sunworshipers. One wall was lined with books from floor to ceiling. In front of them stood a huge antique desk that I had thought of marrying the girl for. There were also a pale-beige carpet, two sofa beds, some good Swedish chairs and a small dining table. The wall along the balcony was all glass and the other two walls were hung with some good prints and some outspoken originals. It wasn't a place just to hang your hat. Somebody lived there.

Fredl placed the drinks on a low ebony cocktail table that seemed to float in the air because of its cleverly concealed legs. She sat next to me on the couch and kissed me on the temple.

"You're getting grayer and grayer, Mac. You're getting old."

"Nothing soon but memories. When all of us old geezers gather around the corner bar in a few years to spend our Social Security checks and start wheezing and drooling to each other about all the girls we've laid, I'll just let that film of memory descend and mutter, 'Bonn, lovely, lovely Bonn.' "

"Whom do you know in the States, Mac?"

I thought a minute. "Nobody, really. Nobody I want to see. A couple of reporters and embassy types perhaps, but I met them over here. I had a doting and dotty great aunt I was fond of, but she died years ago. That's where I got the money to open the saloon. Or part of it."

"Then where's your home now?"

I shrugged. "I was born in San Francisco, but, hell, that's nobody's home town. I like New York and Chicago. I like Denver. I even like Washington and London and Paris. Padillo thinks Los Angeles is Paradise-west. If he had his way he'd have the Autobahn run right through the heart of Bonn and plant palm trees along the verge."

"How is Mike?"

"Fine. Off on a trip."

"And how was Berlin, rat? You knew I had a couple of days off."

"A pure and unsuccessful business venture, laced with too many Martinis—and an assassination waiting for me when I got back."

Fredl had nestled her head on my shoulder. Her blond hair tickled my ear. It smelled clean and feminine and fresh. I didn't see why it needed washing. I let the comment sink in and she sat up with a jerk. I almost spilled my drink.

"You're kidding me again."

"Well, it happened like this. Two men came in and shot another one. Dead." I sat back and drew on my cigarette. Suddenly Fredl was all reporter. She fired questions and didn't take any notes either, and I had a hard time deciding whether Fräulein Doktor Arndt or Lieutenant Wentzel knew more about the killing. It was probably a draw.

"Does Mike know?" she asked.

"I haven't seen him today," I lied. "He'll probably think it's good for business. And God knows the correspondents will descend on us tomorrow at lunch. By the time they stagger out there'll be a dozen theories and inside stories ranging from a political assassination to a grudge killing by a couple of superannuated SS members."

"It depends upon the paper they work for," Fredl said.

"And the number of drinks they've had."

"It might be interesting at that. Buy me lunch tomorrow?"

"Sure."

"Now you can kiss me again."

"I haven't kissed you for the first time yet."

"I'm too proud to admit it."

I kissed her and, like always, it was as if I were kissing her for the first time—as if everything were new and we both were very, very young but had been born into the world with a postgraduate degree in technique.

"Get the light, darling," Fredl whispered.

"Both of them?"

"Just the one. You know I like to see what I'm doing."

I left Fredl reluctantly at four A.M. She was sleeping, a slight smile on her lips, her face slightly flushed but relaxed. The bed looked warm and inviting. For a long moment I was tempted to lie down again. Instead I padded barefooted and buck-naked into the kitchen, groped for the Scotch bottle, took a long drink, and moved back into the living room, where I dressed quietly. I leaned over and kissed Fredl gently on the forehead. She didn't stir. That irritated me, so I kissed her again, this time on the lips. She wriggled and opened her eyes and smiled.

"I just wanted you to know what you're missing," I said.

"Are you leaving, darling?"

"I must."

"Come back to bed. Please."

"Can't. I have to see the police again. Don't forget lunch."

She smiled and I kissed her again. "Go back to sleep," I said. She smiled again, drowsy and content. I let myself out, rode the elevator down, and got into the car.

At four in the morning Bonn seems like an abandoned Hollywood

26

set. In fact, most of the good burghers have bolted the doors by ten, unmindful of—even indifferent to—the fact that theirs is one of the world's most important capitals. In some respects, Bonn is very much like Washington. So I made it from Fredl's place to mine in something less than ten minutes, a new kind of record, considering that we lived a good six miles apart. I parked the car in the garage, closed and locked the overhead door, and walked up the steps to my apartment.

After five moves in eight years I finally had an apartment that suited. Up in the hills outside Muffendorf, it was a duplex built by a bicycle manufacturer from Essen who had struck it rich in the early 1950s, when bicycles were the major form of personal transportation in post-war Germany. He had a penchant for contemporary architecture, but as a widower he spent most of his time following the girls and the sun. I think he was in Florida then, or it may have been Mexico. His frequent and prolonged absences gave me the privacy I wanted, and even when he was in Germany he spent a great portion of his time gossiping with cronies in the cafés of Düsseldorf—or just watching the girls walk by. He was a Social Democrat, and sometimes we would sit around, drink beer, and speculate on how long it would be before Willy Brandt was Chancellor.

The house was a two-level affair, built of dark-red stone with a shake-shingle shed roof, and it had what my parents would have called a veranda running the full length of two sides. The owner had the smaller, lower flat; I had the upper one, which consisted of a bedroom, a small study, a kitchen and a large living room with a fireplace. I had to walk up twelve steps to reach my front door. I climbed the steps and put the key in the lock and turned. The voice came from the deep shadows to my left.

"Good morning, Herr McCorkle. I've been waiting for you for quite some time."

It was Maas.

I shoved the door open. "The cops are looking for you."

He moved out of the shadows. In one hand he carried his familiar briefcase, in the other he held the Luger. It wasn't pointed at me. He just held it loosely at his side.

"I know. A regrettable affair. I'm afraid that I must invite myself in."

"That's nice," I said. "The bath's on the right and there are fresh towels in the linen closet. Breakfast is at ten, and if there's anything special you want, just tell the maid."

Maas sighed. "Your English is very fast, Herr McCorkle, but it seems you are making a joke. I think it is a joke, *ja?*"

"I guess so."

Maas sighed again. "Shall we go in? You first, if you do not mind."

"I don't mind."

We went in—me first. I walked over to the bar and poured myself a drink. Maas watched with a disapproving manner. Perhaps it was because I didn't offer him one. To hell with him. It was my booze.

I drank the first one and then poured another. Then I sat down in an easy chair, put one leg over the arm, and lighted a cigarette. I thought I was putting on a very good show. Calm, nonchalant. The epitome of the sophisticated barkeep. Maas stood in the middle of the room, fat, middle-aged and tired. The briefcase was clutched in one hand, the Luger still dangled from the other. The brown suit was rumpled; his hat was gone. I said: "Oh, hell. Put the gun down and go fix yourself a drink." He looked at the gun as if he had just grown a second thumb and tucked it away in his shoulder holster. He fixed himself a drink.

"Please, may I sit down?"

"Put your feet up. Make yourself at home."

"You have a very nice apartment, Herr McCorkle."

"Thank you. I chose it for its privacy."

He sipped his drink. His gaze wandered around the room. "I suppose you're wondering at my presence."

That didn't seem to call for an answer.

"The police are searching for me, you know?"

"I know."

"That unfortunate occurrence of the afternoon."

"It was especially unfortunate because it happened in my bar. Just for the sake of curiosity, who selected the rendezvous—you or your late friend?"

He looked at me thoughtfully. "This is excellent whiskey, Herr McCorkle."

I noticed his glass was empty. "Help yourself."

He walked over to the bar and turned his back on me as he poured. I looked at it and thought it would make a fine target for a knife, if I had a knife and could remember how to throw it. Or I could slug him with the poker. Or throw a hammer lock on him. There were a lot of things I could do, but I kept sitting in the chair, sipping the Scotch, smoking the cigarette, the perfect picture of inaction stemming from indecision. Maas turned; glass in hand, and walked wearily across the room to sink back into the easy chair. He took a sip of his drink and sighed his appreciation. He seemed to be full of sighs that evening.

"It has been such a long day," he said.

"Now that you bring it up, I must agree. I'm also sorry to pull the 'here's your hat, what's your hurry' routine, but I'm tired. I've got a date downtown this morning with the police, who want to ask me some questions. Then there's the question of running the saloon. That's how I make my living. So if you don't mind, I'd appreciate it very much— you don't know how much—if you would just kind of bug off."

Maas smiled wanly. "I'm afraid that's impossible. At least for a few hours. I need a place to sleep, and your couch here will do nicely. I shall be gone by noon."

"Fine. I'll be with the cops by eleven hours. I'm not the silent type. I like to talk. I won't mind telling them that you're curled up on my couch in a tight little ball."

Maas spread his hands in apology. "But I'm afraid that's impossible. As I said, much as I wish to accommodate you I'm afraid that I must stay here until noon. My appointment is not until then. It is safe here."

"It won't be when I blow the whistle on you."

"You won't do that, Herr McCorkle," Maas said softly. "You won't do that at all."

I stared at him. "You have a hole card, huh?"

"I have sources, Herr McCorkle. Within the police. These sources have access to certain conversations, certain files. In one of these files was a copy of the report the police lieutenant filed this evening. You told what happened quite faithfully and in detail with one exception. You neglected to mention that your partner—Herr Padillo, is it not?— was also present. That, Herr McCorkle, was a serious omission."

"That won't buy you bed and board here for two seconds. I'll just tell them I forgot. I'll even tell them I lied."

Maas sighed again. "Let me put it another way—and may I have another drop of your excellent whiskey?"

I nodded. He got up and waddled across to the bar, again turning his back, and again I thought about the knife, the poker or the hammer lock. Or just a swift kick in the rear. And again I sat comfortably in my chair, watching the fat German drink my whiskey, the thought of violence heavy and distasteful, the guilt of inaction rationalized by a growing curiosity.

Maas turned from the bar and went back to the chair. "As I said, it seems that I must put it another way. You failed to report that your partner was present at the lamentable affair. I could report this to the police through a telephone call—not even a disguised voice—just a word or two. That, in chess terms, is check." Maas leaned forward in his chair, his round red potato face shiny and a little flushed from the drink and fatigue. "But this I know, too, Herr McCorkle. I know where Herr Padillo is going and why. And that, I think you will agree, is checkmate."

CHAPTER 6

If it was a bluff, I decided not to call. I gave Maas a blanket, told him to go to hell, and went to bed. It wasn't the most restful night I've ever had.

Next morning I met Lieutenant Wentzel in his office. He seemed much the same. He sat behind a yellow oak desk that was decorated with a telephone, a blotter, and an in-and-out file that had nothing in either tray. He was wearing the same clothes except for a fresh white-on-white shirt and an apple-green tie. His fingernails were still clean and he had shaved again.

He indicated the chair in front of his desk. Another man, whom I did not meet, sat in a chair by the window. He didn't look at me. He looked out of the window. The view was the brick wall of some kind of factory or warehouse. He may have been counting the bricks.

I made a statement to a stenographer Wentzel called in. I kept it short and as brief as possible. Wentzel excused himself, and I sat there in the chair smoking cigarettes and putting them out on the floor. There was no ash tray. The room was painted the same green that map makers use. The floor was of oiled dark-brown wood. The ceiling was dirty white. It was a room where a government's work is done by the people it hires. It also had that sense of impermanency that most lower-echelon government offices have, probably because their occupants are on the way either up or down or out and they know that this job, this project, is only temporary. So there are no pictures of the wife and kids in the folding leather case, no personal items to make the office assume an air of permanency.

Wentzel came back with the secretary as I was finishing a cigarette. He read my statement to me. I had made it in German, and it seemed longer, more detailed, pedantic and methodical than I had thought. It had the peculiar sound of your own voice coming out of another's mouth.

"So does that seem correct to you, Herr McCorkle?"

"Yes."

"Your employees, the bartender and the waitress, have already been with us and have made similar statements. Would you like to read them?"

"Not unless they vary a great deal from mine."

"They do not." I took the pen he offered and signed three copies. The pen scratched a little. I handed it back to Wentzel.

"I assume you have not heard from the man Maas."

"No."

Wentzel nodded. He seemed neither surprised nor disappointed. "Your colleague, Herr Padillo. Was he overly concerned about yesterday's incident?"

There was no sense in being trapped. "I haven't talked to him yet. I imagine he will be concerned."

"I see." Wentzel stood up. I stood up. The man in the chair by the window remained seated, absorbed in the brick wall.

"If further developments occur that concern you, Herr McCorkle, we'll be in touch."

"Of course," I said.

"And should the man Maas make any attempt to reach you, I am sure you will let us know."

"Yes. I will."

"So. I believe that is all we need. Thank you." We shook hands. "*Auf wiedersehen.*"

"*Auf wiedersehen,*" I said.

"*Auf wiedersehen,*" said the man in the chair by the window.

Maas had been curled up asleep on the couch when I left my apartment that morning. For all I knew, he was still there. It was not yet noon, the time for his appointment. I walked out of the police station in downtown Bonn, around the corner, and into a *Bierstube.*

I stood at the bar with the rest of the morning drinkers and had a glass of Pils and a Weinbrand. I looked at my watch. It was eleven twenty-five. My appointment with Wentzel had taken less than twenty minutes. The Weinbrand was gone, but my beer glass was almost full. I decided on another brandy. "*Noch ein Weinbrand, bitte.*"

"*Ein Weinbrand,*" the bartender droned, and placed it before me with a flourish and a murmured "*zum Wohlsein.*"

It was time for sober reflection, for cunning and for foxylike wiliness. Here was McCorkle, the friendly saloon-keeper, pitted against some of the most fiendish minds in Europe. Maas, for example. He would have a fiendish mind. I thought of the short fat man and couldn't bring myself to dislike him, much less hate him. If I had worked at it, I probably could have found some excuses for his behavior. Then there was Padillo, off to God knows where. How well did I know Padillo? No better than the brother I never had. There were a lot of questions whose answers seemed not to lie in the bottom of a glass, so I went out into the street, got into my car, and headed for Godesberg.

The routine of opening the place, checking the menu, going over the accounts, and writing up purchase orders occupied the next half hour. Karl was at the bar, a trifle morose.

"I never lied to the fuzz before."

"You'll get a bonus."

"A lot of good that'll do me in jail."

"You're not going to jail. You're not important enough."

He ran a comb through his long blond hair. God knows who he was trying to look like that week. "Well, I've been thinking it over and I don't see why we have to lie about Mike."

"What do you mean 'we'?" I asked. "Have you been gassing with the help again?"

"I took Hilde home last night and she was upset and started asking questions."

"Was that before or after you laid her? I told you to keep away from the help. You're part of management." That made him feel good. "If she says anything again, just tell her Padillo's got woman trouble."

"That's no lie," Karl said.

"Tell her he's out of town because of a jealous husband. Tell her anything, but keep her quiet. And keep out of her pants."

"Ah, Christ. I told her already, but she's still worried."

"Tell her some more. Look, I'll tell you what. In Berlin I met this guy who knows where you can pick up a 1940 Lincoln Continental. It's in Copenhagen. It was shipped over just before the war and the owner hid it from the Krauts. You get Hilde off my back, and I'll finance it for you."

Karl was an old-car nut. He subscribed to all the magazines. He was driving a 1936 three-window Ford coupe that he had bought from an American GI for fifteen hundred DM. I think he was applying its eleventh coat of hand-rubbed lacquer. It had an Oldsmobile engine and could easily outdrag my Porsche. If I had offered him a gold mine, he wouldn't have been more pleased.

"You're kidding," he said.

"No. I'm not kidding. I ran into an Air Force captain who told me about it. The guy wants a thousand bucks or it. When this thing cools down I'll give you a thousand bucks and you can run over and bring it back by ferry. It runs O.K., he said."

"You'll loan me the dough, huh?"

"If you keep Hilde quiet."

"Sure, sure. What color is it?"

"Mix the Manhattans."

Karl wandered off in a happy daze and I sat down at one of the tables and lighted a cigarette. I thought about having a drink but decided against it. The time was a little after noon, too early for customers. I began to count the cigarette burns in a four-foot square on the left side of my chair. Then I counted them on the right side. There were sixteen in all. I thought about how much a new carpet would cost and decided it wasn't worth it. There was a firm in town that patched carpets, putting in little plugs of almost matching fiber over the burns. The drinks spilled would make the patches blend quickly enough. I decided to give them a ring.

I heard the door open from the street and saw the flash of sunlight as two men came in. One was vaguely attached to the U.S. Government. I didn't know the other. They didn't see me sitting there at the table, off to their left. They made the usual remarks about the catacombs as they made their way to the bar.

They ordered beer. When Karl served it, the one I had met asked, "Is Mr. McCorkle here?"

"He's sitting right over there, sir," Karl said.

I turned around in my chair. "May I help you?"

They picked up their drinks and came over. "Hell, McCorkle. I'm Stan Burmser. We met at General Hartsell's."

"I recall," I said, and shook hands.

"This is Jim Hatcher."

We shook hands.

I asked them to sit down and called to Karl to bring me coffee.

Nice place you have here, Mr. McCorkle," Hatcher said. He had a clipped, brisk voice that sounded like upper Michigan. I was probably wrong.

"Thanks."

"Mr. Hatcher and I would like to have a talk with you," Burmser said. He sounded like St. Louis. He looked around the room as if a dozen people were trying to catch his words.

"Sure," I said. "We have an office in back. Just bring your drinks with you."

We got up and paraded single file back to the office, which was a small room containing a desk, three filing cabinets, a typewriter, and three chairs. There was also a calendar of more than usual interest supplied by a Dortmund brewer.

"Sit down, gentlemen," I said, lowering myself into the chair behind the desk. "Cigarette?" Burmser took one. Hatcher shook his head. Then we all sat back sipping our drinks with Burmser and me blowing clouds of smoke toward Hatcher. He didn't seem to mind.

"Haven't seen much of you around the embassy circuit," Burmser said.

"A saloon makes a hermit out of you."

Hatcher was apparently convinced that we had observed enough of the social amenities. "The reason we're here, Mr. McCorkle, is to discuss with you what happened here yesterday."

"I see."

"Perhaps our identification would help." They both produced little black identification books, and I read them one at a time. It wasn't the CIA. It was better—or worse—depending upon your point of view. I passed them back.

"How can I help you?" I said pleasantly.

"We happen to know that your partner, Mr. Padillo, was here yesterday when the shooting took place."

"Yes."

"I think you can talk frankly with us," Burmser said.

"I'm trying to."

"We're not so much interested in the man who got killed: he was a small-time agent. We're more interested in the man he met here. A Herr Maas."

"What about him?"

"You met him on the plane coming back from Berlin yesterday," Burmser recited. "You struck up a conversation and then offered him a ride to your restaurant."

"I told all that to the police, to Lieutenant Wentzel."

"But you didn't tell Wentzel that Padillo was here."

"No; Mike asked me not to."

"I supposed you know that Padillo occasionally does some work for us?"

I took a long drink. "How long have you been in Bonn, Mr. Burmser?"

"Two and a half—three years."

"I've been here thirteen, not counting my time with MAAG. Look in your files. You should know how this place was opened. I was blackjacked into taking Padillo on as a partner. I'm not sorry I did. He's a damn good man when he's not studying airline schedules. I know he works for one of your outfits, but I never asked which one. I don't want to know. I don't want to get tangled up in *I Spy*."

I think Hatcher blushed a little, but Burmser kept boring in. "We're concerned about Padillo. He was to catch a flight yesterday. To Frankfurt. And then from Frankfurt to Berlin. But he went to Frankfurt by train; he wasn't on the flight to Berlin."

"So he missed a flight."

"This was a very important flight, Mr. McCorkle."

"Look," I said. "For all I know he was on Flight 487 to Moscow with a connection to Peiping. After he got the plans, he was to disguise himself as a coolie and take a sampan down to Hong Kong. Or maybe he met a broad in Frankfurt, bought himself a couple of fifths of Martell, and shacked up in the Savigny. I don't know where he is. I wish I did. He's my partner and I'd like him back. I never got used to the idea of being in business with a guy who caught more planes than a traveling salesman. I'd like him to get out of the spook business and help write up the menus and order the booze."

"Yes," Burmser said. "Yes, I can understand all that. But we have reason to believe that this man Maas had something to do with the fact that Padillo missed his flight to Berlin."

"Well, I think your belief is founded on faulty reasoning. Maas was at my place at four o'clock this morning carrying a brief case and a Luger and drinking my Scotch. When I left shortly before eleven he was still there snoring on my living-room couch."

Maybe they send them through a special school where they are taught not to express surprise or emotion. Perhaps they stick pins in each other and the one who says "ouch" gets a black star for the day. They showed no more surprise than if I had told them that it was nice this morning, but it looks like rain this afternoon.

"What did Maas say to you, McCorkle?" Hatcher asked. His voice was flat and not particularly friendly.

"I told him why I was going to boot his ass out and then he told me why I wasn't. He said he knew where Mike was going and why and that he'd let the Bonn police know that plus the fact that Mike was here when the shooting took place unless I let him spend the night. What the hell—I let him spend the night.

"He said he had an appointment at noon today. He didn't say where, I didn't ask."

"Was there anything else—anything at all?"

"He thanked me for the Scotch and I told him to go to hell. That's all. Absolutely all."

Hatcher started to recite. "After Padillo arrived at the Frankfurt Hauptbahnhoff he had a glass of beer. Then he made a phone call. He spoke to no one in person. He then went to the Savigny Hotel, where he checked into a room. He went up in the elevator and stayed in his room for eight minutes and then came down to the bar. He sat down at the table of a couple who have been identified an American tourists. This was at eight-fifteen. At eight-thirty he excused himself and went to the men's room, leaving his cigarette case and lighter on the table.

He never came back from the men's room, and that's the last trace we've had of him."

"So he's disappeared," I said. "What am I supposed to do? Just exactly what is it you want?"

Burmser ground his cigarette out into the ash tray. He frowned, and his tanned forehead developed four deep wrinkles. "Maas is important to Padillo," he said in the voice of the patient teacher to the mayor's retarded son. "First, because only he—besides us—knew Padillo was to catch that plane. And, second, because Padillo did not catch the plane."

He paused and then continued in the same patient voice. "If Maas knows of the particular assignment that Padillo is on, then we want to call it off. Padillo is of no use on it. His cover is blown."

"I take it you'd like him back," I said.

"Yes, Mr. McCorkle. We would like him back very much."

"And you think Maas knows what happened?"

"We think he's the key."

"O.K., if Maas drops by, I'll tell him to call you before he calls Lieutenant Wentzel. And if Padillo happens to give me a ring, I'll tell him you've asked after his health."

They both looked pained.

"If you hear from either, let us know, please," Hatcher said.

"I'll call you at the Embassy."

They not only looked pained but they seemed embarrassed.

Hatcher said, "Not at the Embassy Mr. McCorkle. We're not with the Embassy. Call us at this number." He wrote it down on a leaf from a notebook and handed it to me.

"I'll burn it later," I said.

Burmser smiled faintly. Hatcher almost did. They got up and left.

I finished my coffee, lighted a cigarette to get rid of its cold taste, and tried to determine why two of the town's top agents so suddenly had revealed their identities to me. In the years I had been operating the bar, none had given me the time of day. Now I was an insider, almost a fellow conspirator in their efforts to unravel the mystery of the vanished American agent. McCorkle, the seemingly innocuous barkeep, whose espionage tentacles reached from Antwerp to Istanbul.

There was also the equally discomforting knowledge that I was a prime patsy. To Maas I was the lazy, easygoing lout to be used as chauffeur and innkeeper. To Burmser and Hatcher I was a sometime convenience, useful in the past in a minor sort of way, an expatriate American who had to be fed just enough line to keep him on the hook. Give the story the ring of intrigue. Throw in the mysterious disappearance of his partner, who should have been bound for Berlin, a cyanide capsule tacked onto his back molar, a flexible stainless-steel throwing knife sewn into his fly.

I opened the desk and pulled out last month's bank statement. There was a zero or two missing, so I put the statement back. Not enough to go back to the States, not enough to retire on. Enough, maybe, for a couple of years in Paris or New York or Miami, living in a good hotel, eating well, enough for the right clothes and too much liquor. Enough for that, but not enough for anything else that would count. I ground out my cigarette and went back into the bar before I started fondling my collection of pressed flowers.

CHAPTER 7

The luncheon crowd had drifted in. The press was monopolizing the bar, killing the morning's hangover with beer, whiskey and pink gins. Most were British, with a sprinkling of Americans and Germans and French. For lunch they usually gathered at the American Embassy Club, where the prices were low, but occasionally they descended upon us. There were no certain dates that they dropped in, but by some sense of radar they all flocked together at noon, and if someone was missing, then he was tagged as the dirty kind of a son-of-a-bitch who was out digging up a story on his own.

None of them worked too hard. In the first place they were blanketed by the wire services. Secondly, an interesting trunk murder in Chicago—or Manchester, for that matter—could reduce a careful analysis of the SPD's chances in the forthcoming election to three paragraphs in the "News Around the World" column. They were a knowledgeable lot, however, usually writing a bit more than they knew, and never tipping a story until it was safely filed.

I signaled Karl to let the house buy a round of drinks. I said hello to a few of them, answered some questions about yesterday's shooting, and told them I didn't know whether or not it was a political assassination. They asked about Padillo and I told them he was out of town on business.

I wandered away and checked on reservations with Horst, who served as the maître d' and ran the waiters and the kitchen with rigid Teutonic discipline. The press crowd was good for another hour at the bar before they ate. Some of them would forget to. I continued to circulate, shook a few hands, counted the house, and moved back to the bar.

I spotted Fredl as she came through the door and walked over to meet her.

"Hello, Mac. Sorry I'm late."

"You want to join your friends at the bar?"

She glanced over and shook her head. "Not today. Thanks."

"I have a table for us in the corner."

When we were seated and drinks and lunch were ordered, Fredl looked at me with a flat, cold stare.

"What have you been up to?" she demanded.

"Why?"

"Mike had someone call me this morning. From Berlin. A man named Weatherby."

I took a sip of my drink and looked at the tip of my cigarette. "And?"

"He asked me to tell you that the deal has gone sour. That's one. Secondly, he said that Mike needs some Christmas help and soon. And, thirdly, he told me to ask you to check into the Berlin Hilton. He'll get in touch with you there. He also told me that you didn't have to stay in your room. He'd try the bar."

"Is that all?"

"That's all. He sounded as if he were in a hurry. Oh, yes, one more thing. He told me to tell you that you had better get this place swept. Also your apartment. He said Cook Baker would know whom you should call."

I nodded. "I'll get around to it after lunch. How about a brandy?"

I signaled Horst for two. One thing about owning your own restaurant: the service is excellent.

"What's it all about, damn you?" she said.

I shrugged. "It's no secret, I suppose. Padillo and I have been thinking about opening up another place in Berlin. Good tourist town. Lot of military. When I was up there I made a tentative deal. It looks as if it might have fallen through. So Mike wants me to come up."

"And the Christmas help? It's April."

"Padillo worries."

"You're lying."

I smiled. "I'll tell you about it sometime."

"You're going, of course."

"Why the 'of course'? Maybe I'll call Mike, maybe I'll write him a letter. I had the deal all set, and if he screwed it up in one day, then he can damn well unscrew it."

"You're still lying."

"Look, one of us has to be here to run the place. Padillo likes to travel more than I do. I'm sedentary. Like Mycroft Holmes, I'm devoid of energy or ambition. That's why I run a saloon. It's a fairly easy way to keep on eating and drinking."

Fredl rose. "You talk too much, Mac, and you don't lie well. You're a rotten liar." She opened her purse and tossed an envelope on the table. "There's your ticket. I'll send you a bill when you get back. The plane leaves Düsseldorf at eighteen hours. You've plenty of time to catch it." She learned over and patted my cheek. "Take care of yourself, *liebchen* honey. You can tell me some more lies when you get back."

I stood up. "Thanks for not pressing."

She looked up at me, her brown eyes wide and frank and tender. "I'll find out sometime. It might be at three o'clock in the morning, when you're relaxed and feel like talking. I'll wait till then. I have time." She turned and walked away. Horst darted over to open the door for her.

I sat down and took a sip of the brandy. Fredl hadn't finished hers, so I poured it into mine. Use it up, wear it out, make it do, do without. Even with booze. On one of the rare occasions when Padillo had mentioned what he termed his "other calling," he had said that one of the drawbacks was having to work with the Christmas help, which might be anything from the Army's CID to tourists armed with two Canons and a Leica and a fascination for the photogenic qualities of Czechoslovakian armament factories. They always seemed to get caught, and they invariably listed their occupation as student.

Circumstances, not will, determine action. I could ignore the airline ticket and Padillo's distress signal and sit there, cozy in my own little saloon, and get unpleasantly drunk. Or I could call Horst over, give him the keys to the cashbox, go home and pack, and then drive to Düsseldorf. I left the brandy and went over to the bar. The customers had gone and Karl was reading *Time*. He thought it was a funny magazine. I tended to agree.

"Where's Horst?"

"Out back."

"Call him."

He stuck his head through the door and yelled for Horst. The thin, ascetic little man marched sharply around the bar and up to me. I thought he was going to click his heels. Our relationship during the five years he had worked for us continued on a completely formal basis.

"Yes, Herr McCorkle?"

"You're going to have to take over for a few days. I'm going out of town."

"Yes, Herr McCorkle."

"How come?" Karl asked.

"None of your goddamned business," I snapped. Horst shot him a look of disapproval. We had given Horst five percent of the net, and he felt a certain proprietary regard toward the decisions of management.

"Anything else, Herr McCorkle?" Horst asked.

"Call up that firm that patches the carpet and see how much it will cost to get the cigarette burns out. If it's not too much, tell them to go ahead. Use your own judgment."

Horst beamed. "Yes, Herr McCorkle. May I ask how long you will be away?"

"A few days; maybe a week. Neither Mr. Padllio nor I will be here, so you'll have to run the place."

Horst almost saluted.

Karl said, "Christ, the way you guys run a business. What about the Continental, anyway?"

"When I get back."

"Sure. Swell."

I turned to Horst. "There will be a man, perhaps two who will be checking the telephones, probably tomorrow. Give them every cooperation."

"Of course, Herr McCorkle."

"Good. *Auf wiedersehen.*"

"*Auf wiedersehen*, Herr McCorkle," Horst said.

"See you around," Karl said.

I got in the car and drove six blocks to a twin of the apartment that Fredl lived in. I parked in an empty slot across the street and took the elevator up to the sixth floor. I knocked on 614, and after a few moments the door opened cautiously. An inch. A panel of a long lean pallid face peered at me.

"Come on in and have a drink." The voice was deep and mellow.

The door opened wide and I went into the apartment of Cook G. Baker, Bonn correspondent for an international radio news service called Global Reports, Inc. Baker was the one and only professed member of Alcoholics Anonymous in Bonn, and he was a backslider.

"Hello, Cooky. How's the booze barrier?"

"I just got up. Care to join me in an eye opener?"

"I think I'll pass."

The apartment was furnished in a haphazard manner. A rumpled day bed. A table or two and an enormous wingback chair that had a telephone built into one arm and a portable typewriter attached to a stand that swung like a gate. It was Cooky's office.

Around the room were carefully placed bottles of Ballantine's Scotch. Some were half full, others nearly so. It was Cooky's theory that when he wanted a drink he should only have to reach out and there it would be.

"Sometimes when I'm on the floor it's a hell of a long crawl to the kitchen," he once explained to me.

Cooky was thirty-three years old that year, and according to Fredl he was the most handsome man she had ever seen. He was a couple of inches over six feet, lean as a whippet, with a high forehead, a perfect nose and a wide mouth that seemed continually to be fighting a smile over some private joke. And he was immaculate. He wore a dark-blue sport shirt, a blue and yellow Paisley ascot, a pair of gray flannels that must have cost sixty bucks, and black loafers.

"Sit down, Mac. Coffee?"

"That'll do."

"Sugar?"

"If you have it."

He picked up one of the bottles of Scotch and disappeared into the kitchen. A couple of minutes later he handed me my coffee and then went back for his drink: a half-tumbler of Scotch with a milk chaser.

"Breakfast. Cheers."

"Cheers."

He took a long gulp of the Scotch and quickly washed it down with the milk.

"I fell off a week ago," he said.

"You'll make it."

He shook his head sadly and smiled. "Maybe."

"What do you hear from New York?" I asked.

"They're billing more than thirty-seven million a year now and the money is still being banked for me."

At twenty-six Cooky had been the boy wonder of Madison Avenue public-relations circles, a founder of Baker, Brickhill and Hillsman.

"I got on the flit and just couldn't get off," he had explained to me one gloomy night. "They wanted to buy out my interest, but in a moment of sobriety I listened to my lawyers and refused to sell. I've got a third of the stock. The more lushed I got, the more stubborn I became. Finally I made a deal. I would get out and they would bank my share of the profits for me. My attorneys handled the whole thing. I'm very rich and I'm very drunk and I know I'm never going to quit drinking and I know I'm never going to write a book."

Cooky had been in Bonn for three years. Despite Berlitz and a series of private tutors, he could not learn German. "Mental block," he had said. "I don't like the goddamn language and I don't want to learn it."

His job was to fill one two-minute news spot a day and occasionally do a live show. His sources were the private secretaries of anyone in town who might have a story. In methodical fashion he had seduced those who were young enough and completely charmed those who were over the edge. I had once spent an afternoon with him while he had gathered his news. He had sat in the big chair, the private-joke smile fighting to break through. "Wait," he had said. "In three minutes the phone will ring."

It had. First there had been the girl from the *Presse Dienst.* Then it was one who worked as a stringer for the *London Daily Express:* when her boss had a story, she made sure that Cooky had it too. The phone had continued to ring. To all Cooky had been charming, grateful and sincere.

By eight o'clock the calls had ended and Cooky had gone over his notes. Between us we had managed to finish a fifth. Cooky had glanced around and found a fresh bottle conveniently placed by his chair on the floor. He had tossed it to me. "Mix us a couple more, Mac, while I write this crap."

He had swung the typewriter toward him, inserted a sheet of paper, and talked the story as he typed. "Chancellor Ludwig Erhard said today that . . ." He had had two minutes that night, and it had taken him five to write it. "You want to go to the studio?" he had asked.

More than mellow, I had agreed. Cooky had stuck a fifth of Scotch into his mackintosh and we had made the dash to the Deutsche Rundfunk station. The engineer had been waiting at the door.

"You have ten minutes, Herr Baker. They have already called you from New York."

"Plenty of time," Cooky had said, producing the bottle. The engineer had had a drink, I had had a drink, and Cooky had had a drink. I had been getting drunk, but Cooky had seemed as warm and charming as ever. We had gone into the studio and he had gotten on the phone to his editor in New York. The editor had started to reel off the AP and UPI stories that had come over the wire from Bonn.

"I've got that . . . got that . . . got that. Yeah. That, too. And I've got one more on the Ambassador. . . . I don't give a goddamn if AP doesn't have it; they'll move it after nine o'clock."

We had all had another drink. Cooky had put the earphones on and had talked over the live mike to the engineer in New York. "How they hanging, Frank? That's good. All right; here we go."

And Cooky had begun to read. His voice had been excellent, a fifth of Scotch apparently having made no effect. There had been no slurs, no flubs. He had glanced at the clock once, slowed his delivery slightly, and finished in exactly two minutes.

We had had another drink and had then proceeded to the saloon, where Cooky and I were to meet two secretaries from the Ministry of Defense. "That," he had said, on the way to Godesberg, "is how I keep going. If it weren't for that deadline every afternoon and the fact that I don't have to get up in the morning, I'd be chasing little men. You know, Mac, you should quit drinking. You've got all the earmarks of a lush."

"My name is Mac and I'm an alcoholic," I had said automatically.

"That's the first step. The next time I dry up, we'll have a long talk."

"I'll wait."

Through what he termed his "little pigeons," Cooky knew Bonn as few others did. He knew the servant problem at the Argentine Embassy as well as he knew the internal power struggle within the Christian Democratic Union. He never forgot anything. He had once said: "Sometimes I think that's why I drink: to see if I can't black out. I never have. I remember every Godawful thing that's done and said."

"You're not shaking very much today," I said.

"The good doctor is giving me daily vitamin injections. It's sort of a crash program. He has a theory that I can drink as much as I want as long as I get sufficient vitamins. He was a little looped when he left today and insisted on giving himself a shot."

I sipped my coffee. "Mike says our place should be swept. My apartment too. He says you know who can do it."

"Where is Mike?"

"In Berlin."

"How soon do you want it?"

"As soon as possible."

Cooky picked up the phone and dialed ten numbers. "The guy's in Düsseldorf."

He waited while the phone rang. "This is Cooky, Konrad . . . Fine. . . . There are two spots in Bonn that need your talents . . . Mac's Place in Godesberg—you know where it is? Good. And an apartment. The address is . . ." He looked at me. I told him and he repeated it over the phone. "I don't know. Phones and everything, I would think. Hold on." He turned to me and asked: "What if they find something?"

I thought a moment. "Tell him to leave them in, but to tell you where they are."

"Just leave them, Konrad. Don't bother them. Call me when you're through and give me a rundown. Now, how much?" He listened and then asked me: "You go for a thousand marks?" I nodded. "O.K. A thousand. You can pick it up from me. And the key to the apartment, too. Right. See you tomorrow."

He hung up the phone and reached for a convenient bottle.

"He does my place once a week," he said. "I got a little suspicious once because of some phone noise when one of the pigeons was calling."

"Find anything?" I asked.

He nodded. "The pigeon lost her job. I had to find her another."

He took a gulp of Scotch and chased it with another of milk. "Mike in a jam?"

"I don't know."

Cooky looked up at the ceiling. "Remember a little girl named Mary Lee Harper? Used to work downtown. She was from Nashville."

"Vaguely."

"She used to work for a guy named Burmser."

"And?"

"Well, Mary Lee and I became friendly. Very friendly. And one night, after X-number of Martinis, right here in this place, Mary Lee started to talk. She talked about the nice man, Mr. Padillo. I gave her some more Martinis. She didn't remember talking the next morning. I assured her she hadn't. But Mary Lee's back in Nashville now. She left quite suddenly."

"So you know."

"As much as I want to. I told Mike I knew, and I also told him that if he needed anything . . ." Cooky let it trail off. "I guess he decided he did."

"What's Burmser besides what it says in his little black cardcase?"

Cooky looked thoughtfully into his drink. "A tough number. He'd sell his own kid if he thought the market was right. Ambitious, you might say. And ambition in his line of work can be tricky."

Cooky sighed and got up. "Since I've been here, Mac, the little pigeons have told me a number of things. You can add them up and it comes out shit. There was this pigeon from the Gehlen organization who talked and talked and talked one night. She—never mind." He walked into the kitchen and returned with another glass of milk and another half-tumbler of Scotch. "If you see Mike—you are, aren't you?" I nodded. "If you see him, tell him to play it cozy. I've heard a couple of things in the last few days. They don't add up and I don't want to be cryptic. Just tell Mike that it sounds messy."

"I'll do that," I said.

"More coffee?"

"No. Thanks for getting the guy to check us out. Here's a key to my apartment. I'll tell Horst to send you a thousand."

Cooky smiled. "No hurry. You can give it to me when you get back."

"Thanks."

"Take it easy," Cooky said at the door, the faint smile threatening to turn into a grin.

I drove home. Nobody with a Luger was in the apartment. There were no fat little men with shabby brief cases and brown trusting eyes or cold-faced policemen with starched shirts and overly clean fingernails. Just me. I picked up my suitcase, opened it on the bed and packed, leaving room for two bottles of Scotch. I started to close it, then walked over to the dresser and took a Colt .38 revolver from its clever hiding place under my shirts. It was a belly-gun. I put it in the suitcase, closed the hasps, went out to my car, and drove off to Düsseldorf feeling like a complete idiot.

By nine that night I was sitting in my room in the Berlin Hilton waiting for the phone to ring or a knock on the door or somebody to come through the transom if there had been one. I switched on the radio and listened to RIAS knock hell out of the Russians for a while. After fifteen minutes of that, and another drink, I decided it was time to get out of the room before I started leafing through the Gideon Bible's handy guide to chapter and verse for times of stress. I wondered if it had one for fools.

I took a cab over to the Kurfürstendamm and sat in one of the cafés watching the Berliners go by. It was an interesting parade. When he sat down at my table, all I said was a polite *"Guten Abend."* He was a bit of a dude, if the phrase doesn't date me: middling tall with long black hair brushed straight back into not quite a ducktail. He wore a blue pin-striped suit that pinched a bit too much at the waist. His polka-dot bow tie had been knotted by a machine. The waitress came over and he ordered a bottle of Pils. After it came he sipped it slowly, his black eyes restlessly scanning the strollers.

"You left Bonn in a hurry, Mr. McCorkle." The voice was pure Wisconsin. Madison, I thought.

"Did I forget to stop the milk?"

He grinned, a flicker of shiny white.

"We could talk here, but the book says we shouldn't. We'd better go by the book."

"I haven't finished my beer. Does the book say anything about that?"

The flicker of white again. He had the best looking set of teeth I had seen in a long time. I thought he must be hell with the girls.

"You don't have to ride me, Mr. McCorkle. I've got instructions from Bonn. They think it's important. Maybe you will too when you hear what I've got to say."

"Have you got a name?"

"You can call me Bill. Most of the time it's Wilhelm."

"What do you want to talk about, Bill? About how things are in the East and perhaps how they would have been better if the wheat crop had shown its early promise?"

The whiter-than-white teeth again. "About Mr. Padillo, Mr. Mc-Corkle." He shoved over one of the round paper coasters that are supplied by German beer firms. It had an address on it, and it wasn't a very good address.

"High-class place," I said.

"Safe. I'll meet you there in half an hour. That'll give you time to finish your beer." He rose and lost himself in the sidewalk traffic.

The address on the coaster was for a café called *Der Purzelbaum*— The Somersault. It was a hangout for prostitutes and homosexuals of both sexes. I had gone there once in a party of people who had thought it was funny.

I waited fifteen minutes and then caught a cab. The driver shrugged eloquently when I gave him the address. *Der Purzelbaum* was no better or worse than similar establishments in Hamburg or London or Paris or New York. It was a basement joint, and I had to walk down eight steps and through a yellow door to reach a long low-ceilinged room with soft pink lights and cuddly-looking little alcoves. There was also a lot of fish net hung here and there. It was dyed different colors. Bill of the shiny teeth was sitting at the long bar that ran two-thirds of the length of the left side of the room. He was talking to the barkeep, who had long blond wavy hair and sad violet eyes. There were two or three girls at the bar whose appraising stares counted the change in my pocket. From the alcoves came the murmur of conversation and an occasional giggle. A jukebox in the rear played softly.

I walked over to the bar. The young man who said his name was Bill asked in German if I would like a drink. I said a beer, and the sad-eyed bartender served it silently. I let my host pay for it. He picked up his glass and bottle and nodded toward the rear of the place. I followed, sheeplike. We sat at a table next to the jukebox, which was loud enough to keep anyone from overhearing us but not so loud that we had to shout.

"I understand the book says that these things can be bugged," I said, indicating the jukebox.

He looked startled for only a second. Then he relaxed and smiled that wonderful smile. "You're quite a kidder, Mr. McCorkle."

"What else is on your mind?"

"I've been told I should keep an eye on you while you're in Berlin."

"Who told you?"

"Mr. Burmser."

"Where did you meet me?"

"At the Hilton. You weren't trying to hide."

I made some patterns on the table with my wet beer glass. "Not to be rude or anything, but how do I know you're who you say you are? Just curious—but do you happen to have one of those little black folding cardcases that kind of outlines your bona fides?"

The smile exploded again. "If I have one it's in Bonn or Washington or Munich. Burmser told me to repeat a telephone number to you." He did. It was the same one Burmser had written on a slip of paper that morning.

"It'll have to do."

"How do you like it?"

"Like what?"

"The uniform. The suit, the hair—the image." He actually said image.

"Very jazzy. Even nifty."

"It's supposed to be. I'm what our English friends would call a spiv. Part-time stoolie, pimp—even a little marijuana."

"Where'd you learn German?"

"Leipzig. I was born there. Brought up in Oshkosh."

I had been close.

"How long have you been doing this—whatever it is you're doing?" I felt like the sophomore asking the whore how she'd fallen.

"Since I was eighteen. Over ten years."

"Like it?"

"Sure. It's for a good cause." He said that, too.

"So what's the story on me? And Padillo?"

"Mr. Padillo had an assignment in East Berlin. He was supposed to have been here yesterday, but he hasn't shown. Now you arrive in Berlin, so we figured that you've been in touch with Mr. Padillo. Simple?"

"Not quite."

"There's really not much more I can say, Mr. McCorkle. Mr. Padillo's actions don't make much sense and don't follow a pattern. Walking off from the two tourists in the Savigny yesterday and leaving his lighter and cigarette case behind: that evasive maneuver puzzled us. Mr. Burmser doesn't understand why you're in Berlin, unless it's to meet Mr. Padillo. You seem to hold the key, and that's why we want to tag along."

"You think Padillo's playing games? Double agent or something like that?"

He shrugged. "He's being too obvious. Mr. Burmser had only a few minutes to brief me. From what I gathered, he simply doesn't understand Padillo's actions. Maybe he has good cause and maybe he doesn't. I'm to keep an eye on you. We don't want anything to happen to you until we find Mr. Padillo."

I got up and leaned over the table. I stared at him for a long moment. Then I said: "The next time you talk to Mr. Burmser tell him this. Tell him I'm in Berlin on personal business and that I don't like being followed. Tell him I don't like his condescension and I don't like him. And tell him that if any of his help gets in my way I just might step on them."

I turned and walked out past the bartender with the violet eyes. I hailed a cab and told the driver to take me to the Hilton. I looked back twice. I didn't think I was being followed.

CHAPTER 8

It was raining the next morning when I awakened. It was the dull, flat, gray German rain, the kind that makes lonely people lonelier and sends the suicide rate up. I looked out over Berlin through my window, and it was no longer a tough, cheerful, wise-cracking town. It was just a city in the rain. I picked up the phone and ordered breakfast. After my third cup of coffee and a glance at the *Herald Tribune* I got dressed.

Then I sat in an easy chair, smoked my seventh cigarette of the day, and waited for something to happen. I waited all morning. The maid came in and made up the bed, emptied the ash trays, and told me to raise my feet while she used the vacuum cleaner. At eleven I decided it was time for a drink. That killed another twenty minutes, and another drink brought me up to noon. It had been a dull morning.

At twelve-fifteen the phone rang.

"Mr. McCorkle?" It was a man's voice.

"Speaking."

"Mr. McCorkle, this is John Weatherby. I'm calling for Mr. Padillo." The voice was English and sounded public-school. He fairly clipped his consonants and savored his vowels.

"I see."

"I was wondering if you'd be free during the next half hour, say. I'd like to pop over and have a chat."

"Pop away," I said. "I'll be here."

"Thanks awfully. Good-bye."

I said good-bye and hung up.

Weatherby was knocking at the door twenty minutes later. I asked him in and indicated a chair. He said he wouldn't mind a whiskey and soda when I asked if he would like a drink. I told him I didn't have any soda and he said water would be fine. I mixed the drinks and sat down in the chair opposite him. We said cheers and took a drink. He produced a package of Senior Service and offered me one. I accepted it and a light.

"Nice place, the Hilton," he said.

I agreed.

"You know, Mr. McCorkle, one sometimes finds oneself in rather peculiar positions. This go-between business may seem a bit far-fetched to you, but—" He shrugged and let the sentence lie down and die. His clothes were English and he wore them well. A brown tweed jacket with dark flannel slacks, not baggy. Old but carefully cared for Scotch-grain brogues that looked comfortable. A black knitted-silk tie. I had draped his mackintosh raincoat over a chair. He was about my age, possibly a few years older. He had a long narrow face with a strong red nose and a chin that jutted and just escaped having a dimple. He wore an RAF-type mustache, and his hair was long and a little damp from the rain. It was ginger-colored, as was his mustache.

"You know where Padillo is?" I asked.

"Oh, yes. That is to say I know where he was last night. He's been moving about a bit, you know."

"No," I said, "I didn't know."

He looked at me steadily for a moment. "No, I suppose you didn't. Perhaps I'd better explain. I formerly was with the government here in Berlin. I came to know Padillo rather well: we were more or less in the same line of work and there were a couple of mutual projects, you know. I still have contacts in the East—quite a few good friends, in fact. Padillo has been in touch with me, and I put him in touch with my friends. He's been staying with them—moving about a bit, as I said. I believe you received a message from him through a Miss Arndt?"

"Yes."

"Quite. Well, my further instructions were to meet you here at the Hilton today, and tonight at ten we're to go to the Café Budapest."

"That's in East Berlin."

"Right. There's no problem. I'll lay on the transport and we'll drive over. You have your passport, don't you?"

"Yes."

"Good."

"Then what?"

"Then, I suppose, we wait for Padillo."

I got up and reached for Weatherby's glass. He finished the last swallow quickly and handed the glass to me. I mixed two more drinks.

"Thanks very much," he said as I handed his drink to him.

"To be frank with you, Mr. Weatherby, I don't much care for any of this. Probably because I don't understand it. Do you have any idea why Padillo is in East Berlin or why he just doesn't come back through Checkpoint Charlie? He's got his passport."

Weatherby set his glass down carefully and lighted another cigarette. "All I know, Mr. McCorkle, is that I'm being paid in dollars by Mr. Padillo—presumably by him—to do what I'm doing and what I've done. I haven't questioned his motives, his objective or his *modus operandi*. My curiosity is no longer as . . . shall we say intense as it once was. I'm simply doing a job of work—one that I'm particularly suited for."

"What happens at this café tonight?"

"As I said, presumably we meet Padillo and he tells you what he needs. If anything." He rose. "I'll call for you at nine tonight. Thanks awfully for the drinks."

"My pleasure," I said.

Weatherby slung his raincoat over his arm and left. I went back to the chair and sat there trying to decide whether or not I was hungry. I decided I was, so I took my raincoat out of the closet and went in search of the elevators. I caught a cab to a restaurant I knew. The proprietor and I were old friends, but he was ill and the food reflected his absence. After lunch I took a walk—something I seldom do; but the long afternoon that lay ahead seemed a dull infinity. I was walking down an unfamiliar street, pricing the luxury goods in the small shops, when I spotted him. It was just a peripheral glimpse, but it was enough. I increased my pace, turned the corner, and waited. A few seconds later he turned it, almost at a trot.

"Got the time?" I asked.

It was Maas: still short and squatty, wearing the same brown suit, although it looked as if it might have been pressed. He carried the same shabby briefcase.

"Ah!" he said. "Herr McCorkle. I was trying to catch up with you."

"Ah!" I said. "Herr Maas. I bet you were."

He looked hurt. His spaniel eyes seemed on the verge of manufacturing a few tears.

"My friend, we have many, many things to talk about. There is a café not far from here where I am well known. Perhaps you will be my guest for a nice cup of coffee."

"Let's make it a nice glass of brandy. I just had coffee."

"Of course, of course."

We walked around another corner to a café. It was empty except for the proprietor, who served us in silence. He didn't seem to know Maas.

"Police ever catch up with you?" I asked pleasantly.

"Oh, that. They will soon forget. It was—how would you say?—a misunderstanding." He brushed it away with a flick of his hand.

"What brings you back to Berlin?"

He took a noisy sip of his coffee. "Business, always business."

I drank my brandy and signaled for another. "You know, Herr Maas, you've caused me a great deal of embarrassment and trouble."

"I know, I know, and I sincerely regret it. It was most unfortunate, and I apologize. I really apologize. But tell me, how is your colleague, Herr Padillo?"

"I thought you might know. I get the word that you have all the information sources."

Maas looked thoughtfully into his empty cup. "I have heard that he is in East Berlin."

"Everybody's heard that."

Maas smiled faintly. "I have also heard that he is—or shall we say has had a misunderstanding with his—uh—employers."

"What else have you heard?"

Maas looked at me, and his spaniel eyes turned hard as agate. "You think me a simple man, do you not, Herr McCorkle? Perhaps a buffoon? A fat German who has eaten too many potatoes and drunk too much beer?"

I grinned. "If I think of you at all, Herr Maas, I think of you as a man who has caused me a great deal of trouble from the moment you picked me up on that plane. You poked your nose into my life because of my business partner's extracurricular activities. As a result, a man got killed in my saloon. When I think about that I think about you, Herr Maas. You've got trouble written all over you, and trouble is something I try to avoid."

Maas called for more coffee. "I am in the business of trouble, Herr McCorkle. It is how I make my living. You Americans are still very insular people. You have your violence, to be sure, and your thieves, your criminals, even your traitors. You wander the world trying to be— how does the slang go?—the good guys and you are despised for your bungling, hated for your wealth, and ridiculed and mocked for your posturing. Your CIA would be a laughing-stock, except that it controls enough funds to corrupt a government, finance a revolution, subvert a political party. You are not a stupid or stubborn people, Herr Mc-

Corkle, but you are an ignorant people, a disinterested people. And I pity you."

I had heard it all before—from the British and the French and the Germans and the rest. Part of it was envy, part of it was truth, and none of it would change anything. I long ago gave up being either guilty or proud of my nationality, and there were plenty of reasons for both. I had a life to live, and I lived it the best I could, adapting to the changing rules, avoiding the ho-hummery whenever possible, escaping a little perhaps, but putting keen value on a few things that still seemed important, although these too seemed to be getting just a bit worn and shabby.

"Herr Maas, I don't need a civics lecture today. I just wish you would get to your point—if you have one."

Maas gave me one of his sighs. "I am no longer shocked, my friend, by what man does to man. Disloyalty does not dismay me. Perfidy I find the rule, not the exception. However, these things can often be turned to profit. It is my business to do so. Look." He pulled his left coat sleeve up, unbuttoned his shirt cuff, and folded it back over his forearm. "See this?" he said, pointing to a series of numbers tattooed on the inside of his pudgy arm.

"A concentration-camp number," I said.

He rolled down his sleeve and buttoned it. He smiled, and there was no humor in it. "No, it is not a concentration-camp number, although it appears to be one. I had it tattooed in April of 1945. It saved my life several times. I have been in concentration camps, Herr McCorkle, but never as a prisoner. Do you follow me?"

"It isn't hard."

"When it was necessary—and profitable—I was a Nazi. When that was no longer fashionable, I became a victim of the Nazis. You are shocked?"

"No."

"Good. Then perhaps we can get down to business."

"We do have some, I take it?"

"Yes, we have some concerning Herr Padillo. You see, it was he who was my primary reason for going to Bonn."

"Who was the other man?"

Maas waved his hand airily. "A minor functionary who was interested in buying some arms. Of no consequence, really. He had little money. But it was Herr Padillo I wished to see. And here is where the irony creeps in, Herr McCorkle, and perhaps the pity too. Your establishment is very dim, is it not? There is little light?"

"True."

"As I said, the little man was of no importance. Your place is dimly lighted, so I can only assume that a mistake was made. The two gentlemen who burst in shot the wrong man. They were supposed to kill me." Maas laughed. It sounded as humorous as the ha-ha's people write in letters.

"The pity, I take it, is that you weren't shot. It's not the funniest story I've heard in a long time, although it has its points."

Maas reached into his brief case and rummaged around. He came up with a long dappled cigar. "Cuban," he said. "Would you care for one?"

"I'd be betraying the fatherland."

Maas got the cigar lighted and took a few experimental puffs. "I had information that I wished to sell to Herr Padillo concerning his current assignment. You see, Herr McCorkle, a man of Herr Padillo's talents is rare. Such men are difficult to come by, and they are to be treasured. In the course of their activities they make enemies because their primary function is to frustrate the opposition's carefully made plans. Herr Padillo, through his language ability and his personal resourcefulness, has been highly successful in his assignments. Has he told you of them?"

"We never discussed it."

Maas nodded. "He is also a prudent man. But, as I said, his successes were notable. In the course of his work he found it necessary to remove some rather prominent political figures. Oh, not the ones who make the headlines, but those who, like Herr Padillo, worked in the shadows of international politics. He is, I'm reliably informed, one of the best."

"He also makes a hell of a good hot buttered rum," I said.

"Ah, yes. The cover of the café in Bonn. Really excellent. For some reason, Herr McCorkle, you do not strike me as the kind of man who would engage in this business of information and politics."

"You're right. I'm not that kind of man at all. I'm just along for the ride."

"Yes. How much do you think that our friends in the East might pay for a topflight agent of the United States—for one who is the *sine qua non* of its intelligence *apparat?*"

"I don't know."

"Money, of course, would be out of the question."

"Why?"

"An ambitious man in the U.S. intelligence organization for which Herr Padillo occasionally does odd jobs, shall we say, would not be looking for money. He would be looking for the coup that would enhance his reputation, for the brilliant stroke that would advance his career. That is what I came to tell Herr Padillo. For a price, of course."

"And you were interrupted."

"Unfortunately, yes. As I have told you before, my sources are excellent. They cost a bit, but their reliability is without question. I learned that a trade was in the offing between our Russian friends in the KGB and Herr Padillo's employers."

"What kind of trade?"

Maas puffed some more on his cigar. It was growing an excellent ash.

"Do you remember two men called William H. Martin and Vernon F. Mitchell?"

"Vaguely. They defected four or five years ago."

"Five," Maas said. "They were mathematicians for your National Security Agency. They went to Mexico, flew to Havana, and caught a

Russian trawler. And then in Moscow they talked and talked and talked. They were most communicative, much to the embarrassment of your National Security Agency. As I recall, virtually every major nation in the world changed its codes and caused the agency and its computer no end of trouble."

"I seem to recall."

"You may also recall that the two were overt homosexuals. It caused quite a furor, eventually leading to the resignation or dismissal of the director of personnel. In fact, certain members of Congress thought that the pair's homosexuality was the real reason for their defection, not their expressed horror at the methods of espionage used by your country."

"Some of our Congressmen have old-fashioned ideas," I said.

"Yes. But it seems that last year two more Americans who worked for your National Security Agency also defected. The case almost parallels that of Martin and Mitchell. This time, however, there seemed to be some kind of tacit agreement between your country and the Soviet Union that the two would not be put on display in Moscow—despite the overwhelming propaganda value. The names of the last pair—also mathematicians, by the way—are Gerald R. Symmes and Russell C. Burchwood. Symmes and Burchwood."

"If you could prove it, you could sell that story to a newspaper for a great deal of money, Herr Maas."

"Yes, I could, couldn't I? However, I was more interested in selling it to Herr Padillo. Or perhaps I should say trading it to him for some information that he may have. But let me continue. The pair of defectors, Symmes and Burchwood, were also homosexuals—there must be something wrong with the family structure in America, Herr McCorkle—and, unlike Martin and Mitchell, neither was suddenly cured, if that's the word, and married a fine strapping wife. I believe Martin did find marital bliss in Moscow. Or so he told the press. No, Symmes and Burchwood continued to live together—on their honeymoon, so to speak—and told the Soviet government all they knew about the operations of the National Security Agency. They were, my sources informed me, somewhat piqued because they did not receive the same publicity and fame as Martin and Mitchell. Yet they told all they knew. Which was considerable."

"You were getting to Padillo," I reminded him.

Maas regretfully tapped an inch and a half from his cigar into the triangular white, black and red Martini & Rossi Vermouth ash tray. "As I told you when you so impetuously thought of informing the Bonn police of my whereabouts, I knew what Herr Padillo's mission was and I knew where he was going.

"It seems that our Russian friends had agreed to send the two naughty boys back home—for a price. Padillo was to arrange the transfer here in Berlin—or, rather, in East Berlin. He was to escort them back to Bonn via an American Air Force aeroplane." That's the way Maas pronounced it. His English was growing increasingly formal and precise.

"I'm no expert, but it seems like a simple enough job."

"Perhaps. But, as I said, Herr Padillo has proved effective over the years in his operations in the various countries which are of the Communist persuasion. Too effective, I would say. The price demanded by the Russians for the two defectors was a bona fide, live U.S. agent. Your government agreed. They offered up Michael Padillo."

CHAPTER 9

Maas studied my face intently after he dropped his bomb. Then he signaled the proprietor, who brought me another brandy and Maas another cup of coffee. He poured a liberal dollop of cream into it, added three cubes of sugar, and sipped noisily, still studying my face.

"You seem speechless, my friend."

"I'm working up to an indignant remark," I said.

He shrugged. "My little lecture of a few moments ago about you Americans' insularity was to prepare you. You don't have to make me a speech. I've heard them all in my time, from one side or another. Herr Padillo is engaged in a business which follows no set of rules or laws. It is a hard, filthy business that goes on in its peculiarly arcane fashion, fed by overweaning ambition, by greed, by intrigue, blundering often, and then blundering again to cover up the original mistake.

"Look at it objectively, if you can. Forget your association with Herr Padillo. Here are two men whose defection, if revealed, could cause the United States the most acute embarrassment. In addition, if they were to be returned, then your government could learn what they have told the Soviets. Corrective measures could be initiated. What do you spend on your National Security Agency? I have seen estimates of up to a half a billion dollars a year. The agency is your code-breaking apparat. It also designs the U. S. codes and monitors a fantastic number of broadcasts and transmissions. You have a considerable investment there at Fort Meade, with its ten thousand employees. It's second in size to only your Pentagon."

"You seem well informed."

Maas snorted. "Common knowledge. What I'm saying is that the two defectors may have thrown this huge mechanism out of balance. It may be breaking purposefully distorted code messages. These messages are considered prime intelligence. They help determine your country's economic and military actions in dozens of countries. Now what is an agent worth in terms of your dollars and cents? They have had full use of Herr Padillo. He's an amortized agent. Their investment in him has paid off manifold. So they sacrifice him, much as you would sacrifice a knight to gain a queen."

"Hardheaded businessmen," I murmured. "That's what made America great."

"But they are making an even better bargain than our friends in the East suspect," Maas continued. "By offering up Herr Padillo, they are offering an agent who has been merely on the periphery of their activities. He has worked on specific assignments, and while he would know the details of these assignments and the names of those he worked with in the specific countries, his real knowledge of your intelligence system is extremely limited. So the Americans are, from their point of view, making a perfectly splendid bargain."

"And you think Padillo knows all this?"

Maas nodded. "By now, yes. Otherwise I would not be relating the details. I would be selling them. I, too, am a businessman of sorts, Herr McCorkle. And I have not yet come to my proposition."

"You have a nice sales talk. It reminds me of a used-car dealer I once knew in Fort Worth."

Maas sighed again. "Your humor often escapes me, my friend. However, let us continue. I suspect that Herr Padillo will be trying to leave East Berlin in something of a hurry. Security, of course, will be at a maximum. The wall, although a clumsy, ugly device, remains fairly effective. I have something to sell. In the words of one of your most prominent Americans, I have an egress for sale."

"Mr. Barnum had a few other homilies that might bear repeating now, too. Just where is your egress, Herr Maas, and how much are you asking?"

Maas fished around in his brief case again and came up with an envelope. "This is a map. Here." He handed it to me. "It is, of course, worthless unless the necessary arrangements have been made with the Vopos who patrol that particular area. They discovered and retained the exit—it goes under, not over, by the way—and they are quite greedy. That is why the price is fairly high."

"How high?"

"Five thousand dollars. Half in advance."

"No deal."

"An alternative proposition?"

"If Padillo wants to get out of East Berlin, and if he's in the trouble you say he is, then it's worth five thousand. But not in advance. Only when he's at the egress, as you call it. I'm looking for a little insurance, Herr Maas. Your presence, if and when the exit is needed, would make me a trifle more confident."

"You, too, are a businessman, Herr McCorkle."

"A most conservative one."

"Twenties and fifties would do nicely."

"No checks?"

Maas patted me affectionately on the shoulder. "That humor! No, dear friend; no checks. Now I must leave. I trust you will arrange for the money. I have a feeling that Herr Padillo will be agreeable to my proposition."

"Suppose he needs to get in touch with you in a hurry?"

"Every night for the next four nights I will be at this number in East Berlin. Between eleven and midnight. Unfortunately I can be there for only four nights. Starting tomorrow. Is that clear?" He rose, brief case in hand. "It has been a most interesting discussion, Herr Mc-Corkle."

"Yes, it has, hasn't it?"

"I will be interested in Herr Padillo's decision. Purely from a businessman's point of view, of course."

"One more question. Who were the hard boys who shot the little man?"

Maas pursed his lips. "I'm afraid that the KGB now knows that I know, if you follow me. I shall have to find some way to make my peace with them. It is distinctly uncomfortable to be an assassin's target."

"It could make you jumpy."

"Yes, Herr McCorkle, it could. *Auf wiedersehen.*"

"*Auf wiedersehen.*"

I watched him leave the café, clutching his worn brief case. It was a hard way to make a dollar, I decided. The proprietor came over and asked if I wished anything else. I told him no and paid the check—something Maas had overlooked. I sat there in the café in what the reporters keep calling the beleaguered city and tried to sort it out. I removed the map from the envelope and looked at it, but I didn't know East Berlin and it was meaningless, although it seemed accurate enough, drawn on a one-inch-to-twenty-meters scale. The tunnel appeared to be sixty meters or so long. I put the map back in the envelope. Maybe it was worth five thousand dollars.

I got up and left the café. I hailed a cab and went back to the Hilton. I checked the desk for messages. There were none. I bought a copy of *Der Spiegel* to find out the current German prejudices and took the elevator up to my room. I opened the door, and the two of them were sitting in the same chairs where Weatherby and I had sat earlier. I tossed the magazine on the bed.

"Privacy is something that I'm beginning to put a very high premium on. What do you want, Burmser?"

Bill or Wilhelm, the dude with the wonderful smile, was with him.

Burmser crossed his long legs and frowned. The four wrinkles appeared in his forehead. It may have been a sign that he was thinking.

"You're headed for trouble, McCorkle," he said.

I nodded. "Good. It's my trouble, not yours."

"You've seen Maas," he said accusingly, and named the café.

"I gave him your message. He wasn't impressed." I sat down on the bed.

Burmser got up and walked over to the window and stared out, his hands turned into fists that rested on his hips. "What does Padillo want from you?"

"None of your goddamned business," I said. It came out pleasantly enough.

He turned from the window. "You're out of your depth, McCorkle. You're messing around in a potful of crap that's going to spill all over you. You'd better take the next plane back to Bonn and run your saloon. Your only value to us is that you could put us on to Padillo before he gets himself into a jam he can't get out of. But you tell me it's none of my goddamned business. Let me tell you that we haven't got time to nursemaid you—and God knows you need one."

"They had a tail on him today," Bill said.

Burmser waved a hand in disgust. "Christ, they've probably had someone on him since he left Bonn."

"Is that all?" I asked.

"Not quite," Burmser said. "Padillo has decided to play it cute, just like you. He knows better, and maybe he thinks he can take care of himself. He's not bad, I'll admit. In fact, he's damn good. But not that good. Nobody is—not when he's bucking both sides." He got up. This time Bill-Wilhelm got up too. "When you see Padillo, tell him we're looking for him," Burmser went on, his voice harsh and scratchy. "Tell him he's in too deep to get out."

"In the potful of crap," I offered.

"That's right, McCorkle: in the potful of crap."

I got up and walked over to Burmser. Bill-Wilhelm moved in

quickly. I turned toward him. "Don't worry, sonny. I'm not going to slug him. I'm just going to tell him something." I tapped my finger against Burmser's chest. "If anybody's in trouble, you are. If anybody's played it cute, you have. I'll tell you the same thing I told your friend here, with just a little more detail. I'm in Berlin on a private matter that involves the partner of the business I run. As far as I'm concerned, I intend to preserve that business by being of whatever assistance I can to my partner."

Burmser shook his head in disgust. "You're dumb, McCorkle. A real dumb bastard. Let's go, Bill."

They left. I walked over to the phone and dialed a direct long-distance call to Bonn. It answered on the first ring.

"Sitting in your favorite chair sipping your favorite beverage, Cooky?"

"Hello, Mac. Where are you?"

"The Berlin Hilton, and I need five thousand bucks by eight o'clock tonight. Fifties and twenties."

There was a silence. "I'm thinking," Cooky said.

"You're taking one straight from the bottle, you mean."

"It helps. There are two possibilities: a pigeon at American Express or another one at Deutsche Bank downtown. I've got plenty in both accounts. I'm rich, you know."

"I know. The bank's closed, isn't it?"

"I'm a big depositor. I'll get it."

"Can you get an evening flight up here?"

"Sure. I'll tell New York I've got a touch of virus."

"I'll get you a room."

"Make it a suite. I know a couple of pigeons in Berlin. We may need room to romp. By the way, my friend from Düsseldorf just left. Somebody had a tap on the phone at your apartment and at the saloon."

"I'm not surprised."

"I'll see you tonight. With the money."

"I appreciate it, Cooky."

"No sweat."

My watch said it was four P.M. I had five hours before Weatherby was to pick me up. I looked at the Scotch bottle but decided against it. Instead I went down to the lobby and reserved a suite for Cooky and cashed a check for two thousand Marks. I went back up to my room, wrote out a check to Mr. Cook Baker for five thousand dollars, put it in an envelope, and sealed it. I took the .38 out of the suitcase and put it in my jacket pocket. Then I mixed a drink and hauled a chair around so that I could look out over the city. I sat there for a long time, watching the shadows deepen from gray into black. The grays and blacks matched my thoughts. It was a long, lonely afternoon.

At eight forty-five Cooky called from the lobby. I told him to come up and he said he would as soon as he checked in and got his bag to his room. He knocked on the door ten minutes later. I let him in and he handed me a tightly wrapped package a little over an inch thick. "I had to take hundreds—ten of them," he said. "Ten hundreds, fifty fifties, and seventy-five twenties. That's five thousand bucks."

I handed him the envelope containing the check. "Here's my check." He didn't look at it and I didn't count the money.

"Was it much trouble?"

"I had to threaten to withdraw my account is all. Where's the booze?"

"In the closet."

He got it and poured himself a drink, his usual half-tumbler.

"Want some ice?"

"Takes too long. I had a very dry trip. I sat next to this pigeon who was afraid of landings. She wanted to hold my hand. She held it between her legs. She's the secretary for a Turkish trade mission. What's new with you and why the suspicious-looking bulge in your pocket? It ruins the drape."

"I carry large sums of money."

"Is Mike in a five-thousand-buck jam? That's respectable trouble."

I turned the chair back from the window so that it faced the room and sat down. Cooky had propped himself up on two pillows on the bed, his drink cuddled against his chest.

"Mr. Burmser paid me a call," I said. "He thinks I'm a dumb bastard. I tend to agree."

"Did he have his boy with him—the toothpaste ad?"

"You know him?"

"We've met. He's very handy with a knife. I understand."

"It's part of his image."

Cooky's private joke played around his lips. "You seem to be running with the fast crowd at the country club."

There was a light tap at the door. I got up and opened it. Weatherby stood there, his face the color of wet newsprint. "Little early, I'm afraid," he muttered, then stumbled into the room and sprawled on the floor. He tried to get up once, shuddered, and lay still. There was a small hole in the back of his mackintosh. I knelt quickly and turned him over. His hands were covered with blood, and when his topcoat and jacket flopped open I saw that his shirt was soaked with it. His eyes were open, his mouth gaped, and his teeth were bared in a smile or a grimace: it was hard to tell which.

Cooky said, "He's dead, isn't he?"

"He must have been holding the blood in."

I felt for the pulse in his neck. It seemed like the thing to do. It wasn't necessary. He was as dead as he looked, as dead as he would ever be.

CHAPTER 10

I stepped back and bumped against the bed. It seemed that I should do something, so I sat on it and stared down at the sprawled body of Weatherby. I tried to think of something else to do besides sit on the bed, but nothing came to mind.

"Who is he?" Cooky asked.

"He said that he was John Weatherby and that he was British and that he used to work with government here in Berlin. He said he was going to take me to the Café Budapest tonight to meet Padillo. He was working for him. He said."

"Now what?"

I stared at Weatherby some more. "Nothing. I'll go to the café alone. You'd better get down to your room."

"No cops?"

"They'll be here soon enough after the maid comes in to turn down the bed. If Mike's in the kind of a fix that gets people killed, he's in a bad way. I can't wait around. There's not enough time."

"I think I'll tag along."

"It's not your show."

"I've got five thousand invested and you might be passing bum checks."

"Tag along and you might not get the chance to find out."

Cooky smiled his private-joke smile. "I want to stop by my room first. Meet me there in five minutes." He stepped over Weatherby's legs and went out.

It was some while after Cooky left before I got up and put on my raincoat and slipped the bundle of money into one pocket and the revolver into the other. It no longer felt ridiculous. I went over to the window and stared out at the lights, and after I felt that five minutes had passed I took the elevator down to Cooky's suite.

"A whore's dream," he said, opening the door to my knock. He walked over to his suitcase, which lay spread open on one of the twin double beds that took up most of the room. He took out a long, thin silver flask and slipped it into his hip pocket.

"Taking only the essentials, I see."

"Emergency rations," Cooky said. "I intend to make do with the local stuff."

He looked down at his suitcase thoughtfully, seemed to hesitate, and then took out a wicked-looking revolver with a short barrel. It was an ugly gun, designed to be used quickly and up close, not for plinking at rabbits off the back porch.

"What's that?" I said.

"This," he said, holding the gun delicately by its two-inch barrel, "is a Smith and Wesson .357 Magnum revolver. Note that the forward end of the trigger guard has been removed. Note, too, that the hammer spur has been eliminated, thus removing the possibility of its snagging the clothing if the weapon has to be produced quickly." He put the revolver carefully down on the bed, fished into his suitcase again, and came up with a short leather holster.

"This was made by a good old boy from Calhoun, Mississippi, name of Jack Martin. It's called a Berns-Martin holster. The forward edge is open, and it has a spring that passes around the cylinder of the gun to keep it snug." He picked up the revolver and snapped it into place. "Thusly. I will shortly demonstrate."

He took off his jacket and belt and threaded the belt through the holster. When he slipped the belt back on, the holster, with the gun, rode high on his right hip. He got into his jacket and tugged at the lapels. The gun was invisible—not even a bulge. "Now, when you wish to produce the weapon rapidly, you just swish it forward. If you'll count to three by thousands . . ."

I counted "one thousand." Cooky's body relaxed like a loose rubber band. His right shoulder dropped slightly on the count of "two thousand," and on "three thousand," he swayed his hips to the left and his hand brushed away the edge of his coat. Before I finished saying "three thousand" I was looking into the barrel of the revolver. It seemed uglier than before.

"You're fast."

"About a half-second, maybe six-tenths. The best there is can do it in three-tenths."

"Where did you learn it?"

Cooky replaced the gun in the holster. "In New York when I was on the flit. I was planning a showdown on Madison Avenue with my two partners. It seemed like a good idea at the time. There was an expert who took advantage of the fast-draw craze a few years back and started accepting pupils. I had it in mind to challenge Messrs. Brickwall and Hillsman of Baker, Brickhill and Hillsman to a duel. I used to lock myself in my office and practice for hours before a mirror. When I got good enough I went up to my farm in Connecticut and started target practice. It was a goddamned obsession. I must have fired fifteen or twenty thousand rounds. And finally I found the perfect target."

"What?"

"Quart cans of tomato juice. I bought them by the case, set them up—with the ends facing me—against the barn wall, and banged away. Ever see a .357 slug open up a can of tomato juice?"

"I never have," I said, "but, then, I'm not much on tomato juice."

"It's bang and wow and shleep. The goddamn stuff explodes all over everything. Looks like blood. Flattens the can out like you had snipped it open with tin shears and pounded it flat with a sledge hammer. Most satisfying."

"But you never got satisfaction from your partners?"

"No. I spent a couple of weeks on a funny farm instead, drying out."

Cooky closed his suitcase and slipped on his topcoat. "Shall we go?"

I looked at my watch. It was nine-twenty. We were to be at the Café Budapest at ten. "You don't have to go, Cooky. You'll probably land in trouble."

His secret-joke smile flickered for an instant. "Let's just say that I think I'd like to come along because I'm thirty-three years old and I've never done anything really all the way down to the wire."

I shrugged. "They threw Christ out of the ball game at thirty-three and He got back in. But you're trying to make it the hard way."

We took the elevator down and walked swiftly through the lobby. Nobody stared or pointed. John Weatherby must have been still alone and undiscovered and dead in my room. I couldn't mourn for Weatherby because I han't known him, although I had liked what had seemed to be a quiet competence. If anything, his death seemed to have been too casual and meaningless, as most violent deaths are. But perhaps they are better than the kind that have the dark, quiet room; the drugged pain; the whispering nurses slopping around in rubber-soled shoes; and the family and the friend or two who give a damn and who also wonder how long you'll hold out and whether there'll be a chance to keep that cocktail date at half-past six.

We left the Hilton and walked toward the Kaiser Wilhelm church.

"When was the last time you were in the East Sector?" Cooky asked.

"Years ago. Before the wall went up."

"How did you go through?"

I tried to remember. "I think I was slightly tight. I recall a couple of girls from Minneapolis who were staying at the Hilton. They were with me. We just caught a cab and sailed through the Brandenburg Gate. No trouble."

Cooky looked over his shoulder. "Things have changed. Now we foreigners go through Checkpoint Charlie on Friedrichstrasse. It could take an hour or so to get through, depending on whether the Vopos liked their dinner. You have your passport?"

I nodded.

"There used to be eighty official ways to get into East Berlin," Cooky said. "Now there are eight. We need a car."

"Any ideas?" I said, and looked over my shoulder.

"Rent one. There's a place called Day and Night on Brandenburgische Strasse."

We caught a cab and told the driver to take us to Brandenburgische Strasse, which was about three minutes away. We picked out a new Mercedes 220. I showed my driver's license.

"How long will you have use for the car?" the man asked.

"Two or three days."

"A two-hundred-Mark deposit will be sufficient."

I gave him the money, signed the rental agreement, and put the *carnet de passage* and other papers into the glove compartment. I got behind the wheel, pumped the brakes to see if they worked, and started the engine. Cooky got in and slammed his door.

"Sounds tinny," he said.

"They don't make them the way they used to."

"They never did."

I turned left out of the *Tag und Nacht* garage and headed for Friedrichstrasse. You can usually ignore the speed limit in Berlin, but I kept to a modest forty to fifty kilometers per hour. The car handled well, but it wasn't especially eager. It was just a machine designed to get you there and back with a minimum of discomfort. I turned left onto Friedrichstrasse.

"What's the form?" I asked Cooky.

"Get your passport out; a GI will want to look at it."

I drove on and stopped when a bored-looking soldier standing in front of a white hut waved me down. He glanced at our passports and then handed us a mimeographed sheet, which warned against carrying any non-American persons in the car, admonished me to obey all traffic regulations because "East Berlin officials are sensitive about their pre-rogatives," and cautioned us about engaging in unnecessary conversation with East Berliners.

"What if I have to ask where the john is?" Cooky said.

"You can pee in your pants, mister, for all I care. Just fill this out first."

It was a form requesting the time we could be expected back at the checkpoint. I put down midnight.

"Anything else?"

"That's all, buddy. Just be nice to the krauts."

A West German policeman nearer the crossing yawned and waved us on and I zigzagged the car through a series of white pole barriers and parked it. After that it wasn't much worse than having a tooth pulled. There was the currency declaration. We lied about that. Then there was the passport inspection. There was nobody else in the line, and the Volkspolizei seemed to have nothing better to do.

"You are a businessman," he said, thumbing through my passport.

"Yes."

"What type of business?"

"A restaurant."

He read some more about me and then slipped the passport through a slot behind him, where somebody else got the chance to find out how tall I was and how heavy and what color my hair and eyes were and what countries I might have visited in the past few years.

Cooky was next. "Herr Cook Baker?" the Vopo asked.

"Yes."

"Is that not a strange name?"

"One gets a comment or two."

"You are a public-relations man?"

"Yes."

The Vopo nodded thoughtfully. "Just what is a public-relations man, Herr Baker?"

"We deal in controlled revelation," Cooky said.

The Vopo frowned. He was a short, wiry man with a foxy face and eyebrows that needed combing. "You are a propagandist?"

"Only for inanimate objects—soap, underarm deodorant shaving lotions. Just the essentials. No government work."

The sharp-faced German read some more about Cooky and decided that his passport didn't need to travel through the slot. He got mine back, shot his cuffs, and prepared for the operation. First the stamp was inked twice on the pad, then it was examined, and then it was applied to the passport with a firm yet flashy bang. The Vopo admired his work briefly and then gave us back the passports after a cursory glance at the car's papers. We got into the Mercedes and drove up Friedrichstrasse to Unter den Linden, about a half-mile away.

I drove slowly. East Berlin was even more drab than I had remembered it, the traffic was spotty, and the pedestrians walked as if they had to and not because they were out for a late-evening stroll. Their faces were stolid and they didn't seem to smile much, even when talking to one another; but, then, I couldn't recall many metropolitan boulevards these days where the pedestrians are noted for their cheerful faces.

"What happens if we don't get back by midnight?" I asked Cooky.

"Nothing. They probably marked our passports somehow so that if we don't show up and somebody else tries to use them they can spot it. But that form we signed about when we thought we'd come back is just routine. Nobody cares how long you stay over."

We turned right on Unter den Linden. "Go through Marx-Engels Platza, straight ahead till you hit Stalinallee or whatever the hell they call it now—Karl Marx Allee—and I'll show you where to turn left. I think."

"Sounds as if you've been here before," I said.

"No. I asked the bellhop at the Hilton. Bellhops know everything. He said it's a dump."

"It would fit in with the rest of the evening."

"How much do you know about the whole thing?"

I lighted a cigarette. "Nothing firsthand. Just from hearsay. I saw Weatherby today and he said he would take me to Padillo, who is in some kind of jam. After Weatherby I ran into Maas, the mystery man, who claims that Padillo is being suckered—that he's up for trade for two defectors from the National Security Agency. For five thousand dollars Maas says he can get Padillo out of East Berlin through a tunnel. He seemed to think Padillo would buy the idea. He wanted half in advance, but I said no deal and then called you for the cash. That's it, except Burmser and his assistant with the big, white smile."

"One thing," Cooky said.

"What?"

"Mass is giving you a deal if he's got a tunnel."

"How's that?"

"Rooms on this side close enough to the wall to make a break are just about nonexistent. But the West Berliners, across the wall, are charging up to twenty-five hundred bucks just for a room to run to so you won't get shot after you jump over."

"There are people who will make a buck whatever the graft—fire, pestilence, famine or war." The apartments we were passing were the ones that had been thrown up in a hurry in 1948. Their plaster or stucco exteriors were flaking off, exposing the red brick underneath. The brick looked like angry red sores. The balconies sagged and clung halfheartedly to the buildings.

"You can still walk back," I said.

"Straight ahead," Cooky directed. "You know how many of them were crossing over just before the wall went up?'

"About a thousand a day."

"That's thirty thousand a month. Working stiffs mostly, but also a boatload or two of engineers, doctors, scientists, technicians of all kinds. It was bad public relations on Bonn's part."

"How?"

"They talked it up too much. They rubbed it in until it stung. Ulbricht went off to Moscow and convinced Khruschchev that he had to seal it off: the GDR couldn't stand the embarrassment. The West kept score, and every time they hit a thousand the newspapers carried it in 'second-coming' headlines. So one hot August day when Ulbricht got back from Moscow the word went out. First there was just the barbed wire. Then they started putting up the wall: concrete slabs a meter square. And when they found that that wasn't enough they topped it off with a yard or so of cinder blocks. A guy I know from Lone Star Cement took a look at it and said it was a lousy job—from a professional viewpoint."

"So what should Bonn have done?"

"Turn left here. They should have known it was going up. Their intelligence was lousy, but no worse than ours or the British. Maybe there wasn't time, but the blocks had to be cast, the cement ordered. Somebody should have buttoned on. You don't set out to build a twenty-seven-mile-long wall through the middle of a big town without a few leaks. If they had known, they could have turned their propaganda guns loose. RIAS could have knocked hell out of the Reds some more. The British and the Americans and the French could have sent what are called 'tersely worded notes.' There were sixty thousand East Berliners working in West Berlin. Some of them could have stayed. Hell, they could have done a lot of things."

"All they needed was a good PR man."

Cooky grinned. "Maybe. At least the East was all set for it with an outfit they called 'The League of the German Democratic Republic for the Friendship Among the Peoples.' The flacks for this outfit started pounding away on three points, all aimed at excusing the wall. First, they cried a lot about how the West was inducing doctors, engineers and others to cross over by the use of what they called 'cunning and dishonorable methods.' It comes out money in the translation.

"Second, those who lived in East Berlin and worked in West Berlin were getting four East German Marks for every Western D-Mark they earned. This meant that a guy could go over to West Berlin, sign on as a common laborer, and make as much as the specialist with a university education who worked in the East. That seemed to bother them some, too.

"And, third, they were all upset about the smuggling. Or maybe the Russians were unhappy. At any rate, the East's flacks claimed that the wall went up to stop the 'illegal export' of such stuff as optical instruments, Dresden china, Plauen laces and the like. They claimed it cost them thirty-five thousand million marks a year—however much that is."

"You may be right that the West bragged too much about the numbers of refugees," I said.

"I'd have probably done the same."

"It was just too good to ignore—especially if you're screaming for unification. But it's academic now—like calling that third-down play on Monday instead of Sunday. And if you want a McCorkle prediction, I'll be happy to make one."

"What?"

"That wall isn't coming down—not in our lifetime."

"You only bet cinches, Mac. We're damn near there—wherever there is. Turn left."

I turned left down a dark, mean street whose name I didn't catch and didn't even look for. We drove a block, and the Café Budapest was on a corner, the first floor of a three-story building with a small electric sign that had half of its bulbs burned out. It was a prewar building, and you could see where it had been patched up with plaster that was newer than the original. Parking was no problem. We got out and walked toward the entrance, which was recessed into the corner of the building, catawampus to the sidewalk.

Cooky pulled open the heavy wooden door and we went in. The

room was about sixty feet long and thirty-five feet wide. It had a high ceiling, and at the far end there was a platform where a four-piece band gave out a weary version of "Happy Days Are Here Again." A few couples moved around the twelve-by-twelve dance floor. Two girls danced together. There were some dark wooden booths along both sides of the room and the bar was at the front, next to the door. The place was a quarter full, and we seemed to have missed the happy hour. We didn't take off our coats.

"Let's try a table," I said.

We sat down at one near the door.

"What time is it?" I asked Cooky.

"Five till ten."

"Let's stick to vodka. I understand it's halfway decent."

A waitress came over and I ordered two vodkas. We attracted about as much attention as a flea in a dog pound. The waitress came back with the drinks and waited to get paid. Cooky gave her some D-Marks and waved the change away. She didn't smile. She didn't say thank you. She walked off and stood tiredly by a booth and examined her fingernails. After a while she started to chew on one of them.

Cooky drank half his vodka and smiled. "Not bad."

I sipped mine. I can't tell the difference in vodka, except for the proof. This was high-octane.

"What do we do now?" he asked.

"We wait."

"What if nothing happens?"

"We go back to the Hilton and I explain what a dead body is doing in my room. You can be thinking something up."

We sat there and drank vodka and listened to the band give its version of "Deep Purple." At exactly ten P.M. the door opened and a girl came in. She wore a belted dark-green leather coat and high-heeled black pumps. Her hair was dark and long and fell to her shoulders in what they used to call a page-boy bob. She moved to our table and sat down.

"Order me a glass of wine," she said in German.

I signaled the waitress. She trudged over and I ordered the wine.

"Where's Weatherby? The girl asked. She pronounced the "w" like a "v" and the "th" like a "z.""

"Dead. Shot."

Persons register shock in many different ways. Some gasp and start saying "no" over and over as if, through denial, things can be changed back to the way they were. Others are more theatrical and they grow white and their eyes get big and they start chewing on their knuckles just before they yell or scream. And then there are those who just seem to die a little. The girl was like that. She grew perfectly still and seemed to stop breathing. She stayed that way for what seemed to be a long time and then closed her eyes and said: "Where?"

I foolishly started to say "in the back," but I said, "In West Berlin, in the Hilton."

The waitress was bearing down on us and the girl said nothing. Cooky found some more money and paid again, this time increasing the tip. There were still no thanks.

"Who are you?" I asked.

"Marta. He was to have a car."

"Who?"

"Weatherby."

"I have a car."

"You're McCorkle?"

I nodded. "This is Baker. This is Marta." Since it was a girl, Cooky gave her his dazzling smile. His German hadn't been sufficient to keep up with the conversation. I wasn't sure that mine had been either.

"Padillo said nothing about another man."

"He's a friend."

She glanced at her watch. "Did Weatherby—did he say anything before he died?" She got it out well enough.

"No."

She nodded. "What kind of car do you have?"

"A black Mercedes—the new one parked just across the street."

"Finish your drinks," she said. "Tell a joke. Laugh and then leave. Shake hands with me, both of you, before you go. He does not speak German?"

"No."

"Tell him then."

I told him.

The girl said, "Go out to your car and start the engine. I will follow in a minute or so."

I turned to Cooky and clapped him on the back. "When I get through saying this see how loud you can laugh. O.K. You can start any time."

Cooky laughed, the girl laughed, and I laughed. We shook hands and said *auf wiedersehen* and went out the door. The girl remained seated at the table.

It had grown cool, and I turned my coat collar up as we hurried toward the Mercedes. A car parked down the block started its engine, flicked on its lights, and spun its tires in its hurry to get away from the curb. It roared toward our corner and I jerked at Cooky's arm. The car was long and dark and looked something like a postwar Packard. It seemed to be aimed at us and we stumbled backward on the sidewalk. The car drew abreast and slowed slightly and I saw that there were two men in the front seat and one in the back. The two in the front didn't look at us. The back door flew open and a man spilled out, somersaulting once before he came to rest on his back in the gutter.

A face looked up at us with open eyes and long black hair that was mussed and dirty. Yet the teeth gleamed as whitely as ever. None were missing, but the smile held no humor. Bill-Wilhelm lay dead in the gutter, and the car kept on going and skidded around the corner, the engine straining, the back door still flapping as the man in the rear seat tried to close it.

"Let's go," I said, and raced for the Mercedes.

I started the engine and pounded the horn ring three times. The girl seemed to have understood, because the café door opened and she ran toward the car as I flicked the lights. When she saw the body she paused slightly but not much. I had the back door open, and the car was moving when she slammed it shut.

"What happened?"

"They dumped an American agent on us. Which way?"

"Straight ahead and then left at the second crossing. He looked dead."

"He was. Is Padillo all right?"

"He was an hour ago."

"That's a long time in this town."

"Where are we going?" Cooky asked.

"I'm just following directions," I said.

"We're being followed," she said.

I caught a glimpse of the headlights in the rearview mirror, "Brace yourself," I told her. "How good are you with that pistol, Cooky?"

"Not bad."

"Can you get a tire?"

"From thirty or thirty-five feet. No more."

"O.K., I'm going to take the next corner fast and then slam on the brakes. Jump out and see what you can do."

I sped up, threw the Mercedes down into second, and yawed around the corner on fat springs. I braked quickly to the curb and Cooky jumped out and ran to the corner. His gun was in his hand. He shielded himself with the edge of the building. The car started the corner fast, the driver making excellent use of gears and brakes. Cooky aimed carefully and fired twice. The car's right front and rear tires blew, giving the gun's blast a double echo. The car slewed toward the curb and I could see the driver wrestling for control, but it was too late, and it bounced over the far curb and crunched nicely into a building. By then Cooky was back in the Mercedes and I had it in low, the accelerator pressed hard against the floor board. It wasn't competition pickup, but it was steady. Cooky took out his flask and drank. He offered it to the girl in the rear seat, but she refused.

"Which way?" I asked her.

"We must take the side streets. They'll have radio contact."

"Which way?" I snapped.

"Left."

I spun the wheel and the Mercedes bounced around another corner. I was hopelessly lost.

"Now?"

"Straight ahead for three streets . . . then right."

I kept the Mercedes in second to provide braking power if we needed to turn quickly.

"I wonder why they dumped him on our doorstep."

"Burmser's boy?"

I nodded.

"Maybe they thought he was a friend of ours."

"I hope they weren't right."

CHAPTER 11

As we threaded our way deeper into East Berlin, the girl Marta said nothing but "right" and "left" and "straight ahead." Both pedestrian and automobile traffic grew lighter as the residential area gave way to an industrial section.

"We're in the Lichtenberg District," she said. "It's not far now. The next right."

I turned right and drove half a block.

"Here," she said; "turn down this alley."

It was between two five-story buildings that had escaped major combat damage. The alley was narrow—just wide enough for the Mercedes. I drove slowly, keeping only the parking lights on.

"At the back there is a shed. You can put the car in there."

"Left or right?"

"Left."

The alley was a cul-de-sac ending against a brick wall. Between the brick wall and the building was a shedlike building with sliding doors. I stopped the car and the girl got out.

"Help her, Cooky."

The girl handed Cooky a key and he unlocked a door and slid it open. I drove the car in and killed the engine and the lights. There was another car parked in the shed—a fairly new Citroën ID-19. It was green or black: I couldn't tell in the dark.

"This way," the girl whispered. She opened a door that led from the shed into the building. "They used to make uniforms here during the war, but the Russians took the machinery. Then it was turned into a sleeping barracks. Then a light-manufacturing concern. And now it is vacant. It will be for another month." She opened her purse and produced a pencil flashlight. "All the way to the top. Five flights." We moved up the stairs, guiding ourselves by the railing. By the time we reached the fifth floor I was gasping a little. The stairs ended on a small landing that had a large door. The girl knocked and it opened quickly. Padillo stood in the door, a cigarette in one hand, a revolver in the other. The girl brushed past him. She said, "There is trouble."

Padillo ignored her. "Hello, Mac."

"Weatherby's dead. Cooky decided to come along."

"Hello, Cook." Padillo never called him Cooky.

"Mike," Cooky acknowledged. "You can point that thing the other way." Padillo smiled and tucked the gun in the waistband of his slacks.

We entered the room. It was at least seventy-five feet long and thirty-five feet wide. From the twelve-foot ceiling hung long cords ending in two sixty-watt bulbs that fought weakly against the gloom. The windows were covered with tar paper. At one end of the room were a sink and a two-burner hot plate. A wooden box of canned goods and dishes and glasses sat on a low bench next to the sink. A long, unpainted wooden table with some nondescript kitchen chairs clustered together under one of the sixty-watt bulbs. At the other end of the room were six cots covered by thick gray blankets. A closetlike cubicle stood in one corner of the room.

"That's the john," Padillo said. "Let's sit over here." We sat at the long table. "What are you smoking?" he asked.

"Pall Malls." I handed him the pack.

"I ran out yesterday. You want a drink?"

"I'm half tight now," I said, "but, now that you mention it, yes."

"Marta, would you mind?" The girl had taken off her green leather coat. She wore a skirt and a frilly blouse. The blouse curved pleasantly. From the sink she brought a bottle of Stolichnaya, one of the better brands of Russian vodka. She poured drinks into water tumblers.

We drank. There were no toasts.

"Weatherby," Padillo said. "What happened?"

"We were in my room at the Hilton. He knocked on the door, stumbled in, and died on the rug. He'd been shot. In the back, if that makes any difference."

"He say anything?"

"He apologized for being early."

Padillo's lips compressed into a thin line and his fingers drummed on the table. "Christ."

I took another drink of the vodka: more high-octane. "So what brings us to East Berlin?" I asked.

"A couple of promoters have a clever one going," Padillo said. "They want to trade me for a pair of NSA defectors and I'm trying to buy up my contract. Weatherby was helping. Now that he's gone, we may have to cancel."

"How many do you need?" Cooky asked.

"Four."

"Weatherby, Mac and you would make three."

"There's another guy due: Max."

"With me you have four," Cooky said.

"You seem anxious for trouble, Cook."

Cooky smiled his half-joke smile. "In for a penny, in for a pound. I don't think we can get back through Checkpoint Charlie. When we came out of the café a big black car dumped a dead one right in front of us. He worked for your outfit, I understand. Then we were followed and I had to shoot the tires off another big black car. I think we're pretty well tagged."

"Cooky's very handy with a gun," I said. "Show him."

Padillo looked at him thoughtfully. "Go ahead, Cook."

Cooky stood up. "Give me a count, Mac."

I counted once more by thousands. Cooky dropped his shoulder, rolled his hip again, and made the draw in a swift circular motion.

"You're fast," Padillo said. "What are you wearing—a Berns-Martin?"

Cooky nodded and reholstered his gun.

"You'd have to be sober for what I have in mind. Or nearly so," Padillo said. "How hard would that be?"

"Hard enough," Cooky said, "but I can cut it."

"You don't know what it is yet."

"Look, either you recruit me or you don't. I thought you needed some help and I volunteered. Now you sound as if you're trying to steer me off."

"I just want to make it plain that you can't change your mind at the last minute because you think you're coming down with a bad case of the nasties. And if something happens, something sticky, just remember that you volunteered. I still don't know why you want in. Did Mac sell you?"

"Nobody sold me," Cooky said. "I thought you were in trouble and might need some help."

"I've known lots of guys in trouble," Padillo said, "but damn few that I'd run the chance of getting shot at for. I'm not in your best-buddy classification, Cook. And if Mac is, that's brand new, too."

I waved a hand. "Tell him what you have in mind, Mike. Maybe he won't want any part of it."

Padillo took a sip of his vodka and studied Cooky over the rim of the glass. "After I tell him, he's in," he said. "What about it, Cook?"

"I told you," he said, and tried his half-joke smile, "I'm a volunteer." The smile didn't come off too well.

"O.K.," Padillo said. "You're in."

"One thing more," I said to Padillo. "I ran into our fat friend Maas again. He said the main purpose of his trip to Bonn was to sell you the information about the trade."

"He give you any details?"

Quite a few. He also has a way out: a tunnel under the wall, which he'll sell for five thousand. That's how Cooky got involved. He brought me the five thousand from Bonn."

"You know how to get in touch with him?"

"He gave me his phone number," I said. "But if he knows about this swap, how many others know—and how did you tumble to it?"

Padillo lighted another cigarette. "They were a little too casual, a little too pleasant when they told me about it. It was their offhand attitude. Sort of 'Why don't you drop over and pick up these two because the Russians are tired of them?' It wasn't my kind of a job, and so I started checking with Weatherby's outfit. They found out that the opposition was expecting a new prize for its zoo: the kind of agent that the States keeps denying exists. It all added up to a swap: me for the NSA pair."

"Maas says you're an amortized agent. They can write you off as a tax loss."

Padillo nodded. "The Soviets haven't had anyone big since Powers. They could use a full-scale public trial if they plan to resurrect Stalin. Our side wants the two NSA guys back without any fanfare, and I was offered up—a little long in the tooth and creaky in the joints perhaps, but serviceable."

Padillo told us that he had crossed over into East Berlin with a spare passport after flying from Frankfurt to Hamburg to Tempelhof. I told him about Lieutenant Wentzel and Maas and the visit from Burmser and Hatcher at the saloon. I went through my chats with Bill-Wilhelm, Maas, and Weatherby, and finally the story seemed to dribble away and my mouth was dry and leathery. "I'm hungry," I said.

Marta rose from her chair. "I'll prepare something. It will have to be from a tin." She walked over to the hot plate and began to open a couple of cans.

"She doesn't talk much," I said.

"I suppose she doesn't feel like it," said Padillo. "She was Weatherby's girl." He got up and walked over to her. They talked briefly in tones so low that I couldn't hear. As Padillo talked the girl shook her head vigorously. Padillo patted her on the shoulder and came back. "She wants to stick with it," he said. "And we can use her. With you two and Max, we may be able to bring it off."

"Bring what off?" Cooky asked.

"A daylight snatch. The two NSA defectors." He looked at each of us carefully. His eyebrows were arched in a quizzical fashion; a wide grin was on his face.

I sighed. "Why not?"

Cooky licked his lips.

"How about it, Cook?" Padillo demanded.

"It sounds like an interesting proposition."

"What happens after we kidnap the two from NSA?" I said.

"We get them over the wall. They buy up my contract for me. And I'm out—finished. I can go back to running a saloon."

"It's not exactly crystal-clear," I said.

Padillo took a sip of his vodka. "The chief reason that the Soviets haven't publicized these new defectors is that they have become increasingly effeminate. At least that's what Burmser told me. If they put them on TV or let them be interviewed by the Western press, then Moscow could be turned into the mecca for the world's disenchanted homosexuals. The two guys are really of the la-de-da variety. They would be laughed at, and so would the Russians. So the KGB comes up with a deal, a quiet swap: me for the two defectors. Burmser is the contact, the go-between. He had to find something to trade and he settled on me because if I vanished one fine spring day there'd be none to cry, no Congressman to go visiting out in Virginia to find out what happened to a valuable constituent. Mac might get drunk for a day, but he'd get over it. After that, nothing—until the propaganda drums started beating in Moscow. Then the Soviets could produce their American agent of the variety which is said to be nonexistent by Washington."

"How can the defectors get you off the hook?"

"It's simple. Their defection is still a secret—one that has been kept by both the Russians and the States. I get them back over the wall, turn them in, and threaten to blow the lid off the whole story unless they turn me loose for keeps."

Marta silently placed a bowl of soup in front of each of us. She also set a platter of bread and cheese on the table.

"Aren't you eating?" Padillo asked.

"I'm not hungry," she said. "I'll eat later."

"I've told them about how it was with you and Weatherby."

She nodded.

I started to say I was sorry, but I knew it would be flat and meaningless. I drank the soup instead.

"Where do you plan to kidnap them?" Cook asked. His forehead glistened with sweat and his hands shook slightly.

"Better have a drink, Cooky," I said.

He nodded and poured himself half a tumbler of vodka and took a large swallow.

"If they fly them in, they'll arrive at Shönefeld, probably on an Army TU-104. Max is trying to check this out now. The guard should be light. If they follow the usual pattern, the guards who accompany them will hand them over at the airport and fly right back to Moscow. Since this is supposed to be a combined effort—the GDR and the Soviets— they'll probably bring them to the MfS on Normenstrasse."

"Not the Soviet Embassy?" Cooky asked.

"No. It's too well watched, for one thing; and the East Germans like to keep their hand in."

Padillo spread a map of Berlin on the table. "They'll drive north from the airport along this route. At this intersection is where we've planned to pull it off: nothing fancy—just a plain, daylight Chicago-style snatch. One car—the one you brought—will be parked here," he said, indicating a side street. "Their car will be traveling north, and you will be on their left on a one-way street. The job is to get your car into the main thoroughfare and make them smash into it—but not enough to hurt anybody, so your timing has to be just right. I'll be right behind them in the Citroën. I'll park so they can't back up. Then all of us out. We get the two pansies in the Citroën, one in front and one in back, and we drive like hell to here. We smash their radio first. It'll take them a few minutes to get to a telephone from that particular spot. By the time they do, we should be back up here."

"You kept saying 'you,' " I said. "You want me to drive the crash car?"

"You or Max."

"How'll I know when to pull out?"

"I've got a couple of miniature walkie-talkies. I'll give you the word. Cooky goes with me. Max goes with you."

Cooky pushed his bowl of soup away and poured himself another glass of vodka. "You don't think they'll be looking for something? Don't forget we've already been spotted."

"They may be. But by the time they get that far they'll have grown a little careless. Secondly, it's the only time the two NSA guys will be out in the open. It's the only chance—unless you can bust them out of the Ministry for State Security. I don't think we're that good—or dumb enough to try."

We heard the door slam five floors down. "That must be Max," Padillo said. We waited until the footsteps reached the door. There was a knock. A pause. And three quick knocks. Padillo moved to the wall by the door.

"Max?"

"Ja."

Padillo unlocked the door and opened it for a tall, stooped man in his late twenties who wore horn-rimmed glasses that rested on a prominent nose that leaned casually to one side. Quick blue eyes flickered over Cooky and me. The man was wearing a greenish-blue raincoat and a gray felt hat. He shook hands with Padillo, who introduced him as Max Vess. We shook hands and he walked over to Marta, who had cleared away the dishes, and embraced her. "I'm sorry," he said in German. "I am truly sorry. He was a good man." She smiled slightly and nodded and turned to the dishes in the sink.

"You heard, then?"

He shrugged. "It's on the West radio. The police are looking for Herr McCorkle. He was last seen crossing at Friedrichstrasse. With Herr Baker. Nothing more than that. They described Weatherby as a British businessman." His eyebrows shot up and he smiled slightly. "An accurate enough description, I suppose."

"How'd you make out?" Padillo asked.

Max took a small notebook out of his pocket. "They arrive tomorrow at noon. A car will met them—a Czech Tatra. They'll be handed over to one KGB operator and two from the MfS. They'll be taken to the Ministry on Normenstrasse. There'll also be a driver."

"How much did it cost?"

"Dear. Five hundred D-Marks."

"Here." Padillo took a roll from his pocket and counted out five hundred West German marks.

Max put them in his pocket. "I'll take Marta home," he said. "She's had enough today."

Padillo nodded and Max helped the girl into her green leather coat. "I'll be back in the morning around nine. I'll bring Marta." He nodded to us and they left. The girl had said nothing.

"Let's go over it again," Padillo said.

We went over it again, not only that time, but ten times more. At two in the morning we'd had enough. I fell asleep on a cot quickly and I dreamed a long dream about locks that wouldn't lock, doors that wouldn't open, and cars that wouldn't move when I pressed the accelerator.

CHAPTER 12

I awakened to the sound of running water hitting the bottom of a saucepan. Padillo was at the sink. He put the saucepan on the two-burner hot plate and turned the switch. I looked at my watch. It was six-thirty in the morning. I wondered whether the sun was shining or it had decided to rain again. It really didn't seem to matter, so I got up and went over to the table and sat down. Cooky was still asleep in the far cot.

"Instant coffee for breakfast," Padillo said. "There's some canned meat of some sort if you're desperate."

"I'm not."

"Tell me some more about your friend Maas and his tunnel."

"For five thousand bucks he'll spirit us out under the wall. Cooky brought the five thousand, as I told you last night. Here's the map." I reached into my jacket pocket and threw the envelope on the table.

Padillo picked it up, took out the map, and studied it. "It could be anyplace," he said. "You have his phone number?"

I nodded.

Padillo turned back to the hot plate, spooned some instant coffee into two cups, poured in the boiling water, stirred both of the cups, and set them on the table. "You want some sugar?"

"If you have it."

He tossed me two cubes and I unwrapped them and dropped them into my cup, stirring them with a spoon.

"If everything goes all right this afternoon, we're going to try to make it over this evening."

"Evening?"

"At dusk. It's the best time, because their lights are least effective. We'll use one of the methods that Weatherby worked out. Marta will arrange it in the West Sector. If it doesn't work, you'll probably have to give Maas a ring. His price isn't bad, by the way."

"That's what Cooky said. You think it'll work?"

"I don't know," he said. "I honest to God don't. It's costing a lot. Weatherby was a special sort of guy. I'm having a hard time getting used to the idea that he's dead just because I got tired of my job."

"I didn't know him, but he seemed like a grown man. He must have added up the risks at one time or another."

"Have you?"

"I don't think about it. If I thought about it, I'd go back to bed and pull the covers over my head. I don't know if I'll even be of much help."

Padillo borrowed another cigarette. "You'll do. I might even get you on permanently, Mac. You show promise."

"No, thanks. This is McCorkle's last case. The fox of Berlin is retiring from the field."

Padillo grinned and stood up. "I'd better rouse Cook." He walked to the far cot and shook Cooky, who rolled out and buried his head in his hands.

"One morning," Cooky muttered. "Just one morning without a hangover."

"Have some coffee," I called. "You might even keep the second cup down." He headed for the cubicle that enclosed the toilet. When he came out he seemed a bit pale. He walked over to the sink and splashed water on his face. Then he slumped at the table. Padillo put a cup of coffee in front of him.

"Sugar?"

"I'll use my own," he said, and took out the long silver flask, shook it to see if it still held a gurgle, unscrewed the cap, and took a long swallow. He shuddered and washed it down with coffee.

He seemed to brighten visibly. "Care for one?" he asked, shoving the flask toward Padillo.

"No, thanks, Cook; I seldom drink before nine."

Cooky nodded and brought the flask back and poured a sizable jolt into his coffee.

"All right, group; it's map-study time," Padillo said. He unfolded the *Falk-Plan von Berlin* again, which had cost somebody DM 4.80, and we went over the route until nine, when we heard the door slam downstairs. It was Max and Marta. She had done her crying for Weatherby during the night. Her eyes were red-rimmed. They sat down at the table.

"We've gone over the route a number of times, Max. It's the same one that you suggested. We're going to cross tonight. That means that Marta will have to get in touch with Kurt and his crew. We'll use plan three. Same time, same place, just as Weatherby and I agreed on. You know it, Marta?"

"Yes."

"When you get over into the West, stay over. Don't come back. If something goes wrong, we'll let you know what we plan next."

"We will be there," she said. "I should go now." She looked at us, her eyes resting briefly on each. "I wish you good luck. All of you." She left quickly, a tall, pretty, sad girl wearing a belted, green leather coat who examined the burden of her grief in lonely privacy. I thought that Weatherby would have liked her for that.

"After the crash," Padillo continued, "get out of the cars normally. Don't run. Cook and I will take the curb side. You two take the driver's side. Max will drive the Citroën back to here. We'll have to use the guns—but just wave them around; try not to drop them or pull any triggers. O.K.?"

We nodded.

"Cook and I will pick them up at the airport. The walkie-talkies are Japanese, and they're supposed to work within a mile's range. Cook will be on one radio, Max on the other. We'll close up just behind them in the block that ends on the street where you'll be parked. When Cook gives you the word, pull out. You can judge how fast you should move by the speed of their car. Clear?"

Max and I nodded again.

"I think it should work if they have only one car, if the walkie-talkies function, if one of you doesn't get hurt in the crash, and if they don't trap us on the way back here. That makes several ifs. I hope not too many. It's ten now. Cook and I will leave here at eleven. You and Max leave at twelve-fifteen. You should hear from us on the radio setup by twelve-thirty—if it works. We may as well check them out now."

The radios were Japanese, and they were called Llyods, and they worked. Padillo went down the five flights of stairs. "Do you read me all right?" His voice came through clear and tinny. "They're working fine," Max said. "Can you read me?" Padillo replied that he could. We waited until Padillo came back up and then we all had a drink. The vodka again.

There wasn't much to talk about, so we sat silently, sipping our drinks and smoking, each engrossed in his own thoughts, each wrestling with his own particular and personal fears.

At eleven Cooky and Padillo left. Max and I talked about the weather, a new act of a Berlin cabaret that I had caught on my previous trip, the cost of living in Berlin as compared with Bonn, and the movie business in general. Max said he went often to the movies. We didn't talk about what was going to happen at twelve-thirty P.M. At twelve-ten we went downstairs. I traded Max the key to the Mercedes for the one to the shed's sliding doors. I unlocked and shoved open the one in front of the Mercedes and Max backed it out. I closed the door, locked it, and climbed in beside him.

"You know they may be looking for this car—the police," he said.

"Probably. Do you think they'll turn it back to the rental-car service?"

Max laughed. "No chance."

"Well, I've just bought a new Mercedes."

Max drove carefully. We left the industrial area of Lichtenberg and began zigzagging our way through narrow side streets. At twelve twenty-eight Max said, "We're almost there. Next block we turn right. We should be hearing from them shortly." He made the right turn into a one-way street that was just wide enough for two cars. Max parked the Mercedes ten feet from the corner. "There is the thoroughfare they will take," he said, and took off his glasses and polished them.

"Let's change places," I said.

"It is not necessary."

"Let's do it anyway. My eyes are better than yours and I've probably been in more wrecks. I used to race a little when I had less sense."

Max smiled. "Truthfully, I am nervous about the accident. If anything should go wrong—"

"It won't," I said with what I hoped was an air of confidence.

We changed places. Max took the radio. A half-minute later it sputtered.

"We're a block behind them—about four minutes away." It was Cooky, his voice as deep and bland as if he were reading the news. "They are in a black Tatra: three in the back, three in the front. One of ours is in the back in the middle. The other's in the front in the middle. There are two cars between us and them. No connection. Over."

"We have it," Max said. "Over."

We waited.

"We're still one block behind—three minutes away now. Same as before. Over."

"We have it. Over."

"Two and a half minutes away. Over."

"We have it. Over."

I gripped the steering wheel to keep my hands from shaking. Max was sweating slightly, and he took out a handkerchief and polished his fogged glasses.

"Two minutes away and we're closing," the radio said. "Over."

"We have it. Over."

I started the engine. Or tried to. The starter ground busily, but nothing happened.

The radio crackled. "One and a half minutes away and still closing. Over."

"We have it," Max shouted, and his voice cracked. "Over."

I let up on the accelerator and waited thirty seconds. It seemed more like thirty years. "Flooded," I said, playing master mechanic. I turned the key and the engine caught.

"One minute away and right behind them. Over."

"We have it. Over."

I took my gun out of my raincoat pocket and laid it on the seat. Max did the same thing. We looked at each other. I grinned and winked. Max managed a weak smile. It probably had more confidence than mine.

"Two and a half blocks from you, thirty seconds away, and approaching at approximately fifty kilometers an hour. It's up to you. Good night and good luck."

I put the car in gear and edged it slowly toward the corner. The traffic on the thoroughfare was light. I counted to five and then moved the car past the corner of the building so I could see the approaching left-hand traffic. A Travant went past. Then I saw the Tatra a half-block away. It looked like the Chrysler folly of 1935. It was moving at around fifty. The Citroën was thirty feet behind it.

I started inching the car out into the thoroughfare past the curb, slowly. The driver of the Tatra gave me the horn and I stopped. He kept on coming, not braking. I waited three seconds and decided that that was the moment. I stepped on the gas and the Mercedes shot out into the path of the Tatra. The driver hit his horn, tried to swerve to the right, and slammed into the rear door and fender of the Mercedes. We bounced and skidded a yard or so.

"Keep your gun under your coat and take it slow," I told Max. He nodded.

We got out, glanced at the traffic, and walked toward the driver. I saw Padillo and Cooky making for the side near the curb. Water streamed from the Tatra's radiator. The driver was stunned by the crash; his head rested on the steering wheel. One of the men in the back seat poked his head out of the window and started to say something. I jumped for the door and opened it and showed him my gun at the same time. "Sit and don't move," I said in German. Then I said in English: "You—the American—get out."

Padillo had the front door open. "Out," he snapped. I could see Cooky's short-barreled Smith and Weston pointed at the men in the rear. Two men got out of the front. "Take him to the car," Padillo told Cooky, indicating the second man. "You. Get back in. Keep your hands in sight on the dashboard."

The young man in the middle of the back seat was scrambling out of the car. "Take him," I told Max. Max grabbed the man by the arm and shoved him quickly toward the Citroën, prodding him in the back with his gun.

Padillo opened the front door again, reached down, and jerked at something. I couldn't see, but I assumed it was the radio. Then he slammed the door.

"Let's go," he said.

We ran toward the car and threw ourselves in. I went in the back with Cooky and one of the Americans. Max was already gunning the car. The Citroën picked up speed and turned the corner too quickly. Max fought the wheel but climbed a curb, drove on the sidewalk for twenty feet, and then bounced back into the street.

"Take it easy, Max," Padillo said. "Nobody's behind us yet."

The two Americans had said nothing, apparently numb from the shock of the crash and the kidnapping. Then the one in the front seat turned to Padillo and said: "May I ask just what you people think you are doing?"

"Which one are you—Symmes or Burchwood?"

"Symmes."

"Well, Mr. Symmes, I have a gun that's aimed right at your stomach. I want you to shut up for the next ten minutes. No questions, no comments. That goes for Mr. Burchwood in the back seat, too. Is all that clear? Just nod your head if it is."

Symmes nodded.

"Is Mr. Burchwood nodding?" Padillo asked.

"He's nodding," Cooky said.

"Fine. Now let's all settle back and enjoy the ride."

CHAPTER 13

Nobody seemed to notice us as we drove rapidly through the side streets of East Berlin. Cooky fidgeted and chain-smoked but kept his gun trained on Burchwood. I glanced at my watch. Four minutes had elapsed since I had pulled the car out into the thoroughfare. Almost three of them had been spent in driving. The crash, the kidnapping, and all had taken less than one.

Max still clutched the wheel tightly, but he seemed less jittery. Padillo was half turned in his seat so that he could watch Symmes, who stared straight ahead. Symmes was tall—over six feet, I judged. He was wearing an American-looking suit of dark blue, a white shirt, and a blue-and-black tie. His hair was long and blond and shaggy. He needed a trim. Burchwood was dark, of average height. His black eyes flittered quickly, and he kept running his tongue over pale lips. He sat with his hands clenched in his lap, staring at the back of Symmes's neck. He wore an odd jacket and gray flannels. His shirt was pale blue and he had on a gray-and-maroon tie. His eyebrows looked plucked, but I gave him the benefit of the doubt.

"Speed it up a little, Max," Padillo said.

Max pressed down the accelerator and the Citroën quickened its pace. "We're almost there," he said.

We made two more rights and I recognized the building. Max turned down the narrow alley and pulled into the space before the shed. I got out and unlocked and pushed open one of the doors. Max drove in.

"I'll take Symmes; you take Burchwood," Padillo said to Cooky.

I closed the sliding door and locked it.

"Up the stairs, gentlemen," Cooky said. "There are five long flights."

We walked up the stairs and into the dimly lighted room. Padillo tucked his gun into his waistband. Symmes and Burchwood stood in the middle of the room close together. They looked around warily. They didn't seem to know what to do with their hands.

"Sit on that bunk," Padillo told them, indicating the nearest cot. "If you yell, there'll be no one to hear you. For the next few hours you're going to be held here. After that, you'll be moved."

They sat down on the cot. Symmes, the tall one with the blond hair and small pink ears, moved like a chorus boy. "You *are* Americans, aren't you?" he asked.

"Most of us," Padillo said.

"Would it be too much trouble to tell us just what you—I mean can't you tell us why you wrecked the car and brought us here?"

Burchwood, the shorter dark one, grimaced and ran his tongue over his lips again. "I suppose you're with the CIA or some other terribly clever organization."

"No," Padillo said.

"Well, who are you?"

"I don't think that matters," Padillo said. "As long as you do as we tell you, you'll be all right."

Burchwood sniffed.

Symmes said, "You apparently know all about us."

"Not all. Just enough."

Padillo walked over and sat at the table. Cooky, Max and I joined him. We stared at Burchwood and Symmes. They stared back at us.

"How's Moscow?" Cooky asked.

"We like it very much, thank you," Burchwood said. "We were treated with great courtesy."

"No press, though," Cooky said. "Not a line anywhere. Not even your pictures in the *New York Daily News*."

Symmes waved his hand gracefully. "We are not publicity seekers. Not like some others we know. And if you're trying to bait us, you can stop right now. We hold certain convictions which I could not possibly expect you to understand or appreciate."

"Knock it off, Cook," Padillo said.

"Oh, that's all right. We've met his kind before, haven't we, Gerald?"

Symmes looked at Cooky thoughtfully. "Often," he said. He smiled at Cooky. "In time we might get to like you, Slim."

"*I* like him right now," Burchwood said. "I think he could be nice, if he'd just let himself."

They reminded me of two cats. They had the same grace and the same unwinking stares. And, like cats, they had quickly accepted their new home after sniffing in the corners and scouting under the bed.

"Why don't you come over here and sit between us?" Symmes said to Cooky, and patted a spot on the bunk. "I'm sure we have just lots in common."

Cooky reached for the vodka bottle and poured himself a full tumbler. He gulped half of it and stared into the glass.

"Come on over, Slim. We both like you and we could—" Symmes's suggestion was cut short by the glass that Cooky threw at him.

"Goddamned queers," he said. His voice was thick—the first time I had ever heard it slur. "Queers and Communists is what it's all about now. If they get hold of you, they never let go; you just keep on and on and on . . ."

"You've been at the sideboard again," Padillo told him.

"We're not Communists, sweetie," Symmes sang out.

Burchwood giggled. Max got a pained expression on his face and looked the other way.

Cooky was on his feet and headed toward the pair, who cowered in mock horror. "Oooh—here comes the big man," Burchwood crooned.

Padillo caught Cooky by the arm and swung him against the wall. "I told you to knock it off. I also told you to keep sober. You're not doing either."

"They bug me," Cooky said.

"They're trying to." Padillo walked over to the cot, where Symmes and Burchwood grinned wickedly at him. They nudged each other as Padillo stood looking down at them with a faint smile.

"He's cute, too," Burchwood said.

Symmes smirked. "I saw him first. After all, he rescued me."

They both tittered.

Padillo grinned at them. "Playtime's over," he said. "When the sun goes down you're going over the wall with us. You'll have a gun pointed at you all the way. If something happens, if you do the wrong thing, that gun goes off. Once you're back in the West, I plan to turn you in. You may as well know that now. I don't know what they'll do with you; I don't really care. But if you don't do exactly as I say, and do it when I say, then you'll be dead."

He turned abruptly and walked back to the table. Symmes and Burchwood seemed to huddle together on the cot, as if they were cold. After a moment they began whispering to each other.

"You think that'll work?" I asked.

"If it doesn't, then I shoot them."

"That simple, huh?" Cooky said. "Everything's as simple as that."

"To me it is," Padillo said.

"Suppose you let us in on how we're going to get over the wall and when and where. Or is that simple, too?"

"How drunk are you, Cook?" Padillo said.

"I'll carry my end."

"Not if you stagger, you won't. I didn't ask for your help. I may appreciate it, but I didn't ask for it. And if you're lushed, you'll get left."

"I asked him," I said.

Padillo turned to me. "Think back. Did you?"

I thought back. "I asked him," I repeated.

"Then you keep him sober. If he's not, he gets left."

"I want to know where we go over the wall and when," Cooky said sullenly. "I have a right to know."

"No, you don't," Padillo said. "You don't have any rights at all. But I'll give an idea of what we're going to do. No places, though. No exact times. Just an idea. There'll be an eight-foot-high wall. We run to that wall at dusk, after we receive a signal. We go up a ladder and down another on the other side. Then we run to an apartment building directly in front of the wall."

"What are the Vopos and Grepos doing all this time?" Cooky asked.

"They'll be diverted."

"How?"

Padillo looked at him coldly. "It doesn't matter how. Let's just say that they will."

"I think we should know," Cooky insisted. His voice was petulant.

"No."

"Our plan worked before—some time ago," Max interrupted smoothly. "The trouble lies in the number who have to go over. Usually there have been only one or two."

"We heard all that," Symmes called. "We're not going; you can't make us. What if you have to drag us? What if we scream? You can't shoot us; you'd give yourself away."

Padillo didn't look at them. "You won't scream," he said in a patient voice, "because I can kill you a dozen ways with my hands before you open your mouth. Or I can slit your throat with a knife. If you go limp on us, that's what I'll do." He turned and looked at them then. "Maybe I haven't made it clear. If you don't bust a gut to get over that wall, you'll die. If you've made up your minds to try to screw up, just let me know. I'll kill you right now." He could have been making an offer to run them down to the corner drugstore so that they wouldn't get wet in the rain.

Symmes stared at Padillo. He swallowed once, and then he and Burchwood resumed their whispering.

Cooky shoved his chair back from the table and stood up. "I don't think any of us are going over the wall," he said.

"Why not?" Padillo asked.

"Because we're going to turn ourselves in."

Padillo rose from his chair. He got up slowly, carefully. "I don't think I understand, Cook. Maybe I should—maybe it's obvious—but I don't understand."

"You've been riding me enough. I think you understand."

"Spell it out," Padillo said.

"I've just said it. We're going to turn ourselves in."

"I understand that part," Padillo said. "That's very clear. But why should we turn ourselves in? Do you want it that simple? Just march down to the nearest corner and call a cop?"

I sat still, my hands resting on the table. Max did the same.

"Something like that," Cooky said.

"Your idea, Cook?"

"My idea."

"Why didn't we do it this morning? Why didn't we turn ourselves in then?"

Cooky tried the half-joke smile, but his face crumpled in the effort. "I didn't know you had such a crazy plan then; you can't get over that wall. You can't even get through the death strip. It's a crazy plan. I don't want to get killed."

Padillo kept his eyes on Cooky. "Did you tell Cook that you were going to meet Weatherby at the Hilton last night, Mac?"

"Yes."

"Tell anyone else?"

"No."

"What have they got on you, Cook?" Padillo asked.

"I don't understand."

"I mean what has the opposition got on you—what kind of blackmail? What have you done that's so bad that you'd kill a man like Weatherby? And you killed him: nobody else could have, because nobody knew he was going there except you and Mac."

"You're nuts. I just don't want to get killed going over that wall."

"I think you're a sleeper, Cook. I think they've just been waiting to use you for something like this."

"You're rambling," Cooky said.

"No. You're not doing it for money: you've got enough. Not out of conviction: you don't have any. It could only be blackmail. What was it, Cook? Pictures?"

"We're going to turn ourselves in," Cooky said, but his voice didn't have much conviction.

"No easy way," Padillo said. "You'll have to make us."

Cooky looked as if he wanted to say something else but changed his mind. He seemed to shrug, but his shoulder dipped quickly and his hip rolled. The gun was almost pointing at Padillo when Cooky's nose disappeared and the ugly red blotch opened in his throat. Then Cooky's gun went off and the bullet smacked into the floor. Padillo had fired twice. The shots slammed Cooky back over a chair. He was dead by the time he fell from the chair to the floor. The gunpowder smell was sharp and metallic and my ears rang. My hands still rested on the table, the palms grew wet, and I felt the sweat gather in my armpits. Padillo shook his head in a gesture of embarrassment or disgust and stuck the revolver back in his waistband.

"I just outdrew the fastest gun in East Berlin," he said. "Except that he was drunk."

"It all went a little quickly for me," I said.

"Search him, Max. Keep the money; burn the rest."

I got up and walked over to one of the cots and got a blanket. I threw it down by the body. "You can cover him up with this," I told Max.

Padillo walked around the table, bent, and picked up Cooky's Smith and Wesson. He looked at it curiously. "Mine shot high," he said. "It's the first time I've used it."

"Well?" I said.

Padillo poured himself a glass of vodka. Then he poured two more for Max and me. He held his glass with both hands and looked down into it. "If you go back far enough, you can dig up something in his past that he thought was God-awful—that he didn't think he could live with." Padillo sighed and took a swallow of his drink. "Maybe that's why he drank too much and lied too much and chased the girls. And, after a while, maybe he blamed it on everything.

"He was sauced when he came to see me one time. He didn't show it, but he never did very much. Until now. He told me that he knew what I was up to and that if I ever needed any help, just to let him know. But he told you that. Cook also said that he had certain connections and so forth. He talked in circles, but it was enough for me to know that I was blown. I kidded him along. Did he tell you that one of his girl friends told him about me?"

"Yes."

"They may get drunk and they may talk in the sack, but they didn't know about me. The only way Cook could have found out on our side was from Burmser or Hatcher—or you. And none of you would talk. He had been tipped off by somebody in the opposition; and if he was tipped off, then he had to be working for them."

"Not for money," I said.

"No, but because they knew all about his horrible secret, whatever it was. Maybe he was drunk when it happened, or maybe he got to be a lush afterward. It doesn't matter now. I had you get him to have the place swept because I wanted to keep tabs on him. When he showed up with you here, I was certain that he was in on it somehow. Maybe they were impressed with the way he could handle a gun."

"He was gay," Symmes said dully. "Maybe you think it's silly, but we can tell. We have to be able to tell."

"There's one expert's opinion," Padillo said.

"One thing bothers me. Cooky had to get rung in on this, but I called him myself."

"Why?"

"To borrow five thousand."

"And who said you needed five thousand?"

"Maas—and the light dawns clearly. Maas set up the tunnel deal so I would have to call Cooky for the money."

"Don't sell your fat friend short," Padillo said. "He just might have a tunnel. I'd be willing to bet that Cook set the deal up with Maas. Cook was the only source that you could get that much money from in a hurry. I'll bet another buck that he was sitting by his phone, the money in his briefcase, just waiting for you to call. I don't care how much he has on deposit: getting five thousand dollars out of Deutsche Bank at four in the afternoon is damn near impossible."

"But why kill Weatherby?"

"It gave him the excuse to tag along, for one thing; and he may have been given instructions to kill him if he got the chance."

"What do you want to do with him?" Max asked.

Padillo shrugged. "Drag him over in the corner. Somebody will find him sometime."

Max went through Cooky's pockets quickly. Then he threw the blanket over him and dragged the body to a corner. It left a smear of blood on the floor. Max got a mop and cleaned it up. Padillo and I watched. Symmes and Burchwood sat quietly on the bed and held hands, their faces white and pinched-looking. Burchwood kept wetting his lips nervously.

Max came back and sat down at the table. He reached for the glass of vodka. "Dirty work," he commented. "He should have waited until the wall tonight. He'd have had a chance."

"Probably afraid to," Padillo said. "He was beginning to crack, and the liquor wasn't helping. But maybe he just wanted all the way out. He didn't have to go through that *High Noon* routine. He could have slipped his gun out when he was sitting at the table."

"There are a number of ways to commit suicide," Max said.

"He seems to have tried them all."

Max was going through the papers that he had taken from Cooky's body. He passed something over to me. It was the envelope containing the check that I had written for the five thousand dollars. I opened it and handed it over to Padillo. He glanced at it and tore it up. Neither of us had anything to say.

CHAPTER 14

Max got up and put on his coat. "I'd better do some checking," he said. Padillo sat slumped in his chair, his feet on the table, his eyes half closed. His mouth was in its thin, hard line. He only nodded. "I'll be back in an hour," Max said. Padillo nodded again. Max left, closing the door quietly.

Burchwood and Symmes were stretched out on two of the cots. Symmes seemed asleep, but Burchwood lay on his back, his arms folded behind his head. He stared at the ceiling. We waited.

Padillo sighed and swung his feet off the table. "There's a good chance it may go sour tonight," he said.

This time I nodded. Then I said, "If anything happens to me, you can have my ties. They were selected with great care."

"The gold cuff links. They're yours," he said.

"You mean the ones with your initials?"

"The same."

"That's thoughtful."

Padillo picked up the vodka bottle and eyed it critically. "We have four more hours to go. We may as well finish this."

"Why not?" I said, and moved a glass toward him. He poured expertly. There was a half-tumbler for each.

"Maybe Max will bring another bottle," he said.

"And cigarettes. We're about out."

"How many do you have?"

I took out my package and counted. "Six."

Padillo counted his. "Four."

We drank and lighted cigarettes.

"There'll be a few odds and ends to clear up if we get over tonight," I said. "Minor items really—such as Weatherby dead in my room, the Mercedes I rented and wrecked, what happened to Cooky—a few details."

"You've forgotten one," Padillo said.

"What's that?"

"I have to get our two friends all the way back to Bonn."

"You're right. I'd forgotten. You have a plan, of course."

"Of course. The wall is a minor problem compared with the zone. First we get them out of Berlin. I'm using the editorial we. We'll go at night. At the edge of Berlin the first thing we have to cross is a three-mile-wide strip where they ask for a special pass if they find you in it. Then there's a strip about fifteen hundred feet wide that's planted in crops—maybe a foot high at the most. Anyway it doesn't provide any cover. Next there are the watchtowers located on the strip that's about four hundred and twenty feet wide. That's what they call the security strip. Every house, tree and shrub has been removed. There's nothing but the towers. Of course we make that."

"We're pretty good, I'd say."

"We're perfect. Now comes a nineteen-foot strip that is constantly patrolled. They have dogs—Dobermans. Then there's a fence that we have to get over—assuming we pull a fast one on the patrol. Now that we're over the fence we go across eighty feet of land mines. But we're still lucky. We avoid getting blown up. Then another fence. I seem to recall that it's electrified. Then there's another hundred and thirty feet or so of plowed land that will show any footprint. After the plowed land there's a thirty-three-foot death strip. Anything that moves in it is shot. But once we make that, all we have to do is go over another fifteen-foot fence that is wired to sound a million or so alarms if it's touched. But we're clever. We get over that, too—all the time helping our two friends here."

"Then what?"

"Nothing much. We make our way through a hundred and ten miles of East Germany and repeat the whole process again at the west border."

"I tell you what. I bought a round-trip ticket on an airplane that flies to Düsseldorf. I'll use that."

"I don't think we'll try going through the zone. We'll have to fly. Maybe charter a plane," he said dreamily.

"Something tells me they might be looking for us—I mean our side."

Padillo scratched his chin. "You know, I think you're right. We'll figure it out later."

In an hour Max returned. He brought cigarettes, vodka and sausage.

"Hear anything?" Padillo asked.

Max shrugged. "They've got the Vopos and Grepos on special alert. They expect a break over the wall tonight, tomorrow or the next day. My source wasn't too communicative."

"I can't blame him," Padillo said.

"But they have twenty-seven miles to cover," Max said. "Tonight is as good as tomorrow. Maybe better. I don't think they expect us to try so soon."

"Everything O.K. on Kurt's end?"

Max nodded. "They're set. They sent word through the usual channel."

"Good. Max, you slice the sausage and the bread. I'll make some coffee."

We ate and gave sandwiches and coffee to Symmes and Burchwood. They sat together again on one of the cots and ate hungrily. They whispered to themselves and ignored us.

All conversation died. Max sat and stared into his coffee. Padillo slumped back in his chair and elevated his feet to the table. He stared at the ceiling. His lips were back in their thin tight line. I put my head down on the table and closed my eyes. The vodka and food helped. I slept.

I awoke when Padillo shook my shoulder. "We leave in fifteen minutes," he said. I nodded, rose and walked over to the sink. I doused my face in cold water. Padillo moved to the cots and shook Symmes and Burchwood awake. "Sit over there at the table," he said. "I'm going to tell you what you have to do."

Max had the map spread out. "You two," Padillo said, "will go downstairs with us and get quietly into the back seat of the car. McCorkle will sit with you. Max will drive and I'll be in the front. We have a twenty-minute ride ahead of us—maybe twenty-five minutes. If we're stopped, say nothing. If you try anything, either Mac or I will shoot you."

They nodded. I think they believed him. I didn't know whether I did or not.

"We will park here," he said, pointing to a spot on the map. "You will get out of the car and follow me. Mac will be right behind you. The four of us will stand in this doorway. When I give the signal you'll run—not walk—to the wall. You'll go up a ladder and down another on the other side. Then you'll run to this doorway. Both times you'll run as fast as you ever have in your lives. If you don't run fast enough, you may get shot by the Germans. If you try any heroics, you will be killed by me. I hope you believe that."

"What happens when we get over the wall?" Symmes asked.

"We'll save that for later," Padillo said. "But nothing so bad as what will happen if you don't make it."

Symmes and Burchwood looked at each other glumly.

Padillo turned to Max. "You know what to do?"

Max examined the fingernails of his right hand. "I drive, park the car and wait three minutes. If you're not back, I leave."

Padillo looked at his watch. "We've got five minutes. We may as well have a drink."

He poured five measures of vodka, held up the bottle, shrugged, and topped off the glasses with what was left. It was a sizable jolt. Symmes and Burchwood gulped theirs down greedily. I wasn't far behind. I looked around the room. The blanket-covered shape in the corner was only a lump. I couldn't feel anything toward it one way or the other. I was numb.

Max turned off the two sixty-watt bulbs and we walked down the stairs guided by his flashlight. In the shed Max flicked the light over the car.

"It's a Wartburg," he said. "The Citroën was too hot."

I walked around the car and got in the backseat on the right-hand side. Padillo stood by the rear left-hand door until both Symmes and Burchwood were in. Then he closed the door, walked around the back of the car, slid the shed door open, and waited until Max backed the car out and had it pointed toward the alley. He closed and locked the door and got in the front seat next to Max. He turned and showed Symmes and Burchwood his gun. "This is just to remind you," he said. "McCorkle has one, too."

I dutifully dragged my .38 out of my raincoat pocket and let them look at it. "It shoots real bullets," I said.

Max guided the Wartburg out of the alley and headed it west. It was about seven-thirty. Still daylight. He drove normally. The traffic grew heavier as we approached the Mitte section of East Berlin.

Padillo sat half-turned in the front seat, his eyes flicking from Burchwood and Symmes to the rear of the car and then to the traffic in front. Burchwood and Symmes sat stiffly in the back, their knees close together. They held hands again. I wished there was somebody to hold mine.

It grew darker. Max switched on his parking lights. It was that time of day when you debate whether you can see better with or without your headlights. We had been driving for fifteen minutes when we stopped for a traffic signal. We waited fifteen seconds, and then the Volkspolizei drew up beside us in a Trabant. There were four of them. The two on the right looked us over carefully. One of them said something to the driver. The light changed to green and Max pulled away. The Trabant dropped in behind us.

"They're following," Max said.

"Don't look around," Padillo warned Symmes and Burchwood. "Talk to each other. I don't care if you repeat the Lord's Prayer. Just talk like you were carrying on a conversation. Give me a cigarette, Mac, and offer me a light."

Symmes and Burchwood talked. I don't remember what they said, but it seemed like nonsense at the time. I produced my last cigarette and tapped Padillo on the shoulder. He turned around and smiled, accepting it. "They're still behind us," he said.

"I know," Max said. "We should turn at the next block."

"How's the time?" Padillo asked.

"We have a three- or four-minute leeway."

"Go up three blocks and then turn. If they still follow, you're going to have to try to lose them."

Max continued to drive at a steady forty kilometers an hour. He made two green lights. I counted blocks. On the third one he signaled for a right turn. He pulled over to the right-hand lane and turned the steering wheel carefully, shifted down into second, and watched the police Trabant in the rearview mirror. He sighed. "They kept on going," he said.

I exhaled noisily. I discovered that I had been holding my breath. Padillo glanced at his watch. "We should be right on time," he said. Max circled the block and drove back the way we had come. He turned left on a side street and parked the car. It was twilight.

"Everybody out," Padillo ordered.

I showed Symmes and Burchwood my gun before I put it into my raincoat pocket. "It'll shoot right through it," I said.

Padillo was out first and around the car to open the door for the pair. I crawled out after them.

"I go first," Padillo said. "Then Symmes and Burchwood. You're last, Mac."

We headed down a narrow passageway between two buildings. I let my left hand drag on the brick wall. My right hand was in my coat pocket, wrapped around the revolver. It was not dark, and I could easily see the three figures outlined before me. Padillo turned right around a corner. I followed after Symmes and Burchwood into the recess of a doorway. The door itself had been bricked up. Directly in front of us was the wall, built of meter-square concrete slabs and topped off with crudely laid concrete blocks. Three or four strands of barbed wire ran across the top. I could also catch the faint glint of broken bottles stuck into dabs of cement on top of cement blocks.

Symmes and Burchwood huddled together in a corner of the recess. Padillo kept his eyes fixed on a seven-story apartment building in West Berlin that lay directly in front of us.

"The third floor from the top," he whispered. "The fourth window from the left. See it?"

"Yes."

"When that Venetian blind goes up we get ready. When it goes down we set the outdoor record for the sixty-foot dash—straight ahead. The wire's been cut between here and the wall. Just push it open. You'll go first this time. Then Symmes and Burchwood." He turned to them. "You understand?" They whispered yes. We waited fifteen seconds. Nothing happened. The blind didn't move. Two Vopos passed in front of us, fifty feet away from our doorway, ten feet from the wall. We waited another five seconds.

To our right there were three sharp explosions. They were followed by bright flashes of light. "That's the diversion on the right," Padillo said. "Now on the left." Two seconds later there were three more blasts followed again by the light. "They're a hundred and fifty yards to our right and left. Molotov cocktails. They should draw the Vopos. Their machine pistols are good for only a hundred and ten yards. Watch the blind."

I watched the building that was 150 feet away. It could have been 150 miles. We could hear the police shouting orders to the left and right, their voices distant but penetrating. Somewhere a siren began. The blind that we had been watching began to rise slowly. It seemed to inch its way to the top of the window, it paused, and then suddenly it dropped.

"Now!" Padillo barked.

Searchlights began to play fitfully on the wall but lost their effectiveness in the dusk. I took my gun from my pocket and ran. A machine pistol chattered from my left. I kept running, scanning the top of the wall. I could hear Burchwood and Symmes panting and scrambling behind me. We pushed through the wire and were at the wall. "Where's the goddam ladder?" I whispered to Padillo. He stared up the rough gray blocks.

Suddenly a blond head poked over the wall. "Be right with you chaps. I had to snip the wire," the head said; "now just let me get the pallet over the glass." A thick brown pallet made of two blankets sewn together, thickly stuffed and padded, was flopped over the top. Then the head reappeared with a reassuring grin. "Just a moment," it said. "Have to straddle the thing to get the ladder up."

He was young, not more than twenty. He got one leg over the wall and sat astride the stuffed pallet. "Embarrassing if any of that glass worked through," he said calmly. "Here comes the ladder." It started up over the wall. "My name's Peter," the blond kid said. "What's yours?"

He had it balanced on the wall when the shout came. It couldn't have been from more than forty feet away. Then the faint, not quite yellow light settled on the kid. His mouth opened to say something more, something casual perhaps, but the bullets slammed into him. He teetered for a moment on the wall as if trying to make up his mind which way to fall. But he was past caring. The ladder balanced crazily for a moment and then tilted up slowly and slid out of sight on the other side. The kid fell forward on the pallet, rolled to his left, and followed the ladder.

Padillo turned and fired three shots at the light, which was still focused at the top of the wall. I got off three more in the same direction. The light went out and there was a yell. More shouts of command were coming from both our right and our left. There was another burst of machine-pistol fire. "Back to the car," Padillo ordered.

"I can't move," Symmes said.

"Are you hit?"

"No—I just can't move."

Padillo slapped him sharply across the face. "You'll move or I'll kill you." Symmes nodded and Padillo shoved me ahead. "You first." I ran back to the building and down the passageway to the street. Max's face, a white blob of pure fear, was peering out of the window. I jerked open the back door and held it for Symmes and Burchwood, who threw themselves in. Padillo paused at the entrance to the passageway and fired three shots. A machine pistol answered him. He darted around the front of the car and lunged for the door as Max raced the engine. Before he had the door closed the Wartburg was at its peak in low gear and Max was noisily wrestling it into second.

"The garage, Max," Padillo said. "It's only a half a mile away."

"What happened?" Max asked.

"They got lucky or Kurt's people got careless. The bombs went off O.K. and they gave us the signal. We got to the wall and there was this blond kid—"

"Very young?" Max asked.

"Yes."

"That would be Peter Vetter."

"He was on top of the wall, pulling the second ladder up and making introductions, when a spare patrol dropped by. They shot him, and the ladder went with him. On the other side. Either Mac or I shot out the light, and we ran like hell."

"My God, my God," Max murmured.

Symmes buried his head in his arms on his lap and started to weep uncontrollably. "I can't do any more," he sobbed. "I don't care what happens—I just can't. You're all awful, just awful, awful!"

"Shut him up," Padillo ordered Burchwood.

Burchwood gestured helplessly. "What do you want me to do?"

"I don't know," Padillo said irritably; "just shut him up. Pat him on the head or something."

"Don't touch me!" Symmes screamed.

Padillo reached back and grabbed a handful of the long blond hair. He jerked Symmes's head up. "Don't flake out on us now, Jack." His voice crackled harshly. His eyes seemed to burn into Symmes's face.

"Let go of my hair, please," the blond man said with a curious kind of dignity. Padillo released him. Symmes slumped back into the seat and closed his eyes. Burchwood patted his knee tentatively.

Max made the half-mile in two minutes. He pulled down a side street and honked the horn in front of a none-too-prosperous-appearing *Autozubehör*. He honked the horn twice more and the grimy door slid open. Max drove the car inside. The door closed behind us. Max killed the motor and rested his head wearily on the steering wheel.

"I'm like our friend in the back seat," he said "I can't do much more. It's been a very long day."

A fat man, wearing dirty white coveralls and wiping his hands on a piece of waste, walked up to Max. "You're back, Max?"

Max nodded wearily. "I'm back."

"What do you want?"

Padillo got out of the car and walked around to the fat man.

"Hello, Langeman."

"Herr Padillo," the man said. "I did not expect you back."

"We need a place to stay tonight—four of us. We also need food, some schnapps, and the use of a telephone."

The fat man threw the waste into a can. "The risk has increased," he said. "So has the price. How long will you be staying?"

"Tonight—maybe most of tomorrow."

125

The fat man pursed his lips. "Two thousand West German Marks."

"Where?"

"There is a basement. Nothing fancy, but dry."

"And the telephone?"

The man jerked his head toward the rear of the garage. "Back there."

Padillo took out his revolver and casually transferred it to his slacks waistband. "You're a thief, Langeman."

The fat man shrugged. "It's still two thousand Marks. You can call me some more names if it makes you feel any better."

"Pay him, Max," Padillo said. "Then take those two down to the basement. Be sure Langeman gets you the food and schnapps. For that price, he can throw in some cigarettes."

Max, Langeman and the two Americans moved toward a door at the end of the garage. I got out of the car and walked around it slowly. I was old and tired. My joints creaked. A tooth hurt. I leaned against the front fender and lighted a cigarette.

"What now?"

"You still have Maas's number?"

I nodded my head carefully. There was danger that it might drop off.

"Let's call him and see if he still wants to do a little business."

"You trust him?" I asked.

"No, but have you got any better ideas?"

"I ran out last night."

"His price was five thousand bucks—right?"

"It was. It's probably gone up, if I know Maas."

"We'll dicker. Let's see the five thousand Cook gave you."

I took the flat, wrapped package out of my coat pocket and handed it to Padillo. I remembered the exchange with Cooky in the hotel room. He hadn't looked at my check; I hadn't counted the money. Gentlemen scholars. I closed my eyes as Padillo ripped open the package. "Blank sheets of paper?"

"Not at all," he said. "Cut-up newspaper." I opened my eyes. Padillo tossed the newsprint into the can where Langeman had thrown the waste.

"Cook knew you pretty well, Mac. He also didn't seem to think you'd have the chance to spend the money."

"There's one consolation," I said. "There's no doubt about the stop payment on the check."

CHAPTER 15

Langeman's garage was a twenty-by-forty-five-foot building with a grease pit; a couple of chain pulleys to hoist cars up; an oil-smeared, cluttered workbench that ran most of the length of the right-hand wall; and a small partitioned-off cubicle in the left rear that served as his office. He waddled toward us from the cubicle, counting a sheaf of Deutsch Marks and wetting his thumb every third or fourth bill. His once-white coveralls seemed to have picked up some more dirt and grease in the few moments he had been gone. He had also acquired a yellow-brown smudge on his wide flat nose, which somebody had broken for him at one time and nobody had yet got around to setting. His breath whistled through it with a bubbling sound that indicated he might do well to blow it once in a while.

"I gave them some food and some schnapps, Herr Padillo."

"How about cigarettes?"

"Cigarettes, too. Yes." Langeman nodded his head vigorously and his three chins danced and lapped around his collar.

"How do we get down to your cellar?"

"Through my office: there is a trap in the floor and a ladder. It's not much, but, as I said, it's dry. There is also light. The telephone is in the office."

"We won't be using it until around eleven."

Langeman bounced his chins around again in a nod. "Any time. I am leaving now and will return at eight hours tomorrow. I have two helpers who will arrive at that time. If you go out, I must send them on errands. The noise of the work here will prevent them from hearing you if you speak normally. For a toilet there's a bucket." He tucked the sheaf of bills into his coveralls and gave a slight shrug. "Not luxurious, but it's clean."

"And expensive," Padillo said.

"There is the risk to consider."

"We're acquainted with the risk. Suppose we have to go out tonight. How do we manage it?"

"There is a door at the rear leading from my office. It will lock automatically as you close it. But to get back in is another problem. You can have someone—Max, perhaps—posted by the door. But you must be back before eight hours tomorrow. My two helpers will be here." Langeman paused and then asked carefully: "Would it not be dangerous for you to go out tonight?"

Padillo let the question wander for a while in search of an answer before he said, "You weren't paid to worry about us, Langeman."

The fat man shrugged. "As you wish. I am leaving now. The light in my office burns all night; the rest I turn off."

Without saying good night Padillo and I walked back to the cubicle. It contained a bill-strewn fourth- or fifth-hand oak desk, a swivel chair with a greasy-looking rubber pad, a wooden filing cabinet, and some automobile-repair catalogues. A light with a green shade hung from the ceiling. The telephone sat on the desk. The office had no window—only a door with a spring lock. A trap door that was in the corner not occupied by furniture was fastened against the wall with a hook and eye. A ladder led straight down. Padillo went first and I followed.

It was a twelve-by-twelve room with a seven-foot ceiling. A forty-watt bulb provided the illumination. Burchwood and Symmes sat on a gray blanket against one wall, chewing on some bread and meat. Max sat on another blanket opposite them, a bottle of some kind of liquor in his hand.

"There's a blanket and there's the food and cigarettes," he said. A foot or so of sausage and a part of a loaf of bread sat on a newspaper on the floor. Four packages of cigarettes, an East German brand I had never heard of, were stacked next to them.

I sat down on the blanket and accepted the bottle from Max. It was unlabeled. "What is it?"

"Cheap potato gin," he said. "But it's alcohol."

I took a swallow. The liquor burned all the way down, clawed at my stomach, bounced a couple of times, and started to move around warmly. "Christ!" I said, and passed it to Padillo. He took a swallow, coughed, and handed it back to Max.

Max set the bottle down on the newspaper. "There's food." I looked at it without interest, trying to make up my mind whether to risk another swallow of the potato gin. I decided against it and opened one of the packages of cigarettes, lighted one, and passed the pack to Padillo. We coughed over the tobacco for a while.

"What do you brilliant people plan to do now?" Burchwood asked. "Drag us through another mess like this evening?"

"Something like that," Padillo said.

"And I suppose we'll be shot at again," Symmes said, "and you'll get mad and take it out on us." He seemed to assume that he wouldn't get hit.

"If it doesn't work this time, you won't have to worry about another try," Padillo said. "In fact, you won't have to worry about much of anything. None of us will."

He glanced at his watch. "We've got a couple of hours before you call, Mac. You and Max might as well get some sleep. I'll stay up."

Max grunted, wrapped himself in his blanket, and rested his head on his arms, which he laid across his raised knees. Padillo and I sat on the blanket and leaned against the wall and smoked. Burchwood and Symmes followed Max's example.

130

It was slow time. I went through a what-in-hell-am-I-doing-here cross-examination, then shifted into a small orgy of self-pity, and finally just sat there and planned the saloon's menus, day by day, for the next five years.

"It's eleven," Padillo said.

"Let's go."

We climbed up the ladder and I dialed the number that Maas had given me. It answered on the first ring. "Herr Maas, please," I said.

"Ah!" the familiar voice said. "Herr McCorkle. I must say that I have been anticipating your call—especially since the accident this evening. That was you, was it not?"

"Yes."

"No one was hurt?"

"No."

"Very good. Herr Padillo is with you?"

"Yes."

"Now, then, I assume that you wish to conclude the business arrangement that we discussed day before yesterday?"

"We'd like to talk about it."

"Yes, yes, negotiations would be in order, especially since there are five now that Herr Baker has joined you. Of course, this makes my original proposal subject to review. You understand that the first cost estimate—"

"I don't need a sales talk," I cut in. "Suppose we meet so we can get down to cases."

"Of course, of course. Where are you now?"

My hand tightened on the telephone. "That's a stupid question, coming from you."

Maas chuckled over the telephone. "I understand, my dear friend. Let me propose this: I would assume that you are within a mile of where this evening's—uh—accident—yes, accident—occurred?"

"All right."

"I suggest a café—where I am known. It has a private room in the back. It should be within walking distance of where you are now."

"Hold on," I said. I put my hand over the mouthpiece and told Padillo.

He nodded and said, "Get the address."

"What's the address?"

Maas told me, I repeated it, and Padillo wrote it down on a scrap of paper on Langeman's cluttered desk.

"What time?" I asked.

"Would midnight be convenient?"

"It's all right."

"There will be three of you?"

"No, just Herr Padillo and myself."

"Of course, of course; Herr Baker must stay with your two American guests."

"We'll see you at midnight," I said, and hung up.

"He knows Cooky was with us, and he thinks he still is," I told Padillo.

"Let's let him think it for a while. Wait here and I'll get some directions from Max." Padillo climbed down the ladder and was back in a few minutes. Max followed him.

"It's about nine blocks from here, Max says. He'll stay on the door until we get back. Our two friends are sleeping."

The café was ordinary-looking. We had made the nine blocks from Langeman's garage in fifteen minutes, passing down dark streets, encountering only a stray pedestrian or two. We stood across the street from the café in the doorway of an office building of some kind.

Maas arrived on foot at fifteen minutes until midnight. Three men had come out of the café separately since we had begun our watch. Maas had been the only one to go in. Nobody else came or went during the remaining quarter-hour.

"Let's go," Padillo said.

We crossed the street and entered the café. The bar was immediately in front of the door. To the left of the door were three booths. The rest of the café was taken up with chairs and tables. A couple sat at one. Three solitary drinkers brooded into their beer and a coffee drinker read a newspaper. The barkeep nodded at us and said good evening.

"We are expecting a friend to meet us," Padillo said. "Herr Maas."

"He is already in the back—through that curtain," the barkeep said. "Would you like to order now?"

"Two vodkas," Padillo said.

I led the way through the main room and pushed aside the curtain. Maas, still clad in his heavy brown suit, sat facing us at a round table. A goblet of white wine rested in front of him, next to a new brown hat. He rose when he saw us.

"Ah! Herr McCorkle," he gurgled.

"Herr Maas, Herr Padillo."

Maas gave Padillo's hand the standard shake and bustled around, pulling out two chairs for us to sit on. "It is a real pleasure to meet you, Herr Padillo. You are a man of considerable reputation."

Padillo sat down at the table and said nothing. "Have you ordered drinks?" Maas asked. "I have told the bartender to give you the best. It is my treat."

"We ordered," I said.

"Well, it has been a busy, busy day for you, I would say," Maas said.

We said nothing and the bartender came in through the curtain and deposited our drinks on the table. "See that we're not disturbed," Maas ordered.

The bartender shrugged and said, "We close in an hour."

He left and Maas picked up his wineglass. "Shall we drink to a successful venture, my friends?"

We drank.

Padillo lighted a cigarette and blew some smoke up into the air. "I think we can get down to business now, Herr Maas. What's your proposition?"

"You have seen the map I gave Herr McCorkle?"

"I saw it: it could be anywhere. Or it couldn't be at all."

Maas smiled blandly. "It exists, Herr Padillo. It does indeed. Let me tell you something of its history." He paused to take a sip of his wine.

"It has romance, treachery and death. It is quite a fascinating melodrama." Maas sipped at his wine again, produced three cigars, offered us each one, smiled understandingly when we refused, put two of them back into his pocket, and lighted his own. We waited.

"Back in September of 1949, a sixty-two-year-old widow whom I shall call Frau Schmidt died of cancer. Frau Schmidt left her single valuable possession, a somewhat-bombed-scarred three-story house, to her favorite son—Franz, I think I shall call him—a mechanical engineer who worked at that time for the American Army in West Berlin. Housing was at a premium in both East and West Berlin, so Franz moved his family, consisting of himself, his wife, and a four-year-old son, to his late mother's house. It was old, but it had been well built back in 1910 or 1911.

"There was virtually free passage between the East and West Sectors in those days and Franz Schmidt continued to work for the Americans. On the weekends he renovated the house. He received a small subsidy for his efforts from an agency of the East Berlin government. By 1955, Herr Schmidt was working for a private consulting engineering firm in West Berlin. Without much difficulty he managed to remodel his house completely, from basement to roof, installing new plumbing and even electrical-heating apparatus. It became his only hobby. Sometimes, I understand, Herr Schmidt considered moving to West Berlin, but he would have suffered a tremendous loss on his house and as long as he could travel freely from the East to the West Sector he saw no real reason to move.

"The Schmidt family made friends in their new neighborhood. Among them was the family of Leo Boehmler, who had been a *Feldwebel* on the eastern front during the war until he was captured by the Russians. He reappeared in East Berlin in 1947 as a lieutenant in the Volkspolizei. By the time that the Boehmler family had become friends with the Schmidt family, it was no longer Lieutenant Boehmler but

Captain Boehmler. But even a captain's pay could not match that of a mechanical engineer employed by a prosperous firm in the West Sector, so I have good reason to suspect that Captain Boehmler was a trifle envious of the Schmidt's fine house, their small car, and the general prosperity that surrounded the household, where the captain, his wife, and their pretty young daughter were often guests for real coffee and cakes.

"Schmidt was proud of his work on his house and insisted on showing it in detail to the captain, who, while devoutly of the Communist persuasion, could not prevent his mouth from watering at the modern trappings and innovations that Franz Schmidt had installed. The Boehmlers lived in a small apartment in one of the hastily built piles of flats that were thrown up in 1948. While it was much better than what most citizens of East Berlin had, it was a slum compared with the Schmidts' fine residence.

"By 1960 or thereabouts, Franz Schmidt's son Horst was a young man in his middle teens, and he was becoming interested in young girls—or, to be more specific, in one girl, the daughter of Captain Boehmler. Her name was Liese and she was six months younger than Horst. The parents of both children looked on the romance as—let me think of the American phrase—puppy love, but by 1961 Liese and Horst were spending most of their time together. Captain Boehmler had no objections to his daughter's making a good match with the son of a prosperous engineer, even though the engineer remained steadfastly disinterested in politics. And while Franz Schmidt was avowedly without politics, he was something of a realist, and when the time came he saw no reason why it could not prove useful to have a daughter-in-law whose father was an ambitious officer in the Volkspolizei. So little family jokes were made about the romance and Liese blushed prettily and young Horst stammered and did all the things adolescents do when they are the butt of an adult joke.

"Then one fine August day in 1961 the wall went up and Herr Schmidt found himself without a job. He talked the matter over with his good friend, Captain Boehmler, who suggested that it would be easy for him to obtain suitable employment in the East Sector. Engineer Schmidt found employment readily enough, but he also found that he was making only a fourth of what he had made in the West. And things that he liked—such as good coffee, chocolates, American cigarettes and what have you—were impossible to come by.

"It is now time to point out that Herr Schmidt's house was fortunately situated. It was on a corner which faced the apex of a small triangular park in the Kreuzberg area of West Berlin. When the wall went up it almost touched the tip of the park's apex. The park itself was no more than fifty meters from the Schmidt doorstep, and it was a pleasant spot of greenery in the midst of the city's dreariness."

Maas stopped his story to sip his wine. He seemed to enjoy the role of storyteller.

"After a few months of working at his low-paying position, Herr Schmidt took to standing in a third-story bedroom and staring out at the small triangle of greenery which lay over the wall. Then he began to spend much time in his cellar, tapping here and there with a hammer. And sometimes he would work late into the night, figuring with a pencil on a tablet of paper and drawing diagrams. In June 1962 he summoned a family conference around the dining table. He told his wife and son that he had decided to take them to the West, where he would regain his former position. As for the house—they would leave it. Neither his wife nor his son argued with him. But, later, young Horst drew his father aside and confessed that Liese was pregnant, that they must get married, and that, if he were to go west, Liese must go with him.

"The elder Schmidt examined this new information in his typically methodical manner. He asked his son how far along the girl was and young Horst said only two months. Schmidt then counseled his son that it would be wise not to marry Liese at once but to take her with them to the West Sector. He told Horst of his plans to tunnel under the wall and to come out in the small triangular park. He estimated that the job of tunneling would require two months of work, both of them digging and shoring four hours at night and eight hours on Saturday and Sunday. He told his son that if he were to marry now the Boehmlers would be in and out of the house constantly. Horst asked if he could tell Liese about the plans for the tunnel so that she would be able to plan for the future and not worry about his intentions. The elder Schmidt gave his consent reluctantly.

"The next night Schmidt and son began the tunnel. It was not too difficult a job except for disposing of the sandy dirt. This was done by loading up their small automobile on weekends and driving to various isolated points in the city, where the dirt was dumped from sacks made by Frau Schmidt from bedsheets.

"The mouth of the tunnel in the basement was concealed behind Herr Schmidt's hand-built tool case, which he mounted on cleverly concealed hinges to swing out from the wall. He illuminated the tunnel with electric lights as it progressed. It was shored with timber that he had accumulated before the wall went up, and he even laid down a rough floor of linoleum. By early August the tunnel was nearly finished. And if Herr Schmidt had been less of a craftsman I would not be telling you this story tonight.

"Schmidt had designed the tunnel to come up in a clump of arborvitae in the small park. It was a thick growth, and he had carefully arranged the exit so that a hard shove would work the earth loose above a circular metal cover. The earth could then be replaced. All of this care, of course, took longer than his original estimate. And Liese, nearing her fourth month, began to fret and to question young Horst about his intentions. Finally he brought her to the house and showed her the entrance to the tunnel. It may have been her pregnancy, it may have been her fear of leaving her parents, but the young lovers quarreled. It was the night before Herr Schmidt planned his escape.

"At any rate, Liese went home and confessed all to her father. Thinking quickly, the good captain told her to patch up her quarrel with young Horst the next day and said that, after all, they were in love and perhaps it would be better for her to have her baby in the West, where she could be with her husband.

"The next night, having smoothed over her quarrel with Horst, Liese packed a small bag, said good-bye to her parents, and walked to the Schmidt house. She arrived an hour before the Schmidts were to depart.

"They had a final cup of coffee at the pleasant dining table. Then, taking only a few possessions, they made their way down to the cellar. As Herr Schmidt opened the tool-case entrance Captain Boehmler appeared at the doorway of the cellar holding a revolver in his hand. He said he regretted that he had to do this to his good friends and neighbors but he was, after all, a servant of the people. He told his daughter to go upstairs and go home. Terrified, she left. Captain Boehmler then told the Schmidt family to turn their backs to him. When they did, he shot them.

"He then dragged them one by one up to the living room. Next he went in search of the Vopos guarding the wall in that particular section and sent them on a mythical errand, saying that he would patrol in their absence. He waited until the Vopos were gone and then dragged the three bodies out of the house and to the wall. He carried out their few possessions and dumped them beside the bodies. He then fired three shots into the air, reloaded his revolver and fired two more. The Vopos came hurrying back, and the captain said he had shot the Schmidt family as they had attempted to escape. He ordered that the house be locked and sealed until he had the opportunity to search it the next day.

"The bodies of the Schmidt family were carted away. Captain Boehlmer himself took charge of the investigation of the Schmidt house the following morning, giving his personal attention to the cellar. In his report he pointed out that the house was dangerously close to the wall and should be either sealed up or occupied by a family whose loyalty to the government was above reproach. His superior pulled a few wires and Captain Boehlmer became the new tenant of the house he had long admired, complete with escape hatch to the West.

Maas stopped talking and finished his wine. "And that is the story of the tunnel."

"What happened to the girl?" I asked.

"A pity," Maas said. "She died in childbirth five months later."

He called for the waiter, who entered a few moments later bearing a new round of drinks.

When he had gone, Maas continued: "And it is a pity about Captain Boehlmer, too. He has been passed over for promotion. Not only that, but the government plans to raze the entire block in which his fine home is located. They are going to build a warehouse, I believe. One with no windows. Captain Boehlmer has decided that he might turn the tunnel—still in good repair, he assures me—to a profit. Just once. Fortunately, his discreet inquiries reached me before anyone else."

"You want five thousand dollars?" Padillo asked.

Maas knocked an inch of Havana ash from his cigar. "I am afraid, Herr Padillo, that the price is somewhat higher than that which I previously quoted my good friend, Herr McCorkle. It has risen, I assure you, only in proportion to the intensity with which you are being sought by your friends here in the East—and, I might add, in the West."

"How much?"

"Ten thousand dollars." He held up his hand like a traffic cop signaling stop. "Before you object, let me say that I will not haggle, but I will extend credit. The ten thousand can be paid to me in cash in Bonn upon your return."

"You're getting awfully generous, Maas. The last time I talked to you, it was all cash and carry."

"Things have changed since then, good friend. I have learned that my popularity here in the East Sector—which is really my home, by the way—has diminished. In fact, you may say that I, too, am the subject of a search, though not as intensive as the one that is being conducted for you."

"How much are they offering for us?" Padillo asked. "Not the public offer—the private one."

"It is a considerable sum, Herr Padillo. One hundred thousand East German Marks. That's about twenty-five thousand DM or seven thousand, five hundred of your dollars. You see I am not being overly greedy."

I took a sip of my vodka and then demanded: "How do we know you won't cross us, Maas? How do we know that we won't waltz straight into the arms of Captain Boehmler and sixteen of his finest?"

Maas nodded rapidly in apparent agreement and approval. "I not only do not blame you for your caution, Herr McCorkle, but I admire it. There are two ways that I will demonstrate my good faith. First of all, I must get out of East Berlin, and it is not easy right now— especially right now. So I plan to go with you. Thus, I gain free egress from the East and, at the same time, I will be able to keep a close eye on my investment.

"Now my second method of showing good faith must be unpleasant news for you, but I am sure that you will bear it with your usual fortitude."

"Go ahead," I said.

"It is with deep regret," Maas said in his formal, almost pontifical manner, "that I must inform you that your friend Mr. Cook Baker is not to be trusted."

Padillo played it straight. He even let his mouth drop open slightly and raised his eyebrows in surprise. "I don't understand," he said.

Maas shook his head sadly. "I must confess that it is partly of my doing. If you recall, Herr McCorkle, you were good enough to allow me to sleep on your couch until my appointment the following day in Bonn. My appointment was with Herr Baker. It's true. I must tell it all. After I failed to make a proper connection with Herr Padillo here, I acted like the businessman I am. I sold my information to Herr Baker."

"How much?" Padillo asked.

"Three thousand dollars, Herr Padillo."

"I was in a good mood that day. I might have paid five for it."

"It was cheap, but the market was limited. Herr Baker was the only other customer."

"Why would he buy?" clever McCorkle asked.

"He was told to. You see, gentlemen, Herr Baker is an agent for your opposition." He let that sink in. "Of course, he has not been active until recently. Apparently he committed some indiscretion of a particularly unsavory nature some few years back. Pictures were taken. The pictures fell into certain hands. Herr Baker has his firm in New York, his financial interests to consider. So when friends obtained his current job for him in Bonn the KGB approached him quietly. He is acting not out of conviction but out of fear. Blackmail, its attendant embarrassment and disgrace—a man of Herr Baker's temperament could not stand it."

Maas sighed. "I may as well tell the entire story. It was Herr Baker's idea for me to approach Herr McCorkle and to devise a story that would necessitate my friend to summon Herr Baker to Berlin. Fortunately, I thought of the tunnel, and since I am a businessman I made a legitimate proposition. The five-thousand-dollar price was worked out by me with Herr Baker. He thought the tunnel was a myth. I saw no reason to enlighten him. But now he poses a problem."

"We'll worry about that," Padillo said. "Just when is your tunnel available?"

Maas looked at his watch. "It is twelve forty-five now. I can make arrangements for five o'clock this morning. Is that satisfactory?"

Padillo looked at me. I shrugged. "As soon as possible."

"I have to make certain arrangements with the captain."

"You mean pay him," Padillo said.

"To be sure. Then I must arrange for a car. It would be better if I picked you up. It is too far to walk, especially at that hour of the morning. You must give me your address."

Padillo took out a piece of paper and wrote the address of Langeman's garage and handed it to Maas. "The back door, in the alley."

Maas tucked it away. "I will be there at four forty-five this morning. In the meantime, Herr Padillo, although I realize you are a man of considerable experience in these affairs, I must urge you to make some arrangements about Herr Baker. He is a danger to us all, and he is also very accurate with a pistol."

Padillo stood up. "He's not any more, Herr Maas."

"*Bitte?*"

"He's dead. I shot him this afternoon."

CHAPTER 16

Our luck ran out on the way back to Langeman's garage. They stepped out of a dark doorway, the pair of them, and shined a flashlight into Padillo's face. One of them said, "May we see your papers, please?" His voice sounded young and it almost cracked on the last word. Padillo said, "Of course," and flicked his cigarette into the face of the one with the flashlight. When the Vopo's hands went up to his face, Padillo hit him hard in the stomach. That left me with the other one. He was as tall as I and seemed broader, but I couldn't be sure in the dark, so I kicked him in the crotch, and when he yelled and doubled over to grab himself I lifted my right knee into his face. Something seemed to break and his teeth bit into my leg. He fell to the pavement and groaned and twitched, so I kicked him twice in the head. He stopped twitching. The Vopo who had asked for the papers lay sprawled on the pavement. His flashlight still burned. Padillo leaned over, picked it up, switched it off, and stuck it in his topcoat pocket. Then he knelt down and examined both men. He rose and said, "Yours is dead, too."

Padillo looked up and down the street. It was empty. "Let's get rid of them," he said. He led the way to the middle of the street and then began to run, zigzagging back and forth until he found what he was looking for. It was a manhole cover—the kind that has three inch-long, half-inch-wide holes for lifting it up. Padillo took out a four-inch pocket knife, unknotted his tie, and made a small square knot around the knife. He slipped it through one of the holes in the cover, fiddled it around until it was crossways with the hole, and started to pull. The manhole cover came up an inch and I got my fingers around it and pulled until it was upright and then eased it back on the pavement.

We ran back to the Vopos and dragged them by the legs over to the manhole. We dumped them in without ceremony. Padillo went quickly back to the spot where they had asked for our papers. He took the flashlight out of his pocket and shined it around. He found their two hats and carried them over to the manhole and threw them in. Then we quietly put the cover back. Padillo slipped his knife into his pocket and reknotted his tie as we walked down the street.

I was still shaking when we got to the alley that ran behind Langeman's garage. I wanted a drink badly and decided that I would even settle for the unlabeled potato gin that Langeman had supplied. Padillo knocked softly on the door that led to the cubicle office. It opened a crack and Max whispered Padillo's name. Padillo replied and we went in.

"They O.K.?" Padillo asked.

"Still sleeping," Max said.

"Close the trap door. We've got some things to talk about."

Max undid the hook and eye and lowered the trap door. I sat on the desk, Padillo sat in the old swivel chair, and Max stood.

"We ran into trouble on the way back," Padillo said. "Two Vopos asked for our papers. We dropped them down a manhole."

Max nodded his head in approval. "They won't find them until in the morning," he said. "But they'll start looking for them in an hour or two when they don't check in."

"There's nothing we can do about that. Do you think you're still clean—enough to get across to the West Sector?"

"If I could get home, shave, take a bath," Max said. "I have the proper papers. They're valid—not even forged."

"The exporter's papers?"

"Yes."

"Did you bring the map?"

Max reached into his inside coat pocket and produced the map that we had used to trace the route of Burchwood and Symmes from the airport. It seemed that all of that had happened sometime last month. Max spread the map out on the floor. Padillo knelt beside it and ran his finger through the Kreuzberg area for a moment. "Here. This park. The one in the shape of a triangle."

"I know it," Max said.

"We're coming out there—in the middle of a clump of arborvitae. There's a tunnel from a house that's located here." And his finger moved to a block shaded in light tan, which indicated, according to the map, a "built-up area."

Max tapped a finger against his lower lip. "I don't remember that block—just the park. But the wall runs right next to the park. It almost touches its point."

"Right," Padillo said. "I want you to be there at five-thirty with a van: a Volkswagen panel truck will do. Park it here. Also set up a place for us to go and get in touch with Kurt's outfit. Now you'd better write this down."

Max produced a spiral notebook and a ball-point pen.

"Four GI uniforms," Padillo said. "One with tech-sergeant's stripes, one with master-sergeant's, one with corporal's, and one with buck-sergeant's. Get hold of two combat infantry badges."

"What sizes?" Max asked.

"What do you take, Mac?"

"Forty-two long," I said.

"One forty-two long, one forty regular, one thirty-eight short—you think that'll do for Burchwood?" I nodded. "And a thirty-eight long for Symmes. And get them some shoes: they can wear ten-B. Anybody can."

"You want this by five-thirty?" Max asked. "It can't be done."

"No, just get Kurt's outfit working on it and tell them to get it to wherever they're going to hole us up. Don't forget the shirts—all fifteen necks and thirty-four-inch sleeves."

"They've got most of this stuff already," Max said.

"How about the identification?"

"No trouble."

"Furlough papers?"

Max paused and thought. "We worked that once before with Passen, if you remember. We may have to cut some new orders, but maybe not. I'll check. Fourteen-day ones?"

"Good," Padillo said. "And four round-trip tickets to Frankfurt. Let them figure out the names, but tell him not to get clever. Just plain names like Johnson and Thompson and Miller. The kind you don't remember."

Max scribbled some more.

"How's the money holding out?" Padillo asked.

Max frowned and shook his head. "Langeman cleaned me except for a couple of hundred Marks."

"How much do we have in West Berlin?"

"There should be twelve or fourteen thousand Marks, plus about five hundred dollars."

"O.K. Tell Kurt to make the plane reservations for tomorrow evening and then have a car for us at Frankfurt. At the airport. Tell him to get us a fast one. He can get it back in Bonn."

Max made another note. "Is that all?"

"That's all I can think of. You'd better get moving."

"I'll go down and get the bottle," Max said. "If they stop me, I'll be tipsy, just getting home from my girl friend's." He opened the trap door and went down the ladder, reappearing moments later with the bottle of potato gin. He uncapped it, took a mouthful, rinsed it around, and swallowed. "My God, that's terrible."

My hand was already reaching for it.

"One more thing," Max said. "How long do I wait at this park?"

"Until six," Padillo said.

"And if you don't show?"

"Forget about us."

Max peered at Padillo through his glasses. He smiled. "We'll see," he said. Then he opened the door to the alley and left.

I handed Padillo the bottle and he took a long drink. He almost got it down without a cough.

"Who's Kurt?" I said.

"Kurt Wolgemuth, Berlin's version of Available Jones. An honest crook. The blond kid who got shot on the wall worked for him. He supplies things in a hurry for a price. You'll meet him. He made his first money in the black market; then he caught the crest of the jump in German stock prices and rode that. He gets people over the wall and furnishes passports, new identities, secondhand clothes, guns—anything that turns a dollar. We've done business before."

"I can follow you on the uniforms and on the stripes," I said. "We'd be a little old to pass as privates. But why Frankfurt? Why not straight back to Bonn?"

"GIs don't go to Bonn—not even to Cologne. They go to Munich or Frankfurt or Hamburg, where there's booze and women. How many GIs have you seen in Bonn?"

"Damn few," I admitted. Then I asked, "How do we get our two sleeping friends on and off the plane?"

"You still have that belly gun?"

I nodded.

"Just keep it in your raincoat pocket and nudge one of them with it every so often. They'll behave. And once they're across the wall, there's no place for them to hide. If they kick up a fuss, they'll wind up where they're going anyhow. It's just a matter of who delivers them. I intend to deliver them."

I reached for the bottle. "I think you'll miss it."

"What?"

"Your other calling."

Padillo grinned. "When's the last time you killed anybody, Mac?"

I looked at my watch. "About twenty minutes ago."

"Before that?"

"More than twenty years ago. In Burma."

"Were you scared just now?"

"Terrified."

"What have you done for the past twenty years?"

"Sat on my ass."

"You like it?"

"It's pleasant."

"Suppose you went back to Bonn and we ran the place for a couple of months and then one day you got a phone call and they told you that you had to do something like this all over again by yourself. Only it might be worse. So you'd come around to see me and you'd tell me you'd have to take off for a week or so, and your stomach would be cramping because you wanted to tell somebody, anybody, where you were going and what you had to do, but you knew damn well you couldn't. And so you'd have a drink with me and then you'd walk out by yourself and catch the plane or train by yourself. You'd be all alone and there'd never be anybody to meet you when you got there and there'd never be anybody waiting when you got back. Try that off and on for twenty years and count the dead ones at three o'clock in the morning and then panic sometimes because you can't remember their names or what they looked like. And after twenty years they don't give you a gold watch and a chicken-and-peas dinner. They send you off on another one and tell you you're damn good and it's just a routine job. But before you're forty you're superannuated and they're writing you off like a tax loss because they think your nerve's going—and they're probably right. And you tell me I like it."

"Maybe I said that because you seem good at it. From what I've seen."

Padillo snorted. "Think back over it. It's been a sloppy show from the beginning. I called you in because you're sentimental enough to think that friendship means something more than a card at Christmas and because you're big enough to be useful in case they start throwing bottles down at the corner bar. I used you to get Cook involved to the point where I could control him so that my chances of getting back to Bonn with our two pansies would be better than sixty-forty. I've used you, Mac, and I can get you killed yet. I managed to do it for Weatherby, and he'd been around a long time and was twice as cautious and careful as most. Put it this way: I've already promised you my gold cuff links. You've got another favor coming. You can call it any time."

"I'll think up something. Meantime, what about our two friends downstairs?"

"They're the insurance," he said. "NSA never announced their defection, and the boys who work in the new building out in Virginia just past the sign that says Bureau of Public Roads aren't going to broadcast the fact that they're back. But unless they clean up everything, including Weatherby turning up dead in your room in the Hilton, and the money we've spent, I'm going to call a press conference at Mac's Place and blow the lid off everything."

"They wouldn't like that."

"No, but the reporters would."

"What'll happen to Burchwood and Symmes?"

"They'll disappear quietly."

"Dead?"

"Possibly, but probably not. Sometime somebody may pick up a rock and start wondering what happened to a couple of the bugs. They'll have to be produced quickly."

"You think it will work out the way you just told it?"

"No, but if I didn't say it and try to believe it then there wouldn't be any reason for any of it. And I'd feel more like a damn fool than I do right now."

I looked at my watch. "We have a couple of hours until our good fairy comes. You want to get some sleep? I caught a nap this afternoon."

Padillo rose from the swivel chair, lowered himself to the floor, and stretched out full length, his head resting over the closed trap door. "Wake me up in a couple of weeks," he said. I took over the chair, leaned back, and put my feet up on the desk. I noticed that I needed a shine—and a shave, and a bath, and six eggs over easy with a dozen or so slices of thick bacon, a stack of well-buttered rye toast, a fresh, red whole tomato and a gallon of coffee. Instead I settled for another swallow of bad gin and a cigarette of doubtful merit. I sat in the swivel chair and waited some more. It was quiet. The telephone didn't ring and nobody knocked on the door. I told myself I was learning patience. I was a poor student.

At four-thirty I poked Padillo with my toe. He was up immediately, fully awake. I told him the time. "I'll rouse them up downstairs," he said. He opened the trap door and went down the ladder. Symmes was the first up, followed by Burchwood, and then Padillo. I closed the trap door.

"In about ten minutes we're going to take another little ride," Padillo told the pair. "You will do exactly as you are told. You will say nothing regardless of whom you see or what you are asked to do. You will speak only if he or I ask you a direct question. Is that understood?"

"I don't care what it is any more," Symmes said. "I just want to get it over. I don't want any more killing and I don't want to be pushed and shoved and ordered around like an idiot. Just get it over with, whatever it is, for God's sake."

"Have you got anything to say, Burchwood?" Padillo asked.

His dark eyes snapped and his tongue ran around his lips nervously. He shook his head in a weary, hopeless manner. "I don't care any more," he mumbled. "I'm just too tired to care."

"In a couple of hours you'll have a chance to rest. Just do as you're told. All right?"

They stood there, disheveled, pale and drawn, their hands hanging loosely by their sides. Symmes closed his eyes and nodded. Burchwood said, "Yes, yes, yes, Christ, yes."

Padillo looked at me and shrugged. I leaned against the wall. Padillo again sat in the chair. Burchwood and Symmes simply stood, weaving a little. Symmes kept his eyes closed.

At four forty-five we heard the car. Padillo took out his revolver and opened the door. I removed my gun from my coat pocket. It was getting to feel like an old friend.

Maas was at the door. He had left the car engine running. "Ah, Herr Padillo."

"Everything ready?"

"Yes, yes, but we must hurry. We should be there at five."

"All right," Padillo said; "get back in the car. We'll load up." He swung around from the door to face us. "You two in the back seat with Mac. Get in this side."

He went out first. I followed Symmes and Burchwood. Outside, Padillo held open the door of a brown 1953 Mercedes 220. Burchwood and Symmes crawled into the back seat. I followed. Padillo closed the door to the office and got in the front seat next to Maas. "Let's go," he said.

Maas drove slowly down the dark alley, using only his parking lights. When he got near the end he stopped. Without saying anything Padillo got out and walked to the corner and looked carefully both ways. He signaled Maas on. The car started up, stopped for Padillo, and we were out in the street. Maas switched on his driving lights.

"Where'd you get the car?" Padillo asked.

"From a friend," Maas said.

"Your friend forgot to give you the key to the ignition."

Maas chuckled. "You are very observant, Herr Padillo."

"For five hundred Marks we could have avoided a hot car," he said.

"It will not be missed until late tomorrow. I chose it carefully, and it is very easy to cross the ignition on this model."

The ride took twenty-one minutes. We passed a few trucks on a boulevard, and then Maas took to the side streets. East Berlin was asleep. At five-nine he pulled up in front of a house.

"Is this it?" Padillo asked.

"No. It is around the next corner. But I will leave the car here. We will walk."

"You take Symmes," Padillo told me. "Burchwood will come with me. Let's make it a group, not a procession."

We walked in a bunch. Around the corner Maas stopped before a three-story house. He went up three white marble steps and knocked softly on the door. It opened and Maas whispered, "In quickly!"

We went in. A tall, indistinct figure stood in what seemed to be a hallway. There were no lights. "This way," a man's voice said. "Walk straight. When you come to a door, be prepared to step down past me on the stairs. When you are all on the stairs, stop and I will turn on a light."

We moved slowly in the dark. I went first, feeling my way, my hands in front of me.

"You are at the stairs," the voice said, right next to me. "The railing is on the right. It will guide you."

I found the railing with my right hand and walked down six steps and stopped. I heard the rest of them follow. I heard the door close and a light was turned on. We were standing on a stairway that led down to a landing and then turned right. I glanced back up. A tall, thin man with a hawk nose and bristling salt-and-pepper eyebrows stood at the top of the stairs, his hand on a light switch. He wore a white shirt, open at the neck. A few tufts of gray hair poked out at his throat. He could have been fifty or fifty-five. Maas was on the next step down from him, and below Maas were Padillo, Burchwood and Symmes.

"Straight down," the thin man said.

I walked down the remaining two steps, turned and walked down five more. The basement walls were painted white and blue, and blue-speckled linoleum covered the floor. A workbench with a vise attached to it ran the length of one side of the room. Above it was a series of cabinets, stained a dark brown. At one narrow end of the basement, at what I judged to be the street side, was a five-foot cabinet of good walnut. It had four small shelves at the top and a series of flat drawers beneath them. Brass knobs were attached to the drawers. I kept my hand on my gun in my coat pocket. Padillo motioned Burchwood and Symmes to one side of the room. He stood next to them.

The tall man came down the stairs and looked at us. "They are Americans," he said angrily.

Maas took his hands out of the pockets of a tan raincoat that I hadn't seen him wear before and spread them in a placating gesture. "Their money is good. It would not be wise to change your mind at this point. Please open the passage."

"You said they were Germans," the man muttered.

"The passage," Maas said.

"The money," the thin man demanded.

Maas took his left hand out of his pocket again and handed over an envelope.

The thin man walked over to the workbench, ripped open the envelope, and counted the money. Twice. He stuffed the envelope and the money into his trouser pocket and moved to the chest. He pulled out the first drawer, closed it; pulled out the third, closed it; and then pulled out the bottom drawer and left it open. There was nothing in any of them, but the pulling and closing were some kind of combination.

He tugged at the chest and it swung open easily. It seemed to have clearance from the floor of less than a fourth of an inch. Behind the chest was the tunnel, its mouth about three feet high by two and a half feet wide. I could see that a reddish linoleum covered its floor. Rough, brown-stained boards framed its entrance. The thin man reached into the tunnel and switched on the lights. Padillo and I knelt to look. When we rose, Maas had a Luger in his right hand. It was aimed at the tall, thin man. I made a motion in my pocket, but Padillo caught my arm. "It's his play."

"Please, Captain, would you hand back the money?"

"Liar!" the thin man yelled.

"Please, the money."

He reached into his pocket and handed it to Maas. The fat man stuffed it back into his pocket. "Now, Captain, would you please put your hands on the top of your head and stand next to the wall? No, turn around so that your back is to me." The man obeyed. Mass nodded in satisfaction.

"You remember, Herr Padillo and Herr McCorkle," Maas continued in German, "that man Schmidt I told you about? His name was no more Schmidt than mine is Maas. But he was my brother and I feel I have a debt to pay. I think you will understand, Captain."

He shot the thin man in the back twice. Symmes screamed. The thin man was knocked against the wall and crumpled in a heap on the floor. Maas put the Luger back into his coat pocket and turned to us. "It was a matter of honor," he said.

"You're through?" Padillo asked.

"Yes."

"Let's go, then. You first, Maas."

The fat man got down on his hands and knees and disappeared into the tunnel. "You next, Mac."

I followed Maas. Symmes and Burchwood scrambled after me. The tunnel was shored with rough lumber, about the size of two-by-fours. In a few spots dirt had dribbled down on the linoleum. The forty-watt electric bulbs were spotted every twenty feet. I counted nine of them. We crawled on our hands and knees. My head occasionally knocked against a piece of the wooden shoring. Dirt got down my neck.

"My brother built well," Maas called back.

"Let's hope he didn't forget the egress," I muttered.

I estimated the tunnel to be sixty meters long. As I crawled I tried to figure out how many square yards of dirt the Schmidt-Maas family had funneled into the sacks made from sheets and carted off in the family transportation. The fractions threw me and I gave up.

Maas stopped crawling. "We are at the end."

I passed the word back to Symmes.

"Is the opening there?" Padillo called.

"I'm trying to move it," Maas grunted. He was standing now. I could see only his legs protruding from his raincoat. I crawled on and poked my head into the opening where Maas's legs were. I looked up. Maas was bowed; his neck, head and shoulders were pressing up against a round piece of corrugated metal that looked like the top of a garbage pail. His hands, palms up, strained against the metal. Nothing happened. He stopped. "It will not move."

"Let's see if we can change places," I said. "I'm taller. I can get more pressure from my legs."

We squeezed past each other. Maas's breath was something that somebody should have told him about. I looked up. The metal plate was about five feet above the floor of the tunnel. I spread my legs as far as they would go. My knees, were half bent. I placed my head, neck and shoulders against the plate. I got the palms of my hands flat against it. Then I started slowly to straighten up, using the muscles in my thighs, calves, and arms. They hadn't been used that much in a long time. I hoped they could remember what they were for.

Nothing happened. I could feel blood rushing through my head. The sweat began to drip from my forehead. I stopped and rested. I resumed the position and started the pressure from the legs up. I felt something give and hoped it wasn't my neck. I gave one last effort and the sweat trickled down my forehead and into my eyes. The metal plate moved. I increased the pressure, slowly straightening my knees. There was the sound of a soft plop and I felt the cold air. I shoved again, this time with my arms only, and the metal plate lifted up and fell away. I looked up. I couldn't see any stars.

CHAPTER 17

I hauled myself out of the tunnel and blundered into a thicket of branches and leaves that scratched my face and stung my hands. The leaves felt soft and scaly. I could hear Maas stumbling behind me. When I broke out of the foliage I could see the wall, 150 feet or so away, where the park met it with the tip of its triangle. The wall seemed to squat, ugly and black and damp-looking against the beginning of a dawn. A hand touched my arm and I jumped. It was Max Vess.

"Where are the rest?" he asked.

"On their way."

"So it did exist."

"Yes."

Maas broke out of the arborvitae wiping his face and hands and brushing off his raincoat. Behind him came Symmes, Burchwood and Padillo.

"The truck is this way," Max said, gesturing to his right.

Maas turned to Padillo. "I will leave you now, Herr Padillo," he said. "I am confident that your associates will be able to transport you and your charges to Bonn. But if you run into difficulty . . . you may reach me at this number." He handed Padillo a slip of paper. "I will be there part of today only. Tomorrow I will drop by your café to settle our account."

"Cash," Padillo said.

"Ten thousand."

"I'll have it for you."

Maas nodded. "Yes," he said. "I am sure that you will. *Auf wiedersehen.*" He walked away and was lost in the dark and the mist.

The truck was a Volkswagen panel. We followed Max to it and climbed in through a side door. Before he closed it, Max said, "You won't be able to see out, but nobody can see in either."

"How far?" Padillo asked.

"Fifteen minutes."

It took seventeen minutes actually. Symmes and Burchwood sat on one side of the panel, their heads cushioned on their arms, which they rested against raised knees. Padillo and I sat on the other side and smoked the last of the East German cigarettes.

The panel stopped and we could hear Max getting out of the driver's seat. He opened the door and Padillo and I jumped out. Symmes and Burchwood followed, not speaking either to us or to each other. They looked pale in the dim light and Burchwood needed a shave.

I looked around. We were in a courtyard of some kind. A tall red brick wall covered with dusty ivy made three sides of the court, with a gate built of rough gray lumber providing the entrance. The pavement was of irregular slate slabs. The wall joined a four-story building stuccoed with gray plaster that had recessed windows. The ones on the ground floor had iron bars over them.

Max led the way into a doorless corridor that ended at a steel panel that had no hinges and no handle. Above it was a round hole covered with fine wire mesh. Max stood in front of the panel and the rest of us lined up behind him. We must have waited fifteen seconds before the panel slid silently open. I could see that it was two inches thick, and it looked as if it were made of solid steel.

Max led on down another corridor. At its end stood a small elevator, it's door open, just large enough for five persons. We entered it, the door closed, and there were no buttons to push if you wanted off on the mezzanine. It rose quickly and I judged that it went to the top floor of the building. When it stopped the door opened again automatically and soundlessly and we stepped out into what seemed to be a reception room whose walls were of plaster that was painted a pastel green. The plaster looked as if it had been brushed with a comb when it was wet. Pictures, oils and pen-and-ink sketches of Berlin, covered the walls above the furniture. There were a couple of matching orange-red sofas, two or three casual chairs with eager Scandinavian lines, and a severe coffee or cocktail table adorned with a thick mottled-green glass ash tray shaped like a kidney. The rug was deep-piled and made up of squares of brown and black and green. It wasn't a restful room and it spoke of money, but its tone was neither restrained nor cultivated.

Directly opposite the elevator door was another door that was covered with the kind of wallpaper that pretends to be wood paneling but never succeeds in bringing it off. Max stood in front of that door for a while and it slid open just like the one downstairs. It also had the round aperture above it covered with the fine wire mesh. I guessed that it shielded a television camera. We went through, walked down a hall and turned left into a long, oblong room that had a fireplace burning at its far end. A man stood before the fireplace warming his back. He held a cup and saucer. I could smell coffee and saw a sideboard along the left-hand wall that held an electric percolator that looked as if it could handle eighteen cups or more. Some other dishes were on the sideboard, resting on a thick white pad that I took to be a warming unit. The room was paneled in a dark wood, and there was a library table with a lamp; some beige drapes; a couple of leather couches; some leather armchairs, two of them wing-backed; a dark-green rug; and a full bookcase. I thought I could smell toast and bacon as well as coffee. The man smiled when he saw Padillo, set his cup and saucer down on a table, and walked toward us. He shook hands with Padillo. "Hello, Mike," he said in English; "it's good to see you again."

"Hello, Kurt." Padillo introduced me to Kurt Wolgemuth, who shook hands with me as if he thought it were the pleasure he said it was. He was in his early fifties and he carried them nicely. His long hair was only touched with gray and it lay brushed and shining and cared for on his well-shaped head. He had dark-brown eyes, a good straight nose, and a small firm chin below a mouth that seemed to have all of its teeth and not too much gum when he smiled. He was wearing a maroon dressing gown with a white silk scarf above dark-gray or black trousers. He stood straight and kept his stomach in most of the time.

"I need some food and a bed and a shower for these two," Padillo said, indicating Symmes and Burchwood. Wolgemuth's dark eyes flicked over them. He smiled again and stepped back to the fireplace and pushed an inset ivory-colored button. The door opened a moment later and two men came in. They had the air of quiet competency that big men often have. "These two gentlemen," Wolgemuth said. "They need to clean up, have some food and some rest. Take care of it, please." The two big men looked at Symmes and Burchwood carefully. One of them nodded toward the door. Symmes and Burchwood walked through it. The big men followed.

"You've prospered, Kurt," Padillo said, glancing around.

The man shrugged and walked to the sideboard. "Let's have some coffee—-and let me apologize for what happened the other night at the wall. We slipped up."

"Somebody did," Padillo said.

Wolgemuth paused by the sideboard, a cup and saucer in one hand, the large percolator in the other. "I have a complete report for you, Mike. You may wish to read it after breakfast."

Max announced that he was worn out and would get some sleep. "I'll be up and around in about four hours," he said, and left.

Padillo and I loaded our plates with scrambled eggs, bacon, cheese and sausage. We ate from small tables that Wolgemuth had placed in front of the two wing-back leather chairs that flanked the fireplace. We gobbled the food without conversation, and when I was on my third cup of coffee I accepted an American cigarette from Wolgemuth with gratitude.

"Could you get all the items we need?" Padillo asked, borrowing a cigarette for himself.

Wolgemuth nodded and waved some of the smoke away with a cared-for hand. "Uniforms per your request, the necessary travel orders, the tickets, and I've laid on transport to Tempelhof for this afternoon. Also a car—a fast one—will meet you at Frankfurt." He paused, smiled delicately, and said: "Since my report indicates that you seem to be free-lancing, Mike, whom shall I send the bill to?"

"To me," he said. "Max can give you a small down payment."

Wolgemuth smiled. "I always had the feeling that you were too sensitive for this business. You can send me a check when you get back to Bonn—if you get back."

"They've really turned it on, huh?"

Wolgemuth picked up two blue file folders from the mantel. He gave one to Padillo and one to me. For your bedtime reading," he said. "It's a rundown of everything we've found out—with a few conjectures thrown in for good measure. But to answer your question, yes, they have indeed turned it on. Even the British are making unpleasant noises because of Weatherby. The only ones you haven't offended are the French."

Padillo leafed through his file. "We'll have to think of something. Right now we need some sleep."

Wolgemuth rang the ivory button again. One of the big men appeared. "Herr Padillo and Herr McCorkle are special guests," he said. "Show them to their rooms. Were they prepared as I instructed?"

The big man nodded. Wolgemuth looked at his watch. "It's six-fifteen now. I'll have you called at noon."

I nodded wearily and got up to follow the outsized guide. Padillo

160

followed me. We walked down the hall and turned right. The big man opened a door, walked into a bedroom, checked the windows to see that they were open, turned on the bathroom light, pointed to a bottle of Scotch and two packs of Pall Malls, and handed me the key. I almost tipped him. I went into the bathroom when he left and looked at the tub. It was white and shiny and inviting. I turned on the water, sat down on the john, and opened the report. I had a carbon copy. It was single-spaced and written in German, and it was three pages long.

FROM: FMS
TO: Wolgemuth
SUBJECT: Michael Padillo and Associates

Michael Padillo, 40, using the name Arnold Wilson, arrived at 2030 hours Wednesday aboard BEA Flight 431 out of Hamburg. He then proceeded to a café at 43 Kurfürstendamm, where he met John Weatherby as scheduled. They talked for 33 minutes, whereupon Padillo left by taxi for the Friedrichstrasse crossing into East Berlin. He crossed, using a British passport and the name Arnold Wilson.

Weatherby returned to his apartment and telephoned Fräulein Fredl Arndt in Bonn, instructing her to contact Padillo's business associate and inform him that he, Padillo, was in need of "Christmas help" (we find no suitable German translation for this phrase).

In East Berlin Padillo stayed at the apartment of Max Vess until dark. They then drove in the 1964 Citroën ID-19 to 117 Kerlerstrasse. The building is a five-story, temporarily deserted light-manufacturing structure. Padillo and Vess remained in the building during the night.

Herr McCorkle arrived at Tempelhof at 1730 aboard BEA Flight 319 from Düsseldorf. He was followed to the Hilton Hotel by agents of the American defense establishment and by an agent from the KGB. At 1820 he registered and was assigned room 843. He remained there for two hours, telephoning no one, and then walked to the Kurfürstendamm, where he sat in a café. He was joined by Wilhelm Bartels, 28, American agent, 128 Meirenstrasse. They spoke briefly and Bartels left. McCorkle finished his beverage and proceeded by taxi to *Der Purzelbaum*, where he met Bartels and again talked briefly. McCorkle then returned to his hotel.

John Weatherby entered McCorkle's room at 1200 the following day as scheduled. He remained for 37 minutes and left. McCorkle took a taxi to *Stroetzel's*, where he lunched. He was under surveillance by Bartels and an unidentified KGB agent. At 1322 McCorkle left the restaurant and began walking. While McCorkle was lunching, the KGB agent was replaced by Franz Maas, 46, alias Konrad Klein, Rudi Salter, Johann Wicklermann, and Peter Soerrig. Maas has worked for virtually all operations (including ours in 1963 in Leipzig) and is regarded as resourceful, intelligent and daring, which he masks with the carefully cultivated manner of a bumbler.

He speaks fluent English, French, and Italian and has a knowledge of the Yoruba dialect indigenous to Western Nigeria, where he spent three years, from 1954 to 1957. He has traveled extensively throughout Europe, South America, and Africa as well as the Near East. He has a concentration number (B-2316) tattooed on his left forearm, but it is false. Nothing is known of Maas prior to 1946, when he appeared in Frankfurt.

McCorkle accosted Maas and they entered a café. They talked briefly (21 minutes) and Maas handed the American a paper prior to departing. Contents of the paper are unknown. McCorkle returned to his hotel, telephoned Herr Cook Baker in Bonn, and asked him to secure and deliver $5,000 to Berlin that evening. Baker agreed.

NOE reports that Baker checked in at the Hilton that evening, made a telephone call that lasted only a few seconds from a house phone, and then telephoned for five minutes from a booth. He then seated himself in the lobby.

When Weatherby arrived, Baker entered the same elevator.

There were no other passengers. The elevator stopped at the sixth and eighth floors. When it returned, NOE commandeered it, passing himself off as an official inspector to waiting passengers.

NOE found a .22 caliber cartridge on the elevator floor. A subsequent search of Baker's room revealed a .22 Colt automatic. We assume Baker shot Weatherby in the back, pushed him off at the sixth floor, continued to the eighth floor and McCorkle's room. Bloodstains indicate Weatherby took the stairs to McCorkle's room, where he died.

At 2121 Baker and McCorkle left the hotel, rented a Mercedes, and drove to the Friedrichstrasse crossing. They went through at 2145. Both used their valid American passports.

They came under immediate surveillance by Agent Bartels in the East Sector. You have already received a report on his death and of the successful kidnapping of the two American defectors by Padillo and associates.

However, we have learned from Max Vess that Padillo shot and killed Cook Baker prior to the attempt at the wall. The body has not yet been discovered.

The accident at the wall was a fluke. A two-man patrol was inadvertently in the area. The diversion of the gasoline bombs worked well, and it is regrettable that this pattern, not used in three years, should be expended on a failure. Max Vess reports that Padillo and associates took refuge in Langeman's garage, where they paid DM 2,000 for bed and board. I suggest that I speak to Langeman about his billing.

Padillo and McCorkle met Maas in an East Berlin café. Maas, for $10,000, offered to get the group into West Berlin through a tunnel. Padillo and McCorkle agreed. On their return to Langeman's garage they were forced to kill two members of the Volkspolizei and dispose of their bodies in a manhole.

Max Vess is to meet Padillo and associates shortly after 0500 this morning and transport them here. You are acquainted with their subsequent needs from the verbal reports received from Max Vess.

Item: All our automobiles used in this operation have been re-
covered. I have sent a special memorandum to accounting informing
them of all overhead charges.

I turned off the water in the tub and walked back into the bedroom.
I put the report down and picked up the bottle of Scotch, uncapped
it, and poured a drink. I took a long, deep swallow and stood there in
the clean little bedroom with the turned-down bed and the picture of
a café scene on the wall and let the liquor spread from the stomach to
the cortex. I topped up the drink and opened the closet door. A Class-
A Army uniform, complete with tech-sergeant's stripes, combat infantry badge, and some ribbons indicating that the wearer had gone
through a couple of battles in the Pacific, hung neatly in the closet. I
closed the door and went back into the bathroom and set the glass
down on the toilet lid within handy reach of the bath. I went back into
the bedroom and fetched a package of the cigarettes and an ash tray
and set them next to the glass of Scotch. Then I stripped off my clothes
and threw them into a corner of the bathroom. I eased myself down
into the water, which was a little short of scalding, and lay there staring
up at the ceiling and letting the muscles unkink themselves.

I soaked in the bathtub, drinking the Scotch and smoking the cigarettes and thinking, but not too hard, until the water grew cool. I ran
some more of the hot and then used the soap and rinsed myself off
with a shower. I shaved and brushed my teeth and smoked a final
cigarette. Then I got into bed.

Beds like that are too good for the common people.

CHAPTER 18

I was running down the long corridor again toward the brightly lighted door at the far, far end which seemed to grow no closer when I stepped in the snake-made noose and it began to jerk my leg. But it was only Padillo in his master-sergeant's uniform, complete with the ribbons, the hash marks, and the gold overseas-duty bars. He looked like the kind who wasn't overly generous with a three-day pass.

When he saw I was awake he quit shaking my foot and turned toward the Scotch. He poured himself a drink and said, "I have some coffee coming."

I swung my legs over the edge of the bed and reached for a cigarette. "The sleep was good—what there was of it. You make a hell of a tough-looking top sergeant."

"You find your uniform?"

"In the closet."

"Better get into it. We have an appointment at the beauty parlor."

I took the uniform out of the closet and started to dress. "This is a comedown for an ex-captain, you know."

"You should have stayed in," Padillo said; "you could have retired this year."

"There seems to be some chance that another institution may make me a free-bed-and-board offer. For twenty years or so, if I play it right."

Somebody knocked on the door and Padillo said come in. It was one of the big men with a large pot of coffee and two cups. He put them down on the dresser and left. I tied my tie and walked over and poured a cup. Then I slipped on the blouse and admired myself in the mirror. "I knew a guy who looked like me twenty-one years ago in Camp Wolters," I said. "I hated his guts."

"No dog tags," Padillo said. "If they start asking for those, we're dead anyway."

"What's next?"

"Wolgemuth is a little skittish about the airport. He's got his expert in to do a make-up job on us. All of us."

"The guy has quite an operation."

"You read the report?"

"Seems as though we had some company we didn't know about."

"So did Weatherby," Padillo said.

"That still bother you?"

"It will for a long time. He was a good man."

I finished my coffee and we went down the hall to the paneled room where we had first met Wolgemuth. He was dressed in a single-breasted blue suit, white shirt, carefully knotted blue-and-black tie, and black shoes that glistened. A white linen handkerchief peeked casually out of his breast pocket.

He nodded at me in a friendly way and asked if I had slept well and seemed interested and happy when I told him that I had.

"If you and Mike will come this way," he said politely, indicating the door.

We followed him down the corridor, past our bedrooms, and into a room lined with closets on one side and a series of dressing tables on the other.

A tall blond woman with a lantern jaw and pale skin was arranging some articles on one of the dressing tables, which had a row of frosted bulbs around its mirror. "This is Frau Koepler," said Wolgemuth. She turned, nodded, and went back to her arranging. "Frau Koepler is in charge of this section."

Wolgemuth opened one of the closets. "Here we have uniforms of every description. The ones located in this closet are a complete range of sizes of those worn by the Volkspolizei. Complete with boots, hats, shirts—the lot." He closed that door and opened the next. "These are military—American, British, French and West German. Also East German—which the Vopos are switching to shortly, I understand. Next police uniforms—Berlin variety. And here are dresses for women—made in New York, London, Berlin, Chicago, Hamburg, Paris, Rome: the labels are authentic, as are the materials. Coats, undergarments, shoes—a complete wardrobe. Next are men's furnishings—civilian variety. Off-the-peg suits from the Fankfurt *Kaufhof*, from Chicago and Los Angeles and Kansas City and New York. Also from London, Paris, Marseilles, East Berlin, Leipzig and Moscow—almost anywhere. Hats and shoes, button-down shirts and wide-spread collars. Three-button suits, double-breasted, dinner jackets, and so forth."

I was impressed and said so. Wolgemuth grinned proudly. "If we have time, Herr McCorkle, I would like to show you our reproduction facilities."

"He means his forged-document shop," Padillo said. "I took a look at it earlier. It's good. Maybe the best."

"I'll take your word for it," I said.

"I'm ready," Frau Koepler said.

"Good. Which of you will volunteer first?" Wolgemuth asked.

"Go ahead," I said to Padillo.

He sat down in the chair before the dressing table and Frau Koepler draped a sheetlike affair around him—the kind that barbers use. She studied his face in the mirror and then covered his hair with a rubber cap that fitted down over his sideburns and neck. She murmured to herself, cocked her head this way and that, and then selected some soft wax. "Our nose is straight and thin," she said; "we will broaden it slightly, flaring the nostrils just so." Her hands flew deftly around Padillo's face. She patted and probed and shaped and molded. When she was through, he had a new nose. I would still have recognized him, but his features were altered.

"Our eyes are brown and our hair is black. We will soon have brown hair, but we shall also have brown eyebrows." She picked up a tube and rubbed some of its contents into Padillo's eyebrows. They became brown—or dirty blond. "Now the mouth: it is one of the most important features of the face. May I see our teeth?"

Padillo leered at her.

"They are very white and contrast nicely with our rather olive complexion. We will stain them ever so slightly, giving them a strong yellowish look—like a nice old horse." She squeezed some paste onto a toothbrush that she had taken from a clear-plastic container and handed the brush to Padillo. "Let's brush our teeth now carefully. It will wear off in a few days." He brushed. "Now for the shape of our mouth and cheeks," she went on. "We will balloon them slightly." She inserted some flesh-colored sponge rubber into her mouth. "Bite down. Now open. Now here and here. Now bite down. Now open. You see we have a slightly pendulous lower lip now, rounder cheeks, and we have become a mouth breather. It is always slightly open, as if we were suffering from a slight respiratory ailment. We will also lighten our complexion and give it some of the heavy drinker's veins."

Frau Koepler opened a small white pot, dipped her fingers into a grayish paste, and began to work the paste into Padillo's face. His skin took on a yeasty, almost unhealthy look, as if he had spent too much time in a hospital—or a bar. Just below the sideburns she fitted a small adhesive-backed stencil; then she dabbed at it with a stick wrapped in cotton, which she had dipped into a small bottle of liquid. She let the liquid dry and peeled off the stencil. Padillo's capillary veins had burst into a curlicue profusion of purples and reds. She did the same to the other side of his face and then began similar work on his nose. "Not too much here," she said; "we have been friends with good schnapps for let us say—oh—fifteen years. A half-bottle a day perhaps." She peeled off the stencil and the tip of Padillo's nose glowed merrily. She whisked off the rubber head cover, reached into a bottom drawer, and produced a hair piece, which she fitted carefully to his head. Instead of a thick, gray-flecked crew cut he had a thin crop of dirty-blond hair, parted carefully on the right. Pink scalp gleamed through near the beginning of the hairline.

She examined her work critically. "Perhaps a small blemish on the chin—a pimple from a sour stomach." She reached into a small box— the size of the ones that aspirin comes in—and applied her forefinger to Padillo's chin. He had a pimple. He also had an unhealthy, puffy face; a drinker's complexion; thinning hair; and a yellow-toothed mouth that never quite closed. He stood up. "Slump," she ordered. "A man of our appearance avoids military bearing whenever possible."

Padillo slumped and shuffled up and down the room.

"The perfect-thirty-year man," I said.

"Think I could pass muster, Sergeant?" Padillo had even changed his voice to a White House drawl.

"Well, you're not pretty—but you're different."

"If we had more time ... but ..." Frau Koepler brushed off the chair and shrugged.

"Next," I said, and sat down. She did a similar job on me, except that I grew tanner but unhealthier looking. She also gave me a neat, well-clipped mustache. New circles grew under my eyes, and they seemed to form deeper sockets than were there before. A slight but livid scar appeared over my right eye. "It is like a picture," Frau Koepler explained. "The eye goes to the upper left-hand corner of a face automatically. That is where we put the scar. The mind registers the scar, scans the rest of the face, and runs into the mustache. Again the unexpected because the previous owner had no scar or mustache. Simple?"

"You're very good," I said.

"The best," Wolgemuth said, and beamed some more. "We did not have to do so much work on the other two because they are known only by pictures. But they will pass. Now, then, we must have the pictures taken for your ID cards."

We said good-bye to Frau Koepler. The last time I saw her she was seated at the dressing table, staring into the the mirror and stroking her lantern jaw reflectively.

After the pictures were taken we had lunch with Wolgemuth. Padillo and I chewed carefully because of the spongy rubber doodads that Frau Koepler had clamped in our mouths. They weren't too much trouble—no worse than the first set of false teeth. They didn't slip and slide around, but they felt strange and foreign. We found that drinking was much easier, and Wolgemuth thoughtfully supplied some excellent wine.

"You know, Herr McCorkle, I have been trying to get Mike here to come to work with us for a long time. He's really one of the best in this rather difficult profession."

"He's got a job," I said. "Between trips, that is."

"Yes, the café in Bonn. That has been a really excellent cover. But I'm afraid that it's completely exposed now—blown."

"That doesn't matter," Padillo said. "After this they wouldn't even send me down to the corner for coffee. That's the way I want it."

"You're still a young man, Mike," Wolgemuth said. "You've got the experience, the firsthand knowledge, the languages."

"I'm not fancy enough," Padillo said. "Sometimes I think I would have been good at running bootleg Scotch during Prohibition. Or perhaps I could still make it as a loner, knocking off suburban branch banks on Tuesday afternoons. I have the languages, but my methods are too orthodox, or maybe it's just that I'm lazy: I won't go into an operation loaded down with hollowed-out coins and fountain pens that unfold into motor scooters."

Wolgemuth poured some more wine. "All right; let us say that your past successes have been derived from the simplicity of your methods. Would you be interested in accepting occasional assignments—well-paying ones, of course?"

Padillo took a sip of the wine and smiled at its taste. His newly yellowed teeth flashed like a warning light. "No thanks. Twenty, twenty-one years is a long time. Maybe years ago I should have gone to UCLA and majored in political science and languages, and when I graduated I could have sent in a Form 57 to the CIA or State and right now I could be an FO 2 or 3 with a house in Fairfax County or explaining Vietnam to the newspaper boys in Ghana. But don't forget, Kurt, the only thing I really know is how to run a saloon. My languages are good, but only because I learned them early and correctly. I don't know the first fundamentals of grammar. I just know when it sounds right. I'm weak in history, poor in political science, and ambivalent about the world power struggle. I respect—even admire—those who do know or think they do. But for twenty years now I've had bad dreams and cold sweats and I've had to concentrate just on how to keep on living." He held out his hand and spread his fingers. They trembled slightly. "My nerves are shot, I drink too much, and I smoke too much. I'm used up and I'm worn out and I'm quitting this time around and there's not a thing in God's world that can stop me."

Wolgemuth listened carefully to Padillo's speech. "You, of course, underestimate yourself, Mike. You have that rare quality that kept them coming back to you year after year to perform just one more task. You have the actor's ability to assimilate an identity, to build a new personality with all its kinks and idiosyncrasies. When you are a German you walk like a German, you eat like one, and you smoke like one. These are little things, but after twenty years of occupation a European can recognize an American by his fat behind and the way it moves when he walks. You are a born mimic, an utterly ruthless rogue, and you have the cunning and skepticism of a successful criminal lawyer—and for that package I would be willing to pay a very high price indeed."

Padillo raised his glass in a mock salute. "I'll accept the compliment but refuse the offer. You should be looking for younger blood, Kurt."

"I couldn't even tempt you with the chance for a little revenge against your present employers?"

"No chance. They thought they had a good business proposition. The Russians needed a blood-and-thunder agent for a full-scale production. My employers, God bless them, wanted to get Symmes and Burchwood back quietly and without fuss. So you trade A for B and C, especially if A seems to be getting a little crotchety. Who set up the deal in the East—the good colonel?"

"So I understand," Wolgemuth said. "He's been back for several months now, supposedly in charge of propaganda."

"He's had some experience in the art of the swap," Padillo said. "But our side is made up of the percentage boys and, as our friend Maas told McCorkle, they have me down as an amortized agent."

There was a knock at the door. Wolgemuth said come in and one of the giant-size messenger boys came in carrying a large Manila envelope. He handed it to Wolgemuth and left. The German tore it open and produced two well-worn billfolds. "Some more of the fancy frippery you object to, Mike. But it might come in handy."

I opened mine. It had ninety-two American dollars, 250 West German Marks, an Army ID card that said I was T/Sgt. Frank J. Bailey, carefully folded travel orders, a couple of dirty pictures, an American Forces driver's license, a letter in bad English from a girl named Billi in Frankfurt that seemed overly explicit, a card that said I was a member of the Book-of-the-Month-Club, and a box of Trojans.

Wolgemuth produced two more billfolds and said: "These are for the other two."

Padillo stuffed them into a hip pocket. "How does this make-up look to you, Kurt?"

"It's good enough. As she said, the whole theory is distraction. The uniforms, of course, are the main thing. Then the faces. If you don't linger around Tempelhof, you should make it all right. And, of course, there'll be a drunken fight to take their minds off you for a few moments."

Padillo shoved back his chair and stood up. "The tickets?"

"The driver has them," Wolgemuth said.

Padillo held out his hand. "Thanks for everything, Kurt."

Wolgemuth brushed the thanks away with a wave. "You'll get a bill." He shook hands with me and told me how glad he was to have met me and sounded as if he really meant it.

"You'll find your two wards downstairs," he said.

Padillo nodded and we left the room. Max was standing by the sliding steel door in the fancy reception room that led to the elevator. He looked at us critically through his glasses. Then he nodded his head in approval.

"I'll see you in Bonn sometime soon," Max said.

"Tell Marta that—" Padillo ran out of words. "Just tell her I said thanks."

We shook hands with Max and walked through the door to the elevator. It took us down to the ground-level corridor. Symmes and Burchwood were there, shaved and dressed in Class-A uniforms. One of the giants leaned against the wall and seemed to admire the ceiling. Padillo handed Burchwood and Symmes the two billfolds.

"You can memorize your new names on the way to Tempelhof. Symmes will stick with me, Burchwood with McCorkle. We go through Pan American without fuss, just like you've done it before. I don't think you need any more lectures. You both look nice. I like your haircut, Symmes."

"Do we have to talk to you?" Symmes asked. His voice was petulant.

"No."

"Then we've decided not to any more."

"Fine. O.K., let's go."

Outside was a 1963 Ford sedan. A tall Negro in an Army uniform with the single stripe of a PFC was wiping its headlights with a dust-cloth. He saw us come out and ran around to open the door. "Yassuh, get ri' in. We fixin' to leave heah in jus' a second. Yassuh."

Padillo looked at him coldly. "You can cut out the Rastus act,

Sambo. Wolgemuth said you picked up our tickets. Let's have them."

The Negro smiled at Padillo. "I haven't heard a Texas accent like that since I left Mineral Wells."

Padillo grinned back. "It's supposed to be from nearer Kilgore," he said in his normal voice. "You ready?"

"Yassuh," the Negro said, and moved around the car to the driver's seat. I got in the front seat. Burchwood, Symmes and Padillo got in the back. The Negro opened the glove compartment and handed me four Pan Am tickets. I selected the one with Sergeant Bailey on it and handed the rest to Padillo.

"What's the plan at the airport?" Padillo asked.

"I'll let you out and park the car quick," the Negro said. "It doesn't matter where, because I'll be coming back with either the police or the MPs. Then while you're checking your tickets there's going to be a nasty racial incident. An American tourist from Georgia will insist that I insulted his wife; he'll smack me one and then I'll light into him with this weapon, which is indigenous to my race." He produced a straight razor and snicked it open. "If that cracker clips me too hard, I just might cut him a little."

"Who's the cracker?"

"One of the guys Wolgemuth recruited from Frankfurt a couple of years ago. He's genuine enough. After the cops stop it and cart me off he won't show up to press charges."

"What's your cover?" Padillo asked.

"Play a little sax in the combo at one of Wolgemuth's dives. Run a few errands. Get in trouble like this when it's needed."

"How about the Frankfurt end?"

"Man'll meet you with a car, give you the keys, and then you're on your own."

"How'll he know us?"

"He won't; you'll know him. He's my twin brother."

CHAPTER 19

An MP captain accompanied by a staff sergeant with a leathery face and squinting blue eyes walked up to Padillo at the Pan American ticket counter just after he had cleared his ticket.

"Let's see your orders, Sergeant."

Padillo slowly unbuttoned his raincoat and started to reach for his billfold in his hip pocket when the woman screamed. It was high and piercing and she put her lungs into it. It seemed to come from about a dozen or so yards to our left. I turned and saw a fleshy man of about thirty in a light covert topcoat take a clumsy swing at our Negro driver, who jumped back gracefully and flicked out his razor. He danced around the white man, making little feinting motions with the razor. The white man looked at him and proceeded to peel off his topcoat. He didn't seem to be in any hurry. A woman stood near the white man and clutched a small black purse to her chin. She was blond and plump and did a good job of looking terrified. A crowd was forming.

The Negro moved around the white man counterclockwise. He shuffled now, no longer dancing. His arms were widespread and the razor glittered, cutting edge up in his right hand. He seemed to know what he was doing.

"Come on, whiboy, come on," the Negro called softly. His accent was pure molasses again. "You ain' in the States now; come on, whi-boy."

The white man seemed to study the Negro as he turned with him. Then he suddenly threw his wadded-up topcoat in the Negro's face. He followed the coat, diving in low at the shuffling legs. He moved fast for his weight. They went down on the floor and rolled around some. The Negro let out a good yell. The MP captain and his sergeant were in the middle of the crowd, trying to untangle the arms and legs. A voice over the loud-speaker announced Pan American Frankfurt-Main flight. Padillo and I prodded Symmes and Burchwood down the passageway that led to the plane.

It was Pan American Flight 675 and it was due to leave Tempelhof at 1630 and arrive at Frankfurt-Main at 1750. It was three minutes late in take-off and we were the last aboard. I thought Wolgemuth's timing had been cut a bit fine, but we managed to get seats near each other. I sat with Burchwood, Padillo with Symmes. Neither of them was talking to us.

It was a dull flight and I kept my raincoat on. The revolver was in the pocket and I kept trying to remember how many shots I'd fired and if I had any rounds left. I decided it didn't matter since I wasn't going to shoot anybody soon anyway. I sat there in the aisle seat and stared at the back of the seat in front of me, and when I got tired of that I admired the hostesses' legs and engaged in some mildly erotic fantasies. It passed the time.

We landed in Frankfurt at 1752 and went down the landing steps with the rest of the passengers. The bastardization of the lyrics to "She'll Be Comin' Round the Mountain" kept running through my head. "There'll be no one there to meet us, there'll be no one there to greet us," then some da-da-da-da-da-da-da-da. The other passengers had their hands shaken, their cheeks kissed, and their backs slapped. All we got was a faint nod from the twin of the Negro who, the last time we saw him, an hour and twenty minutes before, had been threshing around on the floor with a straight razor clutched in his right hand.

Padillo walked up to the Negro and said, "Wolgemuth sent us. We just left your brother in Berlin."

The tall Negro looked us over carefully. He seemed to have a world of time. He wore an open white shirt with long points, a black cashmere coat sweater buttoned only at the last two buttons, lightweight gray flannel slacks without cuffs, black ribbed socks that looked silk, and a pair of burnished-black loafers with cute little tassels. His hands were like his brother's: big enough to fit around a basketball comfortably. He held a long slim cigar in one of them. It was fitted with an ivory holder. He drew on it thoughtfully and let some smoke find its way out of his thin straight nose.

"I just talked to Wolgemuth," he said. "You're to have my car. It's the fastest one we could lay our hands on. The only thing is I'd kind of like to get it back. In one piece."

"Something special?" I asked.

He nodded and blew some more smoke out of his nose. "It is to me. I got about 122 hours of my own time invested in it."

"You'll get it back," Padillo said. "If you don't, Wolgemuth'll buy you a new one."

"Uh-huh." He turned and we followed. Outside the airport he led us to a new Chevrolet Impala two-door hardtop. It was black and its rear end seemed to squat. It had no hubcaps. A big fish-pole aerial adorned the rear end. The Negro took the keys out of his pocket and handed them to Padillo, who handed them to me.

"You didn't spot any action around the airport?" Padillo asked.

"Couple of MPs more than usual, but that's normal this time of the month, right after payday. None of the Christians in Action around that I know by sight. I checked real good."

Padillo shook his head and frowned. "O.K., Mac, let's go. You drive. You two in the back seat."

Symmes and Burchwood climbed in. Padillo got in the front.

"What's so special about this boat?" I asked the Negro.

He smiled. It was as if I'd asked how it felt to win DM 400,000 on

Lotto. "It's got the four-twenty-seven under the hood and a Hurst four on the floor. It's got a Schiefer clutch, Jahns twelve-to-ones, and an Isky kit. It's got high-speed shocks and traction masters. Plus the Pittman arm's down to two-to-one steering."

"Sounds like a bomb," I said, getting in.

He placed his big hands carefully on the door and leaned down to look at me. "You done any driving before?"

"Once or twice around the Nürburgring. Sports stuff mostly."

He nodded. "I'd sure like to get this back in one piece."

"I'll see what I can do."

He nodded again, glumly this time. He didn't have much faith. He patted the door affectionately. "Yeah," he said. "See what you can do. Well, take care now." I think he was talking to the car.

"You do the same," I said, and fitted the key into the ignition, threw the clutch out, started the engine, backed out, and headed for the Autobahn.

"What have we got here?" Padillo asked.

"A hopped-up Chevy with a police radio that'll probably hit a hundred and twenty-five—maybe a hundred and thirty downhill. How fast you want to try for?"

"Keep it around eighty. If we pick up somebody who wants to play tag, use your own judgment."

"O.K."

I concentrated on driving. I had to. The clutch was stiff and the special springs eliminated the royal American bounce. Something special had been done to the steering. It felt like rack and pinion. The accelerator pedal was a massive chrome and rubber affair and I had to keep hard pressure on it. It was a car that was meant to be driven at high speed, and the only power assists it had were locked in the V-8 engine. I got it up to between eighty-five and ninety and kept it there, drifting past the double-trailered trucks that streamed out of Frankfurt, headed north.

About twenty miles out of Frankfurt we stopped at the German counterpart of a Howard Johnson and picked up some cigarettes and a bottle of Weinbrand. We let Symmes and Burchwood go to the bathroom by themselves.

Back on the Autobahn, Padillo said: "Something's gone sour."

I let the car slow down to seventy and then to sixty. "How's that?"

"There should have been something at Frankfurt. I'm not sure what, but something was missing."

"The reception not warm enough for you?" I asked, and moved the speedometer back up to eighty-five.

"Somebody must have tumbled to us by the time we got there."

I pressed the accelerator, and the Impala moved quickly up to ninety-five. "If you'll take a look behind you, I think somebody did. They've got a big green Cadillac, and it's been pacing us since we picked up the booze."

Padillo turned and looked. So did Symmes and Burchwood.

"Three of them," Padillo said. "As long as they keep that far behind, keep it around eighty. If they start to move up, then see how fast this thing will go. What's our best bet?"

I glanced in the rearview mirror at the green Cadillac, which had fixed itself a measured hundred yards behind us. "It depends on what they want to do," I said. "If they want to crowd us off, they're going to have to get alongside, and I don't think they've got the speed or the driver for that. If they just want to follow, they can probably keep up pretty well, considering the traffic. If it's tuned right, that Cadillac can hit a hundred and ten—maybe a hundred and twenty if it's blown; but I don't know of many that are.

"Our best chance is when we turn off to Bonn. That's up and down hill and they haven't got the springs for the curves. This thing does. We can probably gain on them there, run up the river to the bridge instead of taking the ferry, and then cut back through Bonn. Any place in mind?"

"We'll figure that out later. Let's see if they've got the steam to keep up."

"He's got seat belts in this thing," I said. "We may as well use them."

"They can cut you in two or make you feel like it," Padillo said. But he buckled his anyway. He turned to Symmes and Burchwood. "Put yours on. We're taking another ride." The two men remained silent but snapped on their belts.

"Shall we?" I said.

"Let's."

I pressed the accelerator almost to the floor board and the Chevrolet spurted past a couple of Volkswagens. The traffic was medium-heavy and I kept to the left-hand lane, flicking the passing-lights switch as we zipped by the slower-moving trucks and cars. The Cadillac moved out into the same lane and its driver began working his lights. He kept the hundred yards between us as if we were linked by a chain.

"What's it say?" I asked Padillo.

"It's bouncing off a hundred and twenty."

I snatched a glance at the special tachometer. Its needle was hovering around red-line. I pressed the accelerator down the last quarter of an inch and held it hard against the floor board. A big blue Mercedes convertible took my passing as a personal challenge and swung out into the left lane to give chase. The Cadillac blew him back over with horn and lights.

The wind noise was almost a scream and, despite its tough springing, the Chevrolet was jumping around. On a hill an Opel moved out two hundred yards in front of us to pass a Volkswagen. It barely got its front fender up to the VW's rear bumper when I leaned on the horn and flashed the lights. It was too late for the Opel to drop back and it didn't have the juice to move ahead. It took the only course available and headed for the dividing strip. The VW made for the shoulder. We roared through, and I still think that my front left fender nicked the Opel. The Cadillac sliced through behind us.

"I haven't done that since I was sixteen," I yelled at Padillo.

Padillo reached into his raincoat pocket and took out his revolver and checked its rounds. I got mine out and handed it to him and he reloaded it from a box of shells and gave it back. I glanced in the mirror and saw that the Cadillac was maintaining its distance. Symmes and Burchwood sat in the back seat, stiffly upright, their eyes buttoned tight, their mouths making little straight lines of fear and disapproval. I supposed that they were holding hands. It was none of my business.

It took us a little under fifty minutes to make the sixty miles from the place where we bought the brandy to the cutoff to Bonn. I double-clutched the Chevrolet and threw it down into third, not using the brake. I did it again and got it down into second. The engine braked the car and, without the rear brake light to warn him, the Cadillac's driver was almost on our bumper before he could figure out what I was doing.

I went into the curve too fast, but the engine was still braking and the Cadillac didn't have a chance. It overshot. I kept the Chevrolet in second and made the curve and shifted up into third again.

"They're going to back up," Padillo said.

"That's a hell of a risk on that road."

We sped through the Autobahn underpass and hit the blacktopped road that led to Venusberg and down to the ferry that crossed the Rhine to Bonn. I kept the car in third, shifting down into second as we scattered a few small children and ducks in a village and started to climb the twisting road to the top of the hill.

"I don't see them," Padillo said.

"We may have picked up a few minutes. We should gain another five or ten on these curves."

The Chevrolet took them on rails, its hard tough springing reminiscent of an old MG-TC I had once owned. I shifted down into second to drift the first bend in an S-shaped curve. The engine was responding nicely on the short straight and I was estimating the rpm's needed for the next bend when we went into it, came out of it, and hit the roadblock.

They had the two junkers parked across the road: a couple of battered but still solid Mercedes of the early-1950 vintage. I was still in second, so I hit the brakes with my left foot and jammed the accelerator down with my right, trying to spin the car into a tight U-turn, but it was too late and the Chevrolet crashed into one of the Mercedes and I was slammed forward against the steering wheel.

There seemed to be dozens of them. They got the Chevrolet doors open and dragged us out. I was stunned, and my stomach ached where the seat belt had cut into it. I felt them lift the gun out of my pocket. I slid down on the ground and vomited. It was mostly wine. I lay there for what seemed a long time, and then I looked up and Padillo was still standing, held by two men in gray felt hats and belted coats whose colors kept changing in the light that filtered through the trees. One of them reached into Padillo's pocket and took out his revolver. They patted some more pockets and found the knife and got that too. I was sick again.

Two of them grabbed me under the arms and helped me to stagger over to a car and then tumbled me into the back on the floor. I lay there panting and trying not to be sick again. I managed to grab the back of the front seat and haul myself to my knees. It took all day. Padillo was sprawled across the backseat, his mouth slightly ajar. His eyes opened and they blinked at me a couple of times and closed again. I knelt on the back floor and looked out the rear window. They had moved the two Mercedes and the Chevrolet over to one side of the road. They were dragging one of the Mercedes off into a clump of trees. It was being pulled by a Ford Taunus. At least it looked like a Ford Taunus, but the light was getting bad. A man climbed into the front seat and aimed a gun at me. He had a sallow ugly face and his long nose was spotted with ripe blackheads.

"Pick up your friend and make him sit up," he said. He spoke German, but it was heavily accented. I couldn't place the accent. I turned and picked up Padillo's feet and swung them down to the floor. Then I pushed and shoved him into a sitting position, but he slumped forward and I had to push him back again. He had vomited over his uniform and there was an ugly dark spot under his right ear that oozed blood. I sat in the back seat beside him and looked at the man with the gun and the blackheads on his nose.

"Nothing foolish, please. No heroics," he said.

"Nothing foolish," I agreed, and spit out one of the sponge-rubber things that had come loose in my mouth. While I was at it I dug some of the wax out of my nose. I didn't have any manners. I didn't need any. I started working on the other sponge-rubber piece with my tongue. It came loose and I spat it out, too. I also peeled off my mustache.

The man with the gun watched me curiously but said nothing. The car we were in was English, I noticed: a Humber with walnut panels built into the rear that let down into tea trays. Or cocktail trays, if you were so inclined. It was an export model with the steering wheel on the left-hand side. Next to that was a two-way radio set made of gray metal. I offered myself nine to two that green Cadillac had one just like it. I looked out the rear window. They were pulling the Chevrolet into the clump of trees. Somebody might find it tomorrow—or next week. The tall Negro down in Frankfurt hadn't had much faith and I wished I had listened to him. We could have gone someplace and talked about cars and drunk beer.

Another man got into the driver's seat. He turned around and looked us over without much interest, grunted, turned back, and started the car. We followed another Humber down the curving narrow blacktop. There were four men in the car ahead. The two in the backseat were Symmes and Burchwood. I couldn't tell if they were speaking to anyone yet.

At the Rhine we turned left and drove along the highway for a half-mile or so before we came to a spot that curved out slightly toward the river. It had a few picnic tables and a trash can and a place to park cars. A stone retaining wall bellied out into the Rhine, and there were steps leading down it to a small dock, where an inboard launch about eighteen feet long was tied up. The green Cadillac was parked in the picnic area, and I decided it must have gone by while I was flat on the ground. I noticed that it was a Fleetwood.

The driver of our car parked, got out, and talked to the driver of the other Humber, which carried Symmes and Burchwood. Then that driver got out and walked over to the green Cadillac and talked to someone in the backseat. The man with the gun stayed with us. There was another man in the front seat of the other car. He probably had two guns.

Our driver came back and said something in a language I couldn't even place, much less understand. But the man with the gun understood it and he told me to get out and to help Padillo out. Padillo opened his eyes and said, "I can walk," but his voice didn't carry much conviction. I walked around the car, opened his door, and helped him out.

The man with the gun was right with me. "Down the steps. Get him into the launch," he told me. I draped Padillo's arm around my neck and half dragged, half led him down the stairs. "You've picked up a few pounds," I said. I helped him into the launch and he sank down on the cushioned seats that ran along the side. It was getting quite dark. Symmes and Burchwood came down the steps to the dock and got into the boat. They looked at Padillo, who was hunched over. "Is he hurt?" Symmes asked.

"I don't know," I said. "He doesn't say much. Are you hurt?"

"No, we're not hurt," he said, and sat down next to Burchwood.

The man who had driven our car walked up to the bow and got behind the wheel. He started the engine. It caught and burbled in neutral through its underwater exhausts. We sat there for five minutes. We seemed to be waiting for something. I followed the gaze of the man at the wheel. A light across the Rhine flashed three times. He picked up a flashlight that had been clamped to the dash, aimed it across the river, and flicked it on and off three times. It was a signal, clever McCorkle decided. The interior light of the green Cadillac flashed on as the back door opened and a man got out and started down the stairs to the dock. He was short and stocky and waddled a bit as he walked across the dock to the boat. It was growing too dark to see his face clearly, but I didn't have to. It was Maas all right.

CHAPTER 20

Maas waved at me cheerfully from the dock and climbed into the launch. One of the drivers let go of the stern line and the launch headed out into the Rhine, taking an oblique course upriver. I nudged Padillo in the ribs with my elbows. "Company's here," I said. He lifted his head and regarded Maas, who smiled cheerfully at us from his seat near the stern.

"Christ," Padillo said, and dropped his head back down on arms folded across his knees.

Maas talked quietly with one of the men who had driven the Humbers. The other two men sat across the launch from us and smoked cigarettes. Each held a gun casually in his lap, pointing at nothing in particular. I decided that they could keep them. Burchwood and Symmes sat next to me and stared straight ahead. It was dark now.

The boat driver reduced his speed and angled the launch sharply to the left. Down river, a half-mile away, I could see the lights of the U.S. Embassy. They looked warm, inviting and safe, but they didn't get any closer. I hadn't really expected them to. The dark outline of a self-powered barge loomed ahead of us. It was anchored in the channel about fifty feet from the riverbank and sat low in the water as if heavily loaded. It was the kind of barge that you see plowing up and down the Rhine from Amsterdam to Basel, the family wash snapping merrily in the breeze. They are almost always family owned and operated. Children get born on them and old men die on them. The occupants sleep and eat and make love below decks in compact quarters located near the stern that are about the size of a smallish American house trailer. The barge we approached was about 150 feet long. The pilot of the launch cut the engine and we drifted, stern first, toward its bow.

Somebody shined a light on us and threw a rope, and the man in the stern next to Maas caught it and pulled us up snug to a rope ladder and wooden rungs. Maas was first up the ladder and he had trouble with one of the rungs. I hoped he would fall, but someone on the barge caught him and pulled him up. The two men with the guns were on their feet and one of them waved negligently at Symmes and Burchwood. They got the idea and went up the ladder after Maas. Padillo had raised his head from his arms and watched Symmes and Burchwood climb the ladder.

"Think you can make it?" I asked.

"No, but I will," he said.

We got up and I let Padillo precede me to the ladder. He grabbed a rung and started to pull himself up. I boosted him from behind and some hands reached down and caught him under the arms and pulled. I started up and the strain knotted and twisted my stomach where the Chevrolet's seat belt had cut into it. Some more hands, not particularly gentle, fastened on and helped me. The barge had its parking lights on for navigational safety and the only other light was from the flash that somebody kept shining around.

"Straight ahead," a voice muttered in my ear, and I put my hands out and started to take some small careful steps in that general direction. A light suddenly appeared from an open door that led down into the living quarters. I could see Maas backing his way down the stairs, holding onto the rails. Burchwood and Symmes followed, then Padillo and I. I heard the launch pulling away. Only the two men with the guns remained, and they motioned for me to follow Padillo.

I turned into the doorway and started feeling for the steps below. I moved down slowly in the narrow passage until there weren't any more steps. I turned around. We were in a room about seven by ten. The ceiling was barely tall enough for me to stand erect. There were two built-in bunks with brightly quilted covers along one side. Padillo stood slumped and listless beside them. I noticed that he was rid of most of the make-up devices and the hair piece. His face was back to normal except for the pallor of his skin. Burchwood and Symmes stood next to him.

Maas was seated at one end of a table that could fold up against the wall. He smiled and nodded at me and his knees knocked together nervously like those of a fat little boy at a party who has to go to the bathroom but is afraid he'll miss the ice cream and cake. At the other end of the table was another chair, and behind that was a door.

"Hello, Maas," I said.

"Gentlemen," he said, and giggled and nodded his head some more. "We meet again, it seems."

"Just one question?" I said.

"Of course, my dear McCorkle: as many as you wish."

"You had a two-way radio working out of that Cadillac into the Humbers—right?"

"Correct. We merely chased you up the Autobahn into our little trap. Simple, but effective, you will admit?"

I nodded. "Mind if we smoke?"

Maas shrugged elaborately. I took out a package of cigarettes and gave one to Padillo and lighted them both from a pack of matches. The small door opened and a man in a gray-and-black hound's-tooth jacket and gray trousers backed out of it. He was talking in Dutch to someone still in the other room. The back of his head was covered with long black shiny hair that almost but not quite met in a ducktail. He closed the door and turned around and his horn-rimmed glasses flinted in the light. He could have been fifty or forty or younger, but there was one thing certain: he was Chinese.

He stood before the closed door for several long moments, staring at Padillo. Finally he said, "Hello, Mike."

"Hello, Jimmy," Padillo said.

Maas had bounced out of his seat and was dancing attendance to the Chinese. "It went very smoothly, Mr. Ku," he said in English. "There was no unexpected trouble. This is Symmes and this is Burchwood. The other is McCorkle, who is the business partner of Padillo."

"Sit down and shut up, Maas," the Chinese said without looking at him. Maas retreated to his chair and his knees started knocking together again. The Chinese sat down in the chair at the other end of the table, took out a package of Kents, and lighted one with a gold Ronson.

"It's been a long time, Mike," he said.

"Twenty-three years," Padillo said. "And you're calling yourself Ku now."

"It was in Washington at the old Willard, wasn't it—that last time?" Ku said.

"You were Jimmy Lee then and you liked Gibsons."

The Chinese nodded absently. "We'll have to talk about the old days in the Oh, So Secret one of these times. I've been out of touch. I understand, though, that you're still working."

"Not really," Padillo said. "Just an odd job now and then."

"Like in Bucharest in 1959—March?"

"I don't remember," Padillo said politely.

Ku smiled. "They say it was you."

"You must have had an interesting wait these last few days," Padillo said. "But it's pleasant along the Rhine this time of year."

"A few anxious moments," Ku said. "And it's been a little rich. I'm going to have a hell of a time with the expense account."

"But you've got what you came after," Padillo said.

"You mean these two," Ku said, jerking a thumb at Burchwood and Symmes.

Padillo nodded.

"It's not every day that we turn up a couple of defectors from NSA."

"Maybe it's your Peiping climate."

"You learn to like it," Ku said. "After a while."

"Don't bother; I've got a place fixed up for you. It's through that other door there." Ku got up and walked over to a door next to the stairs. He unlocked it with a key and held it open. "It's not big, but it's quiet. You can get some rest." One of the men with guns had come halfway down the stairs. He was sitting on a step, the gun pointed nowhere and everywhere. He waved it at the door that Ku held open. I led the way; the rest followed.

Ku reached into a cupboard and brought out a bottle and handed it to Padillo. "Dutch gin," he said. "Have one for me." We went through the door into a room with two bunks along the walls and heard the lock click behind us. A red light shielded by a metal network burned overhead. It didn't give off a cheery glow.

"That horrid little fat man is here again," Symmes said to nobody in particular. Maybe we were all speaking again.

"You are now on what may very well turn out to be a slow barge to China," Padillo said. "Sorry," he added; "I couldn't resist."

"I take it that the lad with the almond eyes is not of the Chancre Jack persuasion," I said.

Padillo and I had taken the floor and Burchwood and Symmes were on the lower bunk. We had done it automatically, as if we somehow owed them a favor. Padillo held up the bottle to the red light and examined it critically. "No, he's one of the mainland types and has probably mixed this gin with some strange new truth serum. In which case I'll volunteer as chief guinea pig." He unscrewed the top, took a long swallow, and handed the bottle to me. "No ill effects," he said.

I took a drink and offered the bottle to Burchwood and Symmes. They looked at each other and Burchwood finally accepted it. He wiped off the neck with his sleeve and took a delicate sip. Symmes did the same and handed it back to Padillo.

"The wily oriental in there is a former classmate of mine from World War Two. We trained at the same funny factory in Maryland. I heard later somewhere that he was sent on some kind of do with Mao's outfit and never came home. He's probably the equivalent of a buck general in their intelligence setup."

"Hard work and dedication to duty have often been known to pay off," I said.

"He is also one bright cooky. He graduated from Stanford at nineteen. And you two," he continued, looking at Symmes and Burchwood, "are probably curious why he happens to be on this Dutch barge on the Rhine."

"Why?" Symmes asked.

Padillo took another swallow of the gin and lighted a cigarette. "Mr. Ku is the key piece in this week's jigsaw. Everything else that's happened falls into place around him. It's been a very slick operation. And it's cost somebody a packet."

"Us, for example," I said.

"We may not have to worry about that. But let's take it from the first, when Maas met you on the plane from Berlin. He had you tagged and he was trying to get to me on the pretense of selling me the information on the trade: me for Burchwood and Symmes here. But he really wasn't supposed to sell me the information. Ku just wanted him to tip me off. But Maas was greedy and he decided to sell it, and before he did he had another small piece of business to conduct with the dark little Coca-Cola drinker that got shot in our place."

Padillo paused and drew on his cigarette. "Ku wanted Burchwood and Symmes. Somehow he had found out about the proposed swap between the Russians and us. He probably got the information from his Moscow source, but that's not important. When he found out that I was part of the swap he got the great idea: Why not tip me off and let me worry about getting Burchwood and Symmes out of East Berlin and back to Bonn? And when we got to a convenient spot, like near Bonn, he could arrange a snatch-and-grab, load us onto a barge, and chug down the Rhine to Amsterdam. There it would be simple to load us onto a ship. Except for one thing."

"What's that?" I said.

"I don't think that you and I are going to make the entire trip. Just Burchwood and Symmes."

"We're not Communists," Burchwood said. "I've told you two men that again and again. We're certainly not *Chinese* Communists."

"That's what makes you such plums," Padillo said. "The Chinese haven't been able to get their hands on anyone good since the Korean thing, and most of the ones they got then have turned out to be stumblebums. They've been recruiting quietly all over the Iron Curtain territory, trying to latch on to some defectors. And they don't want them for just propaganda reasons. They need them to teach English, to do broadcasts, to check translations—all the little onerous tasks that need the attention of the native-born American.

"Now suppose they see the chance to pick up a couple of welleducated guys who have defected to Russia, whose defection has been kept under wraps by both Moscow and Washington, and who just happen to have worked in one of the code sections of the National Security Agency.

"You can almost see the 'tilt' sign light up in their minds. One: they can parade them around as real live defectors who've seen the true Holy Grail rising out of the mists of the Yangtze. It might take a little therapy, but that they've proved they can do. Two: they get all the code stuff that Burchwood and Symmes know. It might be a little out of date, a little old, but it's better than nothing, and you can bet that there's been no trade-off between Moscow and Peiping. Third—and this is the real gem: they've got a two-edged propaganda device going for them. Two National Security Agency employees get fed up with the U.S. and defect to China. If the Moscow flacks send up the cry that they had them first, then the Chinese come back with the charge that it's a double defection: first from the home-grown imperialism of the U.S. and then from the deviationist brand of the backsliding Muscovites. After they've milked Burchwood and Symmes dry of their propaganda value and their knowledge of NSA, they can put them to work teaching English to an advanced kindergarten or being Shanghai Sam, disc jockey for the Marines in Vietnam."

"You draw a nice clear picture in the center," I said, "but it's fuzzy around the edges. For instance, how did Cooky get on stage?"

"Cook was a KGB patsy. No money, no beliefs, just blackmail. Maas knew this, and when he missed out on me he went to Cook and sold him the information about the trade. Cook checked in with his resident in Bonn and told him what he had. The resident told him to tag along through you. The problem then came up about how to get you to get Cook to Berlin. The KGB called in Maas and he came up with the tunnel and the idea of five thousand dollars cash ante. So Maas was double-agenting. His main job was to get me to spirit Symmes and Burchwood over the wall for Jimmy Ku. But the KGB called him in to work on you so that you'd call Cook to Berlin with the five grand. Where else would you get that much money on short notice? The Russians were depending on Cook and his fast draw to keep the thing from going too far. Then they'd have Burchwood and Symmes *and me* and they could thumb their nose at any deal they'd previously cooked up with our side."

"When did you figure all this out?" I asked.

"When I saw Jimmy come through that door a few minutes ago. Most of it anyway."

"Pass the bottle," I said. He passed it and I took a swallow and offered the bottle to Burchwood and Symmes, but they declined. Politely this time.

"Wasn't the KGB a trifle suspicious of Maas since he had sold the information about you and the trade to Cooky?"

"They would have been—if Cook had told them where he'd bought it. But he didn't. Or they'd have never used Maas. Cook was being threatened. He hadn't been producing anything; he'd been drinking too much. This was a chance for him to play big shot. So he paid Maas for the information that Maas wanted him to have anyway. And from there on you and I and Max and poor old Weatherby started raking the chestnuts out of the coals."

"I wonder if Ku knows about Maas and his various deals. Our fat friend could very well hand us over and then trot up the road aways and blow the whistle on Ku to the Russians."

"I seriously doubt that Jimmy's going to let Maas off the barge until it's tied up alongside some freighter in Amsterdam. Like I said, Jimmy's no dope."

"You don't figure Maas has worked for our side yet—providing we still have a side left?"

Padillo frowned. "That's what was bothering me at Frankfurt. I thought they'd have met us there. In fact, I was toying with the idea of just driving on down to the I.G. Farben building and dumping the whole thing in their laps. Maybe the uniforms and the make-up really did fool them. Maybe they still think we're in East Berlin and they're waiting for us to come back through Checkpoint Charlie. Don't forget: we came under the wall at five o'clock this morning. The only people who know we made it are the guy who owned the house and the tunnel—and he's dead—plus Wolgemuth's people—and they're not saying anything. I owe them too much money."

I lighted another cigarette and leaned back against the wall. My stomach still hurt, but the Dutch gin was helping. "I hate to give up so close to home," I said. "If we could find a taxi we could be sitting at the bar in fifteen minutes with a couple of tall cold ones while we counted the day's receipts."

"That's a nice thought."

"It's the only one I've had lately. You have a plan, of course."

Padillo rubbed a palm across his forehead wearily. He held his hand out straight in front of him and looked at it carefully. It shook. "I'm in lousy shape. I think a couple of ribs are cracked. But you're wrong. I haven't any plan—just an idea or two—and we'll need some help."

He looked at Symmes and Burchwood. "How does China sound to you two?"

"What do you expect us to say?" Burchwood said. "Peachy keen?"

"They do that brainwashing," Symmes said. "We heard all about that in Moscow. They turn you into zombies."

"They wouldn't do that," Padillo said. "You'd just have to make a few speeches, a few tape recordings. Tell them what you remember about NSA, and then they'd give you a job. Teaching, probably."

"No, thank you," Symmes said.

"How do you expect to avoid it?"

"You got us into this mess; you can just get us out of it. We're your responsibility," Burchwood said.

Padillo studied them for a moment. "I'll make you a deal."

"What kind?"

"You help McCorkle and me, and if we get off this tub, all bets are off. You can go wherever you want. The Russian Embassy's about a mile from here. You can ask for political asylum. Of course, they offered to trade you for me and you might prove just a little embarrassing for them, but that's your risk. Or you can turn yourselves in and I'll do what I can. It would be a kind of blackmail, but I think our side might pay. They'd almost have to."

"What do you mean blackmail?" Burchwood asked.

"As you've gathered, my former employers and I don't quite see eye to eye. Either they give you a break—and I get good evidence of it every six months—or I call in the press and then they can explain how come two top staff members of NSA defected to the Russians."

"We weren't top staff members," Symmes said.

"The way I'd tell it you would be."

Symmes and Burchwood looked at each other and their mental telegraphic systems seemed to be functioning as well as ever. They nodded their heads simultaneously.

"Do we have to hit anybody?" Burchwood asked.

"It might come to that. If it does, hit as hard as you can. If there's something lying around, like a bottle, use that. There're four of them—Ku, Maas and the two Albanians."

"I was wondering what they were," I said.

"There's also somebody in the room that Jimmy Ku came out of— probably a Dutch couple who owns the barge."

Padillo outlined his plan. Like most of his ideas, its merit lay in its simplicity. We wouldn't have to sink the barge or set the Rhine on fire. All we had to do was run an excellent chance of being shot and dumped over the side.

"How about it?" Padillo asked Burchwood and Symmes.

"Isn't there some other way?" Symmes asked. "All that violence."

"If you've got something better, lay it on."

Symmes and Burchwood telegraphed their messages to each other. They nodded agreement. I shrugged.

"O.K., Mac, here's the bottle."

"No sense in waste," I said, and took a drink and gave it back. "Hand it up to me." I heaved myself up to the top bunk. Padillo took a drink and passed me the bottle. I poked its neck through the metal-wire mesh that covered the red light and smashed the bulb. I turned and lay lengthwise along the bunk, which was only eighteen inches or so from the ceiling. The door was to the right of the bunk and I held the bottle in my right hand.

"O.K.?" Padillo whispered.

"Ready," I said.

"Go ahead, Symmes," Padillo said.

I could hear but not see Symmes moving toward the door. He let out a scream, a good loud one that ranged up and down the scale. He began to pound on the door with his fists. I took a tighter grip on the bottle.

"Let us out!" Symmes yelled. He made his voice crack. "He's vomiting blood. Let us out, for God's sake; let us out!" He moaned and whimpered. He was very good.

"What is it—what's going on?" It was one of the Albanians calling through the door in German.

"This man—this Padillo is sick—he's getting blood all over everything. He's dying."

Some voices murmured in the other room. A key turned in the lock. The door opened and light from the other room shafted in to show Padillo bent over in a corner, his head cradled in his arms. The Albanian came through the door, gun drawn, his eyes on Padillo. I swung the bottle in a flat sidearm, backhand motion. It hit the back of his neck and shattered. The pieces tinkled as they fell to the floor. Padillo sprang from the floor and chopped the Albanian across the throat and grabbed his gun. The Albanian crumpled. I rolled out of the bunk and snatched Symmes's left arm and bent it backward behind him until it almost touched his neck. He screamed and this time it was sheer pain. I jabbed the broken shard of the bottle against his neck with my right hand. Padillo had the Albanian's gun up against Burchwood's neck, just below the right ear.

"We're coming out, Jimmy," he called. "Just stand there. If you blink, I'll shoot Burchwood and Mac will slice Symmes's throat."

Looking over Symmes's shoulder, I could see Ku and Maas through the doorway, standing by the table. Maas's mouth was slightly open. Ku's hands were in his jacket pockets, his face impassive except for a slight, bemused smile. "How'd you fake the blood, Mike?" Ku asked.

We moved out into the room slowly, turned, and backed toward the stairs.

"I didn't," Padillo lied. "I just stuck my finger down my throat and it came up. I've got a couple of cracked ribs and something's bleeding inside. Call your man down from topside, Jimmy."

Ku called him and the other Albanian clattered down the stairs backward. Padillo clipped him hard across the back of the neck with the barrel of the gun. He fell forward on the stairs and then bumped down the steps to the floor. He didn't move.

"That wasn't necessary," Ku said.

"I evened the odds," Padillo said.

"You know I have a gun in my hand?"

"I don't doubt it. But shooting through a coat pocket is tricky, Jimmy. You might hit me, but more likely you'd hit Burchwood here. And anyway I'd pull the trigger and he wouldn't have any ear left or any face. As for Mac, he'd probably cut the big vein or at least make Symmes whisper for the rest of his life."

"Shoot," Maas whispered to Ku, his eyes bulging a little. "Shoot, you fool."

"I would just as soon shoot you, Maas," Padillo said, "and make my deal with Jimmy alone."

Ku's smile grew broader and he exposed some very good teeth or an excellent cap job. "Make your proposition, Mike."

"We'll leave these two on deck for you after we bolt the door from the outside."

Ku shook his head slowly from side to side. "Not good enough. You'd spill on us, Mike, once you got off this barge. One way or the other, you'll have to try to shoot your way out."

I could feel Symmes's Adam's apple move against the broken neck of the bottle that I held pressed to his throat. I gave a small jerk to his left arm and he gave out a little cry, like a kitten's whimper.

"Please," he said, "please do what they say. I know they'll kill me. I've already seen them kill too many people."

"Shoot them," Maas pleaded. Ku's hand moved slightly in his jacket pocket.

"No more, Jimmy. I don't have to aim, but you do."

"Shut up, fat man," Ku told Maas.

"Let's go," Padillo said to me, and started to back toward the stairs. He kept the gun pressed against Burchwood's neck, his eyes on Ku. I watched Maas and gave Symmes's arm a tug. We backed after Padillo and Burchwood.

The door next to the table banged open and a chunky, blond man jumped into the cabin. He held a shotgun in his hands and he was waving it around the room when Padillo shot him. I knocked Symmes to the floor and dived for the stairs. I could see Maas fumbling for his

Luger. Padillo fired again, but nobody yelled. There was another shot and Padillo grunted once behind me but kept scrambling up the stairs. I was outside and Padillo stumbled through the doorway of the stairs. He fell and sprawled on the deck. I picked up his gun transferring the broken neck of the bottle to my left hand. I flattened myself against the cabin housing, and when Ku came through I chopped the wrist that held his pistol with my gun barrel. He yelled and dropped the gun, stumbled over Padillo, and sprawled into the darkness. Padillo got to his knees. His left arm hung limply by his side. He turned and looked at me. "Take care of Maas," he said. He got painfully to his feet and Ku jumped him from the edge of the pool of light. I couldn't get in a shot. Ku's left hand, palm up, jabbed at the base of Padillo's nose. Padillo blocked it with his right and kicked out with his left foot. The kick was low and caught Ku on the thigh. Ku jumped back into the darkness and Padillo dived after him. I started to move toward them, but I heard a clatter on the stairs. I flattened myself against the cabin housing. The noise on the stairs stopped. I could hear a thumping out in the darkness, and then I could make out two figures struggling tight together against the low railing that ran around the stern of the barge. There was a scream and they disappeared over the side. There was a splash, smaller than I expected. And then there was no noise at all. Nothing. I ran to the railing and the shotgun blasted behind me. The blast drilled a thousand or so burning needles into my left thigh. I stumbled and fell to the deck, twisted around, and saw Maas framed in the door of the stairway. I lifted the gun and took aim and pulled the trigger and it clicked.

Maas smiled and walked toward me carefully. I threw the gun at him and he dodged. It was no trouble. He held the shotgun casually, just aiming it enough to make sure it would blow off my head. I looked at the shotgun and then at Maas.

"So, Herr McCorkle, it is only you and I."

"That's a bad line, Maas, even for you," I said, dragging myself up so my shoulders rested against the stern railing. My thigh was wet and warm and covered with liquid fire.

"You are hurt," he said, and sounded as if he were really concerned.

"Just a nick—nothing really. No need to panic."

"I assure you, Herr McCorkle, I am far from panicking. Everything has worked out even better than we had planned."

"What happened to Symmes and Burchwood?"

"They are comfortably asleep for the moment. A slight, carefully placed blow. Perhaps they'll have a headache, but no more."

"The blond man with the shotgun?"

"The owner of the barge? Dead."

"So now?"

"So now I simply make other arrangements for the transfer of Herr Symmes and Herr Burchwood in Amsterdam. Where Ku failed, I shall succeed, and I assume that I shall be adequately compensated."

"You can pilot a barge?"

"Of course not. I will merely transfer them to an automobile and drive to Amsterdam. There will be no trouble at the border. I checked their excellent papers that you so thoughtfully provided."

"That takes care of everyone but me," I said.

"I'm afraid, Herr McCorckle, that this is the end of our association."

"And we were becoming such friends."

Maas smiled faintly. "Always the joke, even at such a time."

"There's one you haven't heard yet."

"So?"

"That's a single-shot you're aiming at me. I don't think you re-loaded."

Maas pulled the trigger and the hammer made a comforting click. He swung the shotgun down at me, but I had already begun to move and its barrel clanged on the steel railing. My right foot caught him in the stomach. It was a hard, satisfying kick. He belched and stumbled forward and fell on the railing. The shotgun dropped into the water. I edged myself around and gave him another kick and he tumbled over the edge, but his arms caught the rail. I hit at him weakly with my right hand. He slipped some more and dangled above the water, clutching the railing with only his hands.

"Please, Herr McCorkle; I cannot swim. Pull me up. Good Jesus, pull me up!"

I crawled to the rail and leaned over and looked down at him. Something scraped against the deck. It was my left hand. It still held the neck of the broken bottle.

I stared down at Maas. He stared back, his mouth making little round O shapes as he tried to make his arms lift his weight. They refused. His head twisted from side to side. His shoes scraped against the barge. He couldn't pull himself up, but he could hang there all night.

"Drown, damn you," I said, and raised the bottle and brought it down on his hands again and again until they were bloody and they didn't clutch the rail anymore.

CHAPTER 21

The attendants were putting me in a strait jacket and chattering away like magpies about what kind of knots they should use when the pain came back and I could taste its bitterness far down into my throat.

But it wasn't a strait jacket, it was only a life preserver, the Mae West type, and Symmes and Burchwood were struggling to get me into it.

"He'll bleed to death," Symmes said severely.

"Well, there's no rowboat and I don't go to all those summer camps without learning something." That was Burchwood.

"I know what you learned," Symmes said, and giggled.

"What town is this?" I said.

"He's awake," Burchwood said.

"I can see he's awake."

"We're going to swim you ashore, Mr. McCorkle."

"That's nice."

"That's why we're putting this life preserver on you," Symmes said. "Russ used to be a lifeguard."

"Good," I said. "Have you got one for Padillo? He's hurt." I knew it was a stupid thing to say before I said it, but it came out anyway.

"Mr. Padillo isn't here," Symmes said. His voice was apologetic.

"Gone, huh?"

"Everybody's gone, Mr. McCorkle."

"Everybody's gone," I said dreamily. "Weatherby gone. Bill-Wilhelm gone. The blond kid on the wall a long time ago. He gone, too? The captain gone, and Maas is gone, and Ku is long gone. And the Albanians gone. And old partner Padillo gone. Goddamn, that's something. Old partner Padillo."

The water woke me up. Someone had me by the neck and was swimming somewhere. I was on my back. My left leg throbbed and I felt lightheaded. I leaned back into the life jacket and looked up at the stars. The water must have been cold because my teeth chattered. But I didn't notice. I was too busy counting the stars.

They dragged me up the bank of the Rhine and flagged down a truck that was bound to the Bonn market with a load of chickens. I had to talk to the driver, because he spoke only German. I was standing there, supported by Symmes and Burchwood, sodden and scraggly, and trying to make up a reasonable lie about how my friends and I had been walking by the river and had fallen in. Finally I gave up and fished out all the money I had from the ruined billfold Wolgemuth had given me. I pressed it on the driver and gave him my address. For $154 he let us sit in the back of the truck with the chickens.

Burchwood and Symmes dragged me out of the truck and up the twelve steps to the front door of my house. "There's a key under the mat. My clever, clever hiding place."

Burchwood found it and opened the door. They half carried, half pushed me in and dumped me into my favorite chair so I could bleed on it for a while.

"You need a doctor," Symmes said. "You're bleeding again."

"Whiskey," I said. "At the bar. And cigarettes."

Symmes went behind the bar and came back with a half-tumbler of whiskey and a lighted cigarette. I clutched the tumbler and managed to get it to my mouth, where it started to play a tune on my teeth. I sloshed some of it down. It was bourbon. I got some more down and then reached for the cigarette and took a long, grateful drag. Then some more whiskey and another lungful of smoke.

"Hand me the phone," I told Burchwood.

"Who are you going to call?"

"A doctor."

He handed me the phone and I dropped it. Burchwood picked it up and said, "What number?" I told him and he dialed it.

It rang for a while and a sleepy voice answered it. "Willi?"

"Ja."

"McCorkle."

"You drunk again, you and that no-good partner?"

"No. Not drunk yet. Just shot. Can you help?"

"I'll be right there," he snapped, and hung up.

I slopped some more whiskey down. The pain wouldn't go away. "Dial 'nother number," I told Burchwood. He looked at Symmes, who nodded. He dialed and the number rang. It rang a long time before it answered.

"Fredl," I said. "S'Mac."

"Where are you?" she asked.

"Home."

When I awoke I was in my own bed between fresh clean sheets and daylight was creeping through a crack in the drawn drapes. Fredl sat in a chair next to the bed smoking a cigarette and drinking a cup of coffee. I moved experimentally and my thigh responded by sending out a wave of pain. My stomach felt as if someone had slammed a bat into it.

"You're awake," Fredl said.

"But am I alive?"

She leaned over and kissed me on the forehead. "Very much so. It took Dr. Klett an hour to pick the shot out of your thigh. He said you got only the fringe of the pattern. Also your stomach is going to be sore for a week or so and you bled a lot. And, finally, what in God's name have you been up to?"

"Too much," I said. "Where are Symmes and Burchwood?"

"Those two!" she sniffed.

"You jealous?"

"No, they just seemed so tired and pathetic—and lost, I suppose."

"They've been through a lot, but they're O.K. I'd hate to see anything happen to them."

"One's asleep in the den. The other's on the couch in your living room."

"What time is it?"

"Almost noon."

"What time did I call you?"

"About three this morning. You passed out right after that, they said. Then the doctor arrived and started to use his tweezers. He said that you lost quite a lot of blood—that you'll be weak for a few days."

I ran a hand over my face. "Who shaved me?"

"I did—and gave you a bath. Since when have you been a sergeant?"

"Since yesterday morning—or afternoon. A long time ago."

"A long story?"

"Long enough. I'll tell you about it while I get dressed."

"For what? Your funeral?"

"No. To go out. Into the world. To take care of things. Earn a living. Run a saloon."

Fredl rose from the chair and walked across the room to the dresser, where she opened a drawer and took out a shirt. She turned, holding the shirt against her breasts, and looked at me strangely.

"It's not there anymore."

"What's not there?"

"Your place. They blew it up the day before yesterday."

I threw the covers back and tried to swing my legs over the side. They refused to obey and I grew weak and a little giddy. I finally learned what that word meant. I closed my eyes and sank back into the bed and the pillow. It was all coming apart too soon. A nice comfortable, quiet, easy world was breaking up and McCorkle wasn't tough enough for any other world.

"Who blew it up?" I said carefully, keeping my eyes closed.

"I don't think they've found out yet. But it was early in the morning."

"What time early in the morning?"

"Around three."

"How did they blow it up? With a firecracker?"

"Dynamite. They seemed to have all the time in the world. They placed it in several areas where it would do the most damage. Herr Wentzel said that he thinks it was because of the man who was killed there the other day. Someone blamed you and Padillo for it, Wentzel said. He said he's looking for you both."

"You talk to him?"

"No. It was in the papers."

"They should tell him to try the river," I said.

"For what?"

"For Padillo. That's where he is: dead in the Rhine."

I opened my eyes and Fredl still stood there, the shirt held tightly against her. She put it down carefully on the bed and came around it and sat down next to me. She didn't say anything. She didn't have to. It was all in her eyes and the way her hands moved and the way her teeth caught her lower lip and held it.

"You want to talk about it?"

I thought about that for a moment and I knew then that there would be only one time that I would tell it honestly, the way I saw it happen, leaving out nothing. And so I told her and in the telling it grew easier and when I came to the part at the end about Padillo there was no reason to hold back the tears.

Afterward we sat there in the dim room, not talking. I asked for a cigarette and she lighted one for me. It tasted all right, so I wondered out loud if I could have some coffee and some brandy. While she went to get them I lay in the darkened room and thought about what I had to do and if I had the strength to do it.

Fredl came back with the coffee and I drank it and sipped on the brandy and then had another one.

"Are they awake?" I asked.

"I think so."

"Why don't you give them some of my clothes? They could use them."

"I already have. They're presentable."

"Then help me get dressed."

It was an effort, but I managed to get into some slacks and a shirt. I left the shorts off. Fredl knelt and worked my feet into a pair of socks and loafers. I ran my hand through her hair. She looked up and smiled.

"Marry me?" I asked.

"Aren't you rather on the rebound from a lot of things?"

"Maybe, but there's nothing else I want."

"All right," she said. "I'll marry you."

I got up shakily. "Let's go in and post the banns."

We walked into the living room. Symmes was sitting up on the divan.

"You'd better get Burchwood," I told him. "There're some things that have to be settled."

"How do you feel?" he asked.

"I feel all right."

"You look positively ghastly—like death warmed over." He left and went into the den to get Burchwood. They both came out and sat on the couch. My clothes looked all right on Symmes. He was tall enough, even if he didn't have the breadth—or fat. But they draped around Burchwood. The two sat close together on the couch, not touching, and they looked very much as they had when they were in the loft in Berlin.

"Would you like some coffee?" Fredl asked. They nodded. She was going to be a help, I decided. I'd never have thought to ask.

Reminded of my manners, I offered them a cigarette even though I knew they didn't smoke. "I want to thank you," I said formally, "for getting me off the barge. You didn't have to, especially after what you had been through."

"We had a deal with you and Padillo—remember?" Burchwood said.

"That's what I want to talk about. You can also talk in front of Miss Arndt. She could be part of your insurance. It all depends."

"On what?" Symmes asked.

"On what you do. You can walk out that door with my blessing and go any place you take a notion to. Or you can turn yourself in and I'll make the deal for you that Padillo promised."

"Can you?" Symmes asked.

"If I can't, you can still go out that door."

They were silent for a moment. Fredl brought in the coffee and placed it on the low table in front of them. Then she sat in a chair near me.

"We've talked it over," Symmes said slowly, "and we've decided to go back. We still think we were right," he added hastily. "We're not two repentant sinners. Don't take that attitude."

"I don't take any attitude at all," I said. "I don't know what I would do in your place."

"You see, Mr. McCorkle, we have no place to go but back. We speak nothing but English; we have no money, no friends; and I doubt that we have any families any more. The thought of going back to Moscow—just the effort alone—is . . . well, we just can't do it. But we don't want to go back to the U.S. just to get killed. And life has grown very cheap these last few days."

"You want me to set it up, then?"

They nodded.

"Is now all right?"

They looked at each other. Now was far sooner than tomorrow or the next day. They telegraphed each other their answers and Symmes did their nodding. I picked up the phone and dialed a number that had been given to me a long time ago. A man's voice said hello.

"Mr. Burmser," I said.

"Speaking."

"This is McCorkle. I have a message from Padillo for you."

There was a silence on the other end. He must have been switching on the tape recorder. "Where are you, McCorkle?"

"Padillo said to tell you he was dead."

I hung up.

It took them fifteen minutes to get to my house, which was pretty fair time. There was a knock on the door and Fredl answered it. I wasn't getting up for anybody.

Hatcher, the man I had met at the saloon, was with Burmser. They came in quickly, wearing nice gray suits and black shoes and carrying their hats. They stopped when they saw Symmes and Burchwood, who just looked at them and then looked away.

"This is Gerald R. Symmes and Russell C. Burchwood," I said. "This man is Mr. Burmser and the other one is Mr. Hatcher. If you want, they'll show you their little black books that tell you who they work for."

Burmser started toward Symmes and Burchwood. "What are you going to do—put the cuffs on?" He stopped and looked at Hatcher.

"Would you like some coffee—or perhaps a drink?" Fredl asked.

"This is Miss Arndt, my fiancée," I said. "Mr. Burmser and Mr. Hatcher."

"I'll take the drink," Burmser said.

Hatcher nodded. "Please," he said.

"Where's Padillo?" Burmser demanded.

"As I said, he's dead. You can fish in the Rhine for what's left of him. Along with a man named Jimmy Ku and a man named Maas. They're all dead, and there are a couple more that are dead on a Dutch barge that's tied up about a mile up the river."

"Did you say Ku?"

"Yes. Ku."

Hatcher reached for the telephone and dialed a number. He started talking into it in a low voice. I didn't pay any attention to what he said.

"Now we come to the problem that Mr. Symmes and Mr. Burchwood face," I said. "Padillo offered them a deal. I intend to see that it's carried out."

"We make no deals, McCorkle," Burmser said. "I'm sorry about Padillo, but he wasn't acting on our authority."

"You're a goddamned liar, Burmser," I said. "Padillo's job was to get Symmes and Burchwood here into West Berlin. Isn't that what you told him? Didn't you tell him that it was just a run-of-the-mill job, that all he would have to do would be to shepherd them through Checkpoint Charlie and they'd be carrying all the necessary papers and passes in their nice new suits? And didn't you work a deal with the KGB to trade Padillo for Symmes and Burchwood—and didn't you do it without getting clearance on it? It was going to be your own coup. Christ, Burmser, you know what a crummy deal you pulled. And Padillo got out of it, or tried to, using whatever method he could get his hands on. He wanted out. He wanted to run a bar somewhere in Los Angeles, but in the end he would have settled for just being left alone. Yet you couldn't let him have that; you had to set him up for the prize-patsy award, and in the end he got killed and you killed him just as if you had put the gun up against his back and pulled the trigger three times, just to make sure he was dead."

Fredl came in with the drinks. Burmser's tight expression didn't change. He accepted the drink but offered no thanks. He took a long pull and set it down. It could have been Pepsi-Cola for all he knew.

"Some of these things, these operations, you don't understand, McCorkle. You couldn't possibly, because even Padillo didn't. I told you in Berlin to keep out of it—that it was a delicately planned thing and depended on exact timing. But you came blundering in—"

"I didn't blunder in; I was asked in by my partner. And, by the way, have you checked out Cook Baker recently? He's dead, you know. Padillo killed him in East Berlin. He killed him when he found out that Baker had shot a man named Weatherby. He also killed him after he found out that Baker was working for the opposition, but I don't think that bothered Padillo too much."

Hatcher grabbed for the phone again and started dialing. He was having a busy day.

"And remember your Berlin spiv—Bill-Wilhelm? Maas and Baker fingered him and somebody shot him and dumped him in front of me just in front of the Café Budapest. Was all that part of your delicate operation?"

Burmser glanced at Hatcher, who signaled that he had heard that morsel, too, and would check it out.

"Now then. Let's get down to the polite blackmail."

"We don't pay blackmail, McCorkle."

"You'll pay this or you'll find this whole sweet mess reported in a Frankfurt paper under Miss Arndt's by-line. She knows it all—every last detail."

A thin film of sweat popped out on Burmser's forehead. He chewed on his upper lip, remembered that he had a drink, and took a big swallow as if he were thirsty.

"What about Symmes and Burchwood?"

"These two young men, against impossible odds, outwitted their fiendish Communist captors and, with a remarkable display of determination and daring, escaped over, under or through the Berlin wall to safety."

Symmes giggled. Burmser had his drink to his mouth again and choked.

"They'd never buy that."

"Why not? They'd have them under lock and key. And it's going to come out. Too many people know about them now. I can name a half dozen who might peddle the story this afternoon for the price of a drink."

"You want us to make them into heroes?"

Symmes giggled again. Burchwood tittered.

"You made their escape possible. You'll get all the kudos you can use."

Burmser's tight expression relaxed. "Possibly something could be developed along the lines you just mentioned—"

"Don't get cute, Burmser. I want to hear from them every three months. I might even insist on visiting rights. The story—the whole story—will be good for years. Especially if you make that phony announcement."

Burmser sighed. He turned to Hatcher. "You understand."

"It could be done," Hatcher said. "We could leak it here and there."

"Call them," Burmser said.

"A few more items," I said. "You might save a telephone call or two. First, this whole thing was expensive. It cost me a lot. And I've a few items hanging over me in Berlin—like Weatherby being found dead in my room. I want that cleared up. And then there's the matter of financing this operation. Somebody blew up my saloon, and with only a little effort I could make a good case against you, but I won't. We were overinsured anyway. Padillo saw to that. But cash out of hand amounts to—" I paused and grabbed a figure out of the air. "Fifteen thousand dollars. Cash. Small bills."

Burmser gasped. "Where do you think I can get that kind of money?"

"That's your problem."

He thought a moment. "All right. Fifteen thousand. What else?"

I looked at him for a full fifteen seconds. "Remember this: I'm going to be around for a long time and, one way or another, I'll keep track of you. And someday I may change my mind, just to do Padillo a favor. It'll be on impulse, an idle whim maybe. But it's something for you to think about at night or when you're thinking about how nicely the career's going and what the chances are for you to make GS 17 or bird colonel—whatever the grade is in your outfit. And especially when you stumble onto a real cute one that might cost somebody more than he wants to pay. Just think of me, the friendly saloon keeper, and wonder how much longer I'll keep my mouth shut."

Burmser got up stiffly. "Is that all?"

"That's all."

"They should come with us," he said, motioning toward Symmes and Burchwood.

"That's up to them. If you think about it, they don't have to unless they want to."

He thought about it and turned toward them. "Well?"

They got up together. I managed to raise myself out of the chair. They nodded shyly at me and at Fredl. I nodded back. We didn't shake hands. They looked very young and tired and I almost felt sorry for them.

I never saw them again.

CHAPTER 22

You can probably find a couple of thousand spots like Mac's Place in New York, Chicago or Los Angeles. They are dark and quiet with the furniture growing just a little shabby, the carpet stained to an indeterminate shade by spilled drinks and cigarette ashes, and the bartender friendly and fast but tactful enough to let it ride if you walk in with someone else's wife. The drinks are cold, generous and somewhat expensive; the service is efficient; and the menu, although usually limited to chicken and steaks, affords very good chicken and steaks indeed.

In Washington you can walk up Connecticut from K Street and turn left after a couple of blocks or so and find Mac's Place. It might have a slight aura of sauerkraut, but the head bartender speaks a very bright line of chatter and cruises around town in a prewar Lincoln Continental. The maître d' is of the old school and runs the place with the firm hand of a Prussian martinet, which he used to be.

The owner, a little grayer and spreading a bit in the paunch, usually arrives around ten-thirty or eleven, and his eyes dart toward the bar, and he has been told that there is a slight look of disappointment in them because whoever he's looking for is never there. And sometimes, on rainy days, he goes to the bar and pulls down the Pinch bottle and has a couple by himself, waiting for the luncheon trade. He usually has lunch with a blonde who looks something like a younger Dietrich and who, he says, is his wife. But they seem to like each other too much for that.

If you went to the bother, you could check the liquor license and learn that it's made out to the owner, whose name is McCorkle, and to a man named Michael Padillo, whose address is listed as a suite in the Mayflower Hotel; but if you call there they'll tell you that Mr. Padillo is out of town.

Once the owner got a postcard from Dahomey in West Africa. All it said was "Well," and it was signed with a "P." After that the same advertisement started to appear in the Personal Columns of the *Times* of London every Tuesday. It reads:

> **MIKE:** All is forgiven. Come
> home. The Christmas Help.

Made in the USA
Las Vegas, NV
15 April 2022

47517015R00134